I0699631

THE ILLUSION *of a* PERFECT LIFE

The Illusion
of a
Perfect Life

LYNN WEST

*Dedicated to my better half, Nicholas, and the A-Team.
And to the family members who generously
helped fund this dream.*

PROLOGUE
October 2015

I stared up at the ceiling, uneasy about what I'd agreed to that day. With concerted effort, I rolled over and squinted to make out the time: 4:52. In my younger years, I would have considered it still nighttime, but now I never slept past five, even if I tried. *Why did you agree to meet this young thing? She is just going to ask you questions you don't want to answer and bring up memories you have worked hard to forget,* a voice hissed. Then came the predictable rebuttal. *You haven't had a visitor since James came last Christmas, and all he wanted to talk about was estate planning. It will be nice to talk to someone who is interested in something beyond the superficial.*

I resented the second, nagging voice. While lighter in nature, I always felt annoyed and slightly chided after letting it speak. It was that voice that had dominated my mind a few weeks earlier, when I received an unexpected phone call.

After introducing herself and explaining the reason for her call, the young, chipper voice asked, "Would you be willing to meet me? I'm in Columbus, Ohio – only about an hour away from Dayton, and your time would significantly help me with my dissertation. I would, of course, drive to you."

Perhaps it was the ache for a deeper connection. Perhaps it was the guilt. Perhaps it was because my own kin hadn't visited me in nine months, two weeks, and four days. Whatever the reason, I responded, "Yes, a visit sounds just fine, as long as it starts before seven o'clock in the morning. Just stop at the Welcome Desk when you get here, and they will let me know you've arrived."

The clock finally read 5:20, and, reaching for my glasses, I sat up to begin my morning routine. After removing my silk hair-protection cap, I carefully unraveled the toilet paper underneath. My hairdresser, Betsy, swore toilet paper helped perms keep their shape, and while I didn't try all of her unusual ideas, I had to admit that her beauty tip of using Preparation H on wrinkles did seem to work.

I put on a pair of printed, tie-waist ankle pants. *Those pants looked so much better on the model in the fall catalogue. Probably because she didn't wear them up to her chest.* I shook my head, as if to shake out the voice, and reached for my black wrap top and silver-toned drop-hooped earrings. In my younger years, I would have finished the outfit off with black heels. Alas, my ninety-one-year-old feet required functional, comfortable tennis shoes. *At least you have a black pair,* I thought, letting out a heavy sigh. *You can still cancel. You don't owe it to this girl, her grandma, or anyone else for that matter to talk about your past.* I considered my options as I finished off my look with my favorite matte lipstick, Faux. At six o'clock sharp, I grabbed my quad cane, opened the door to my room, 5A, and started the long walk down the hall to the cafeteria to swallow another mass-produced breakfast and burnt coffee.

CHAPTER 1
1944

It was a warm summer day, and despite the rain, most of the windows were open. I was studying in the library – my favorite part of the house. I loved the smell of all the old books, Grandma's handwoven rug on the floor, and the picture of Johnny that hung on the wall. He looked dashingly handsome in his Army uniform. Beneath his thick head of chocolate brown hair, his piercing green eyes matched the sincerity of his closed-mouth smile. We were all proud of him for fighting in the war, not least because the Japanese had killed my cousin David when they sank the *Oklahoma* during the attack on Pearl Harbor. More than any of us though, Johnny had been deeply affected by his death. I saw a fire in his eyes whenever it was mentioned; it was what had impelled him to enlist. Johnny would have been exempt, too, as he fell just under the height requirement, but he managed to be granted an exception. I'd spent a lifetime wishing I could have convinced him otherwise.

That afternoon – the day my life was flipped upside down and turned inside out – my mother was cooking beef stew in the kitchen and my father, a doctor, was home but on-call.

Even with Tommy Dorsey and Frank Sinatra's "I'll Never Smile Again" playing on Daddy's Philco radio, through the open window I could hear the faint footsteps of someone walking up the cobblestone path. I couldn't recall Mother saying she'd invited anyone over for supper, and it was nearing supper time. When I peeked out the window, my heart started racing. The blood pumped hotter through my body, my palms suddenly sticky with sweat, my breathing ragged.

As I stood in the doorframe surveying the living room, the doorbell rang. Daddy had fallen asleep again in the recliner. Mother went to answer it, untying her white apron as she blithely strolled toward the door. I picked up my pace, wanting to plant my body between her and the door, to stop her from the inevitable. Too late. I caught Mama as she fainted in front of the Western Union courier. I dropped to my knees, her limp body dragging me down. Daddy abruptly woke to the scream I didn't know left my lips, and then he saw the courier.

The next few minutes passed in a blur. My father thanked the solemn, uniformed man, opened and then dropped the telegram, and walked over to the kitchen to light a cigarette. With Mother still in my lap, I reached for the telegram. The chilling, standardized words read, "I regret to inform you that your son . . ." I couldn't read the rest through my tears.

Johnny was a prisoner of war.

Months passed. Nursing school discharged me so I could spend time with my parents, with the understanding that I would return when able. Mother spent most waking hours perfecting the art of distraction: baking, knitting, cleaning, praying, weeping. Daddy was a master at compartmentalizing, and I wondered sometimes if he had forgotten my big brother was probably being tortured while he ate a home-cooked meal. For me, what began as anger toward Johnny's helpless situation turned to rage. I hated those bastards who were holding him captive. Like Mother, I prayed, but felt nothing but frustration and heard nothing but silence in reply. I concluded that God, if He even existed, did not care.

Thanksgiving came and went. We cut down our Christmas tree a few weeks before Christmas and kept it up until it was brown, because Mother held on to a desperate hope that somehow the Christmas season would bring good news. Ironically, that same December, Johnny drowned on the *Oryoku Maru*, an unmarked Japanese ship, struck down by a U.S. Navy plane. At least that is what the next, and last, telegram read. Not long after, my mother took solace in the bottle, my father took on more hours at the hospital, and I took to my nursing books. Thankful to not have to apply again, I resumed nursing school, desperate for a distraction.

CHAPTER 2
1946

Graduation Day was nerve-wracking, to say the least, but it turned out to be better than I expected.

I tried going into the weekend without expectations because, as the saying goes, "expectation is the root of all heartache." Although eighteen months had passed since Johnny's death, Mother was still convinced her son was alive, and if she didn't have a porcelain mug in hand, which she claimed was only tea or coffee, she clutched the fountain pen she used to write letters to him. Father told her he took them to the post office, and she believed him. He knew as well as I did she was not only losing her bloody mind and a fool to hold out hope, but also damaging her body.

Like usual, I woke early that morning so I could have some alone time. While outgoing, I found people draining, and I needed those precious minutes before my parents were awake to refuel. I took my time in the shower and in front of the mirror. I wanted to make sure my hair was pulled back just right and my bumper bangs were perfect. As I lightly applied my vanishing creme, I wondered how long I would live under this roof. *Many girls are married by now or at least engaged. Despite your attempts, you aren't going to turn any heads.* I silenced the critic's words and carefully applied my rouge, using the tri-dot system Mother had taught me years ago, and I finished my face off with powder. After checking to make sure my profile looked flawless, I reached for my new sterling silver ear clips. They were a gift from Daddy and matched the sterling silver brooch I'd wear on my graduation gown.

Once in the kitchen, I started the coffee maker and put a piece of bread in the chrome toaster. The newspaper on the kitchen table displayed headlines about the Tokyo War Crimes Tribunal and the trial of the Japanese military and political leaders for war crimes. *Those damn Japs better get what they deserve*, I thought to myself, sitting in the judgment seat and hoping they received the harshest punishment possible. *Stop thinking about them and what they did to your brother and family*, I redirected, flipping the newspaper over and finishing off my breakfast.

It was time to get ready. Since my brother's death, I had steadily lost weight and I had nothing that would fit my slender frame. Thankfully, Daddy had offered to buy me a new dress. Carefully, so as not to wrinkle the delicate fabric, I stepped into the white laced and beaded dress I'd chosen for the occasion. I was certain Mother wouldn't even notice; sometimes it felt like she looked right through me. But, while I was slipping on my white short heels to leave, she asked, "Margaret, would you like to wear my pearls? I think they would complement your new dress nicely."

Shocked, I answered, "Yes, Mother, that would be marvelous!"

I let Mother put her treasured saltwater pearls around my neck. Her fingers felt frail, almost childlike, and I noticed the simple platinum wedding band on her left hand. Her hands used to be so strong; with them she had raised two children, managed the affairs of the household, cooked every meal, kept the house clean, tended the garden. With those hands, she had welcomed me and Johnny into this world, changed us, fed us, comforted us when we were upset or fighting, wiped tears from my eyes when Sugar, my Siamese cat, couldn't get down from the tree, or from Johnny's eyes, when he broke his leg falling down the basement stairs. She also taught us how to fold them in prayer, telling us, "Prayer is the most powerful thing these two hands can do."

I scoffed at the last childhood memory. *A lot of good prayer had done.*

"Princess, it is time to go," Daddy said, interrupting my thoughts. When he dropped me off, he promised to do his best to be at the ceremony on time and with a sober wife.

"Thanks, Daddy," I replied, thankful for one reliable parent. Daddy's face had noticeably aged in the last two years, his once strawberry blonde hair now almost completely white. But while his skin and hair showed clear signs of age, he still was in good shape physically from his daily long walks. Come rain or shine, he walked at least two miles every evening, sometimes more. I couldn't help but wonder if he did it as much for his health as he did to escape.

I arrived at the ceremony early, and before I stepped out of Daddy's Cadillac, I applied and blotted my lipstick. The Victory Red added an exclamation point to my look. After saying bye to Daddy, I looked around the parking lot and saw only a few other cars. *Good, you won't have to make meaningless chit chat, at least not yet.* I approached the outdoor stage where the graduation ceremony would be held, brought a Chesterfield cigarette to my lips, lit it, and took a long drag, trying to calm my mind. The air was crisp that morning; a few clouds feathered the blue sky, and the sun was brilliant. Out of the corner of my eye, I noticed Dr. Kettle approaching me.

"Good morning, Margaret, and congratulations on graduating," he said cordially, lifting a bright white handkerchief to his large, prominent nose. The handkerchief, embroidered with a red caduceus, was almost as white as the wisps of hair crowning his head.

Dr. Kettle, likely in his sixties and close to retirement, had been my anatomy professor. My lips curved into a smile as I recalled his classes. It was not just his clear mastery of the subject that made him my favorite teacher, but his humor, humble demeanor, and kindness. Moreover, he had been empathetic when the Japs captured Johnny.

"Thank you, Dr. Kettle. I am excited to start at Miami Valley in the coming weeks, and I know my parents are thankful I will continue to call Dayton my hometown," I replied.

"I knew you would secure a position there. You will be serving in the maternity wing, correct?" he asked, stuffing his used handkerchief in the pocket of his khaki pants.

"Yes, sir." And before I could stop myself, I continued, "It will be nice to be around new life, especially after the war and losing my brother." I felt my face redden as I looked down at the freshly cut grass, wishing I hadn't said so much.

Dr. Kettle responded with grace and in his usual sincere tone. "Yes, it will, Margaret. Again, I am very sorry for the loss of your brother. I can certainly relate to what you are going through. Can I grab you some coffee?"

"Yes, please. Black is fine," I quickly replied. I felt like a total imbecile. Of course, he knew what I was going through! He had lost both his sons on D-Day, around the same time we found out about Johnny's capture. Dr. Kettle returned with my coffee, and I thanked him as I cradled the steaming paper cup, excused myself, and walked away. I didn't want to talk to anyone else.

From underneath a weeping willow tree, I stood sipping my coffee and noticed how perfectly the white chairs were lined up. Most of the graduates had arrived, and, like me, they were dressed in their Easter best. I fingered the pearl necklace Mother had given me, wondering what state she would be in when she arrived with Father.

My mind became a battlefield. *Mother was having such a great morning – of course she will be supportive, on time, and sober.* Then, *Don't get your hopes up. She has done this to you before, remember? For heaven's sake, she ruined your last two birthdays! If it wasn't for Daddy, she would've forgotten it altogether last year, and just a few weeks ago, after another good morning, she forgot your birthday lunch.* Snapping back to the present, I decided to stick with my original plan – no expectations. I finished my coffee and went to put on my white robe.

Thankfully, my parents arrived on time, dressed nicely, and Mother looked beautiful – and sober; if only she would spend the same amount of time with me that she did to perfectly curl her chocolate brown hair. I felt mixed emotions when my name was called – pride, for what I accomplished, tinged with sadness because my brother wasn't there to whistle and clap for me. Quickly burying the negative feelings, I smiled and accepted the diploma. I had spent enough time that morning thinking about the past.

The three of us went to Culp's Cafeteria for a late lunch, joining a line of at least twenty people along the sidewalk. I was happy to wait, eagerly anticipating their homemade bread and pastry selection. While we waited, I glanced across the street and noticed the theater was still showing *The Best Years of Our Lives*. While I wouldn't mind seeing Dana Andrews on screen, I fixated on the title, wondering if – and when – I would ever have the best years of my life.

"Now, Mags, you get whatever you want," Daddy said, bringing me back to the present.

I smiled and took a step forward into the establishment, willing myself to believe that things were normal again.

～

May 12, 1946

Happy Mother's Day to me. Ha! Some mother I am.

I want to be a good mother for Margaret, though. And a good wife for Thomas.

Yet every morning when I wake up – today included – my mind is consumed with thoughts of my boy. I earnestly try to replace the thoughts with a Bible verse or song from my youth, but inevitably my mind drifts back to him. My chest tightens, my heart rate increases, and I feel like vomiting or passing out from shortness of breath. And worse, Thomas, and even Margaret, think I am crazy to hold out hope that Johnny is missing, not dead. The Army can't be 100 percent certain he was on that ship, after all.

The pain from missing him is worse than any physical pain Thomas inflicts.

In the days leading up to Margaret's graduation yesterday, Thomas warned me to be on my best behavior. He took her out one evening to buy a new dress, and I vowed that I would try to be excited for her when they came back. However, it had been an emotionally draining day because I'd spent the afternoon folding and packing Johnny's clothes – as I had till the end of the month to donate them, per Thomas's insistent instruction – and my voice lacked my intended sincerity. Exhausted, physically and mentally, I was sitting at the kitchen table when they returned, elbows on the enamel topped table, my forehead resting heavily in my hands, and my eyes staring at the piece of cold buttered toast I couldn't bring myself to eat.

"Mom! Look at this dress Daddy bought me for graduation! Isn't it lovely?" Margaret eagerly asked as she unzipped the dress bag.

I looked up from my uneaten dinner and gazed in her direction, the bourbon in my coffee mug hindering my ability to focus. "Yes, darling. You will look beautiful," I replied, trying to smile and hoping my eyes were not as puffy and bloodshot as they were the last time I'd checked.

The excitement faded from her face, and she turned to head toward her room, shoulders slumped. "Thanks, Mother," she quietly said. "And thanks for the dress, Daddy," she smiled as she made eye contact with her father.

I am such a failure. I wonder if they would be better off without me.

After she left, Thomas shot me a stern look, and I slowly walked down the long, carpeted hallway to our bedroom. I berated myself as I undressed, feeling awful for discouraging my daughter. Thoughts swirled in my head. I remember telling myself, "Snap out of it, Violet. Be thankful you still have a child left. Some mothers buried all their children."

I stared at myself in the mirror, still naked, knowing that my inward depression showed outwardly as well. I have more than a few new gray hairs and wrinkles, after all. My eyes reflect no joy, and my lips have no color without lipstick. My body is thinner than before because I have lost my regular appetite. Thomas has complained he doesn't have as much to grab onto around my hips, but he still seems to enjoy my chest well enough. Despite nursing two children, they managed to maintain a round, fairly perky shape, and the weight loss actually accentuates them.

If only Thomas still loved me. If only he understood my heartache.

Anyway, later that night, after I had slipped on my light pink nightgown, I found myself backed up against our bedroom wall.

"You will not ruin her graduation," Thomas sneered between his yellowed teeth. Ever since the last telegram, he had smoked at least a pack a day. My mind started to wander, and I wondered if Johnny had picked up smoking, and if he had, if the nicotine brought him any sense of relief.

My teeth unexpectedly grinded together when he hit me; my hand flew up to my cheek, and pain pulsed through my jaw from the impact. I steadied myself against the wall as my vision spun. Pressing his large hands against my shoulders, he practically yelled, "Pay attention to me, woman!"

He turned around and walked to his twin bed where so much love had been made. I had once considered it a sanctuary. Resting his face in his bear-like hands, he looked defeated.

Despite the pain he has caused me, I feel sad for him; I know his heart is hurting. It has to be. But he won't let me inside his heavily guarded soul. Instead, he lashes out. I wonder if he doubts the Army too. I know he doubts God, as his Biblical namesake had.

After I regained my balance, I went over to him, knelt down, and placed my weathered hands on his knees. I whispered, "Dear, I am sorry for spacing out again. I promise I will be on my best behavior for graduation and will make you proud."

He looked up at me and the rage left his eyes.

The war and John's death have changed him; he is bitter and angry. I hoped to see a flicker of regret or a twinge of guilt from hitting me – again – but I didn't.

"Good," he flatly said, and then pulled me up gently – but strong enough that I knew I could not object – and slid down the straps on my nightgown. I buried my face in his neck, kissing it, because I didn't want him to see my hesitation. Picking me up like a ragdoll, he laid me down on the bed and pulled off my night-gown. I faked a smile as he undid his belt and pushed his pants to the hardwood floor.

At least graduation went well. I even curled my hair in victory rolls. Off to bed. Night.

Violet

Autumn came – my favorite time of year. I enjoyed the crisp, cool air on my face, still tan from the summer, and the way the leaves instinctively knew to change from green to all shades of yellow, orange, and red. Finally, I felt like I was in a rhythm. Serving new mothers and their babies was such a joy, and I relished the daily opportunities to help sustain and support new life. I soon developed the nickname "Eager Beaver" for being so willing to help, but I didn't mind. I *was* eager!

The American Nurse Association endorsed the eight-hour workday that year, and while I was tired by the end of each week, I never dreaded going to work. Not only did I love my job, but I also found companionship with the gals I worked with. Martha became the opinionated sister I never had, and we spent most lunch breaks together. She was shorter and slightly plump, and her hair reminded me of Little Orphan Annie's. I am not sure why she picked me to be her friend; Martha was boisterous and intimidatingly confident, and she lived a much more exciting social life compared to my reserved, fairly boring one. She was always talking about a different handsome guy and their exciting weekend day trips or their "killer-diller" nights, as she called them. And besides always being dressed in the latest atomic prints outside of the hospital, she seemed to know all the breaking news.

"So, did you hear we now have a picture of Earth from space? Wild, isn't it?" Martha asked me one day over lunch.

"Are you serious?" I responded, unaware but interested.

"America is taking the credit, but the Germans made it possible. It was their rocket, after all," she replied, her face flushing a little at the mention of the Germans.

I didn't know how to respond. She had this strange, love-hate relationship with the Germans. Her father and brother had both been killed in the war by the Germans, but much of her extended family still lived in Frankfurt, at least what was left of that city. And, she was all about peace and love, or some boloney like that. How she could find it in her heart to feel anything but pure malice left me mystified. I could say with one hundred percent certainty that I had only a hate relationship with the Japanese.

She switched topics. "I was always against the war, but once we dropped the A-bomb, I knew I had to do something," she said, chewing her egg-salad sandwich as she talked.

"What did you do?" I asked.

"Well, I felt helpless at first, but then I met some others who thought like me, and we decided to meet regularly as a group. We get together every other Sunday night and talk about a whole host of issues, from how to defeat the *real* enemy facing our country – racism – to how we can defuse the Cold War."

Not sure what to think, I took a sip of water and managed a long "*hmmmm*" in response.

"You should come this weekend, at least to check it out. We eat while we talk, and afterwards the group hangs out and relaxes. You may even leave with a good buzz," she insisted, laughing slightly. She quickly added with a wink, "And, you can meet some guys!"

⌒

That Sunday, I grappled with what to do about the gathering Martha had mentioned. As well-to-do Republicans with traditional views about a man's duty to fight for his country, my parents would not, in any way, support my attendance, and I didn't want to rock the boat after a good morning together. Ever since I'd started working, Mother had been making a concerted effort to not drink and be her old, cheery self.

We went to church that morning and listened to the minister talk about trust. Still angry at God, if He existed, I attended only to please my parents. The minister, dressed in all black, opened his sermon with the two centers of decision-making: the head, where decisions are made based on logic, and the heart, where decisions are based on emotion. Although I was interested in what he had to say, I felt tricked when he quoted Proverbs 3: "Trust in the Lord with all your heart and lean not on your own understanding; in all your ways acknowledge Him, and He will make your paths straight." I would be a millionaire if I had a dollar for every time I'd heard that scripture quoted, from either my mother or my late grandma; I just rolled my eyes because I didn't understand how the Lord could have Johnny's path lead to the bottom of the Pacific. Yet, his message was intriguing, and I found myself wanting to make my decision about the evening based on both my heart and my mind. My emotions told me the evening with Martha and her friends would be fun, entertaining, and relaxing. My head cautioned me, warning bells ringing because of how Martha had mentioned boys and getting buzzed.

In the end the head won, and I decided to stay home and hopefully do something enjoyable with Mother and Father. My decision made, I wandered to the kitchen for a snack. In recent weeks, Mother had resumed baking banana bread on Sundays like she did before the war. But that day the kitchen did not smell like bananas and there was no bread to be found. There were, however, three ripe bananas on the counter, so I decided to give it a try.

"Mother?" I called out, as I opened the pantry door to find the flour, sugar, almond extract, baking soda, and salt. I eyed the chocolate chips, wondering if they would be a tasty addition.

After not hearing an immediate answer, I walked past the bathroom and toward the bedroom, chocolate chips in hand. No reply. *She might be out in the yard*, I thought, pulling open the sliding door. Sure enough, she was sitting on the antique wrought-iron bench by the massive red oak tree. Towering at least fifty feet, the old oak was still a beautiful crimson color, shading most of the lawn. Scattered rays of sunlight slipped through the leaves, which stubbornly clung to the branches. A well-worn tire swing still hung from one of the branches, triggering childhood memories.

I saw myself with braided pigtails and lacey white socks under my favorite patent leather Mary Janes. Johnny was pushing me on the swing, and I clung on for dear life, squealing as he launched me higher and higher. I didn't dare complain; the last thing I wanted was for him to think I was a coward, or worse, stop playing with me. Father was sitting on that wrought-iron bench, reading the paper with a pipe lazily dangling from his mouth, and Mother was in her element, the aroma of freshly baked banana bread escaping from the kitchen as snippets of Frank Sinatra's "My Way" wafted on the breeze. *Oh, to go back!* I thought to myself, smiling at the memory.

"Hi, dear," Mother said apathetically, jolting me back to the present.

"Hello, Mama," I replied cheerfully, hoping I'd heard her tone wrong. "I saw some bananas on the counter and wondered if you wanted to help me make banana bread. You know I have a hard time gauging when the bread is done. I don't want the middle to sink in like last time. Oh, and I had an idea to add—"

I held out the bag of chocolate chips to show her when she cut me off. "I am tired." Tears welled in her eyes.

"Mother, I didn't mean to upset you," I sighed, silently chiding myself for bothering her, but also certain my ask did not cause her distress.

"You are fine, dear," she managed to say, dabbing her eyes with an embroidered white handkerchief. And then, on her lap, I noticed the source of her distress: a letter Johnny had sent while stationed in the Philippines.

"Mama, you know those letters only upset you," I pleaded, but she was no longer listening. Unashamed, she reached for one of Daddy's flasks in her sweater pocket and, bringing it to her lips, tilted her head back, finishing off the contents.

Knowing there was nothing more to say or do, I walked back toward the house. Suddenly, my evening plans included Martha, boys, and booze. The heart had won after all.

I met Martha outside her apartment at a quarter to six. As she grabbed her things and locked the door, I soaked in the warmth of the evening sun. In a few weeks, we would be welcoming the moon around this time rather than begging the sun to slow its descent.

"You ready to go? George's place is just a short walk away," she said as she jumped to the sidewalk, hopping over two concrete steps.

"Let's go!" I said, trying to mask my nervousness with enthusiasm.

As we started down the path, Martha began, "My mother called today. I hate it when she calls me on Sundays, and she does almost every week! I disappoint her each time." Her voice changed a little as she impersonated her mother, "'Did you attend mass today, sweetie?' She knows I left the Catholic church years ago. I was sick to death of the rituals and rules. I haven't told her how much I admire Mahatma Gandhi and how fond I am of Hinduism. She would flip."

Martha continued on about Gandhi and her respect for his views on religious harmony and peace until we approached a brick house with a large front porch. Although the lawn and garden looked a little shabby, the porch was well swept. Two guys sat on a swing, chatting away. One wore an untucked, loose-fitting Hawaiian Aloha shirt over a white undershirt, and the other, a green knit shirt with a horizontal yellow stripe.

"Martha! What's buzzin', cousin?" The one in the green shirt welcomed her, standing up. "Who is your friend?"

"This is Margaret," Martha said, smiling as she looked back at me.

"Welcome, Margaret. I'm George. Let's head on in and grab some food. You two are the last ones I was expecting," he said and ushered us through the front door, following us into the house.

Martha headed to the kitchen after announcing to the group of people in the living room, "Everyone, this is Mags. Mags, this is everyone."

Mags? Only my father uses that nickname for me, I thought as I gave a fake, slightly irritated smile. *Well, you can't correct her now.* Despite the poor lighting, I could see stains in the green velvet couch. The curtains were mismatched, the walls were covered with handmade anti-war and pro-peace posters, and there was an unfamiliar, musky smell in the air.

"Where is the bathroom?" I asked those sitting on the velvet couch, my hands fidgeting behind my back.

A strikingly handsome guy spoke up. "It's down the hall, second door on the left," he answered, looking me up and down, and then winked.

I didn't actually have to use the restroom; I just needed a minute to myself, especially after being gawked at. No one had ever looked at me in such a bold, sexual way before, and while my parents had raised me to value sophistication and respect, I had to admit that something about him was alluring – almost dangerously so. After a quick glance around the peach-tiled bathroom, I decided it was clean enough to use if I actually needed it. I shut the door and was immediately taken aback by a poster of a topless woman.

"Oh my gosh!" I exclaimed a little too loudly. My hand flew to my mouth, and I hoped no one had heard me. I had never seen anything like it before. Trying to erase the image in my mind, I quickly fixed my gaze on the mirror and gave myself a mental pep-talk. *You will have fun. Just relax.* I focused instead on the matching peach towels, the large, fuzzy peach rug on the floor, and the little lamp on the bathroom counter. Then, I flushed the toilet and turned on the faucet to let the water run for a minute. Averting my eyes, I reached for the door handle, keeping my gaze fixed on the matching peach tile floor.

"Mags, there you are," Martha said as I stepped out. She handed me a plate with some bread, cheese, and vegetables on it. "We are starting, come on."

After a long shower, I finally slid into bed at 1:38 a.m. Lucky for me, Mother and Father were not waiting up, likely because they'd had yet another fight about the resurrected letters. I lay there staring into the darkness, unable to sleep. My buzz and bravado had worn off, and fear and anxiety pushed aside the blithe personality I had displayed only a few hours before. *Did Joe really sense a connection? Would I see him again? What if my parents found out?*

I replayed the evening in my head. The meeting portion had been far more interesting than I expected. It was complete with an agenda, a different person speaking per topic, and action items for the next two weeks.

After the meeting, the guy who had caught me off guard earlier introduced himself.

"Hi, Mags. I'm Joseph, but you can call me Joe," he said confidently. "You know, I think you took offense to how I looked at you earlier when you asked about the bathroom. I am sorry about that. It just isn't every day that a girl as pretty as you shows up at one of our meetings. I mean, wow – you have beauty and heart."

"Oh. Well, thank you," I managed, looking up to meet his gaze. His eyes were a grayish blue, and his shaggy dark hair complemented his handsome face. His pants were a shade of dark red, and over a white crew neck he wore a short-sleeved, collared zip-up jacket. Dog tags hung around his neck.

"So, tell me a little about yourself," he said, as he brought what looked like a cig, but wasn't, to his mouth.

I watched him take a long inhale, pause, and then exhale. He must have noticed the confused expression on my face and answered the question I didn't verbalize. "Yes, this is marijuana. And no, it is not like *The Devil's Harvest* portrays it. A puff won't turn you into a reckless harlot." He laughed slightly. "Want to try it?"

Maybe it was his seductive smile. Maybe it was a deep-seated desire to let go and relax. Maybe it was my burning anger toward God, my mother, the Japanese, the world. Whatever it was, something in me screamed, *yes*, drowning out the small voice whispering, *no.*

Without answering him, I reached for the joint, knowing full well it was illegal, and inhaled. Instead of pausing and exhaling, though, I started coughing almost immediately.

"Don't worry. Everyone coughs their first time or two. You'll get the hang of it," he said reassuringly, as if I were learning to ride a bicycle.

I blushed, embarrassed.

"Give it another go," he coaxed, holding it out for me again. I went for it, and by the third time, I didn't cough. He watched me with a sly smile, applauded my success, and opened another drink.

After a few inhales, I felt as if physical weights had been lifted off my shoulders, and I didn't have a care in the world. As I reached for another slice of cheese and a piece of bread, I started sharing things about my family I wouldn't have otherwise. We talked for hours, learning about one another and laughing. Joe was a nature enthusiast and worked as a gardener to pay the bills, but he was most passionate about his side work as an aspiring artist and photographer. He lived with his younger brother, who had been wounded in the war, in a small two-bedroom apartment close to Miami Valley Hospital. The dog tags were his brother's, and Joe said they were a constant reminder of what is actually worth fighting for. And while against the war, he had actually enlisted with his brother, but was turned away due to a heart murmur. When I asked about other family members, he shared that his only other relatives lived further south, in Lexington, Kentucky. His father had died in the trenches during WWI, and his mother never woke up from the Twilight Sleep the doctor put her under during the delivery of his brother.

As the hour clock circled, we sat closer together. Eventually, his arm was around me and I was leaning against him, hand on his thigh.

"I'll be right back," I giggled as I stood up, looking back at him, smiling as my extended hand let go of his.

What are you doing? Be careful, I thought as I walked to the peach restroom. The battle ensued. *Calm down, you are just having fun. He is handsome, funny, and a good listener! You're really hitting it off with him. Have fun. You haven't had the chance to be yourself in, gosh, years!*

I stared at my reflection in the mirror, scrutinizing my appearance. My skin was flawless and had a slight sheen from perspiration. My rich brown hair lay perfectly – I'd made sure of it before I left that evening – and I had unbuttoned another button on my blouse earlier when I was chatting with Joe, revealing more skin than my mother would've approved of. I couldn't remember if I felt hot from the room or because he made my insides tingle and my face flush in an unfamiliar way. Still, my inner critic taunted me. *Yeah, sure, you are pretty. But you certainly don't look as good as the model pinned to the bathroom door.* Slightly discouraged, I brushed down my skirt and reached for the knob. To my surprise, Joe entered, gently pushing me back into the bathroom as he shut the door behind him.

He grabbed my face and kissed my lips passionately. For a split second, I was caught off guard. But my shock quickly evaporated, and I kissed him back hungrily, my hands instinctively resting on his firm chest before unzipping his jacket. Still kissing me, he slid one hand to my back and pressed me up against his body, as his other hand reached for my bare left leg. Desire shot through my entire body like lightning.

Stop him, now, Margaret! Alarm bells sounded, and I pulled away slightly. He took a step back.

"Mags, if you don't want to, it's fine. I just feel this strong attraction to you and thought it was mutual." His eyes burned with intensity, and I knew he didn't want to stop.

For the same reasons I took the grass, I acquiesced. I *was* attracted to him, and a large part of me did in fact want him.

I answered him by turning on the small light on the counter, turning off the overhead light, and then unbuttoning my white blouse. Staring at him, I untucked it, letting it hang open. Smiling, he gently pushed the blouse off my shoulders and down my arms. As he unhooked my bra and tossed it on the floor, he glanced at the poster on the back of the bathroom door.

"She's got nothing on you," he whispered, his breath hot on my face.

CHAPTER 4
2015

The young girl was mesmerized by every word I shared. And even with the glow of the recorder's red light, I felt comfortable. More than comfortable, in fact. The more I spoke, the freer I felt.

When I first saw her, however, promptly at quarter till seven, I wanted to turn around and run; the likeness was undeniable. Dressed in khaki pants and a navy, short-sleeved blouse with white polka dots, she had familiar blue eyes and blond, curly hair. From the moment I saw her, I could see the relation. A wall went up during the simple introduction. As if she knew what both my stomach and soul were craving, she asked if I'd be opposed to going to a local coffee shop. Despite my initial hesitation, the simple gesture slightly softened my heart. Then, during the short drive in her black Volkswagen Jetta, I heard my mother's voice plead, *Give her a chance, Margaret. She is not your enemy.*

I relished the heavenly aroma of the coffee shop – a welcome respite from the stale, institutional smells of the assisted living facility. I ordered a large black coffee, and Megan ordered a small black one. Before I could protest, she quickly handed the barista a credit card to pay for both drinks. I smiled my thanks, then followed her to two worn, camel brown leather chairs. Carefully, I sat down on top of the firm pillow I had laid on the seat, as she excused herself to add cream and sugar. As I watched her stir her drink and smile as she passed the container to another patron, I tried to put all my preconceptions aside. Instead, I focused on cradling the porcelain mug, enjoying the warmth against my wrinkly skin. *I wonder what she knows about me*, I thought, and then cringed at the possibilities.

I soon discovered that Megan was almost thirty, married, and pursuing her doctorate at The Ohio State University. She was drafting her dissertation on the topic "generational wounds and the healing power of story." I wasn't sure why anyone would want to write such a long paper, and at the beginning of our conversation, I didn't see how a story could be therapeutic, but her warm smile, my mother's encouraging voice, and a strange tug at my heart persuaded me to be a willing participant.

Sincere and understanding, Megan continued to ask questions about my parents, the hospital, my first lover, and my relationship with my mother. While I hadn't thought back to the 1940s in quite some time, I continued to allow myself to remember. And the more I spoke, the more the memories came flooding back, clear as day.

CHAPTER 5
September 1946

To avoid my parents that morning, I dressed and ate early. Father walked into the kitchen as I was about to open the door to leave.

"Good morning, Margaret." His voice was groggy, as he ambled over to the counter to fill his coffee mug.

Before he could ask or say anything else, I responded, "Bye, Daddy. I am going in early today." And with that hurried farewell, I headed out the door.

Once at the hospital, I went straight to the women's locker room. Each girl was assigned a blue locker for her personal belongings, and even though most new girls received a locker on the lower level, mine was on top – a small privilege that I was secretly proud of. With ample time to spare, I decided to organize my locker. Since overtime was not permitted, it seemed like a good way to pass the extra hour. My mind still spinning with the events of the previous night, I had to do my lock combination three times before I could get it to open. And, despite my best attempt to focus on stacking my toiletries and extra pairs of socks, my thoughts wandered. Would I see Joe again?

After he had taken my virginity, he kissed me quickly and said with a wink, "I'll slip out first, so we don't become the talk of the town." I flushed the toilet to make it sound like it was used, combed my hair with my fingers, and adjusted my skirt. Out of the bathroom, I rounded the corner to the kitchen looking for Joe but found Martha instead.

"There you are! Come on, let's go. It's late, and we both work tomorrow," she said, eyeing me suspiciously.

As she led me out the front door, I couldn't help but glance furtively around, in hopes of seeing Joe. But to my disappointment, he was not in the living room or on the porch.

I wanted to shower as soon as I returned home; a twinge of guilt made me feel dirty, but I didn't out of fear I would wake my parents. Instead, I'd slipped into bed and fell into a restless sleep.

What were you thinking? that familiar voice scolded me. *Even if he would call on you, you shouldn't see him again. What would your parents think if they found out? You went against everything you were taught about relationships with men!* I took a deep breath to clear my head, steadying myself against my locker. *Stop. You did nothing wrong. It was fun. Besides, it's not like your parents are a poster example of how to act. And . . . you did enjoy yourself. You only live once, and if you've learned anything from the war, it's that you need to enjoy life while you're still breathing.*

"Well, good morning, Mags," Martha sang, bringing me back to the present. She was chipper and full of her usual morning spunk. Lowering her tone and shimmying right up next to me, she asked, "Is it safe to assume you lost your virgin card last night?"

"Martha!" I gasped.

"Oh, come on. No one else is around. You seriously think I wouldn't figure it out? Joe is such an interesting guy too. Not to mention, a dream to look at!" she said wistfully, raising her eyebrows up and down, smiling ear to ear.

I rolled my eyes and punched in my timecard. "Yeah? Well, we will see if I see him again," I responded, trying to sound strong and indifferent.

September 30, 1946

Margaret left for work so early this morning, and she was out well past midnight last night. Odd. I suppose it is good for her to be out socializing with people her own age. I just hope they are good people. She hadn't noticed me sitting in the corner when she walked through the living room. It was dark, but in the moonlight, I could see her hugging herself like she was cold; perhaps it was chilly outside.

I decided it was best to stay silent, mainly because I didn't want her asking why I was up, although I am sure she would've guessed it – another fight between me and Thomas. Last night's argument, however, was different.

I had broken my word again about reading Johnny's letters. I'd like to say I was quick to apologize for breaking his trust, but my pride told me I was right, and this time I actually fought back.

"There isn't a problem with me reading these letters!" I screamed, alcohol on my breath and letter in hand.

"It isn't that you re-read them. I am disappointed you broke your promise – again," he answered, raising his hands in a gesture of frustration, his tone defeated. "I really thought this time was different. I just wanted you to wait till you were stronger, and we agreed that the next time you read them was going to be with me," Thomas continued, his voice increasing in volume. "For heaven's

sake, you simply can't handle your emotions, and you spiral out of control each time!"

I looked down, my pride quickly replaced with self-loathing. Then came the low blow. Without even turning around to face me, Thomas added a stinging question, "Do you have any idea the damage you have done to our marriage or the relationship – what's left of it – with Margaret?"

His words hung in the air. He was right, of course. Everything he said was right, but I wasn't willing to admit it.

"I am sorry you feel that way," I finally answered flatly. My mind was still fixated on how I felt and how he had treated me over the last year. I then added a damning shot to his heart: "You don't even miss John!"

As soon as the words left my mouth, I regretted them. I braced for him to slap me, but he didn't. He just looked at the ground and walked away. It was almost worse than if he had hit me.

I tried to connect with him later, physically at least. I showered, did my hair and makeup, and sat in my bed wearing only a satin robe so he could see the shape of my body through the thin material. He kissed me politely, turned off the light, and crawled into his own bed. I waited for him to come over, but he never crossed the divide between our beds.

I don't know how I am going to fix this mess I created. What am I going to do? I wish I could talk to Mother. Oh, I wish I had the wisdom she did. She would probably be disappointed in me too though.

I need to stop and make Thomas breakfast. Maybe that will help a little. I doubt it though.

Violet

At the end of my shift, I managed to grab my things and slip out of the locker room without seeing anyone. I was glad not to have to make small talk. As I hurried out of the hospital, I decided to stop for some ice cream before heading home. Much to my surprise – and delight – Joe was outside the ice cream parlor, a backpack slung over one shoulder and a cigarette in his mouth.

"Well, hello beautiful. I like the uniform." A flirtatious smile painted Joe's face, and he gave me a quick eyebrow raise as he leaned in for a hug.

"Hi!" I gushed, thrilled and relieved to see him. *You see? He does like you. Don't worry so much and try not to act so eager.*

"You mentioned you stop here sometimes after work, so I figured I would see if Mondays are ice cream days for you or not. Let's grab a cone."

His invitation sent sparks off in my heart. As we walked inside, I was struck by the heavenly smell of sweet cream. Framed pictures of ice cream adorned the walls and there were a few vacant chairs. We looked over the flavors as we stood in line, and I decided on my regular one scoop of vanilla in a waffle cone. He ordered a bowl of strawberry ice cream, and I smiled when he offered to pay.

We sat down at one of the glass tables. The table's frame was the same turquoise color as the chairs, and along with the abundant lighting, the place was bright and cheery. Joe dipped his spoon into his bowl and raised it up, as if to toast.

"To our first date."

I followed suit, raising my cone.

I told him about my workday, leaving out how I'd arrived early and what Martha had said to me. He shared at length about his research on the Japanese Americans who had been relocated to internment camps during the war. One such individual, Toyo Miyatake, happened to be a photographer, and he covertly captured his experiences while in camp through a makeshift camera. He was Joe's latest inspiration. Despite my strong feelings about the Japanese, I was interested in what Joe had to say and couldn't help but feel sympathy for those who had been mistreated simply by virtue of their ethnic background.

Once we had finished our ice cream, Joe reached for my hand. "Want to get out of here? We could go to the park nearby?" he asked.

"I can go, but just for a little while. I have to be home for dinner," I answered, stealing a glance at the clock on the wall. "I have an hour until I need to head home."

Holding hands, we sauntered down the street to a nearby park. There were a few other couples walking along the path, a few men fishing at the pond, and an older gentleman tossing a frisbee to his dog. We guessed at their stories, each building upon what the other said. As we walked, we came to another pond, free of fishermen, and soaked in the landscape.

Joe opened his backpack and laid out a checkered blanket under a large willow tree. *He must have planned a trip to the park*, I thought, and my mind flashed back to graduation. For a moment I felt the familiar rush of nerves that I'd experienced that day wondering whether my mother would be sober or not. This time, however, it was nervous excitement that coursed through me as I sat down with him beneath the willow, his legs cradling me, my back resting against his chest. He wrapped his arms around me, and we sat there for a while in comfortable silence. All we heard were the birds, the rustle of leaves, and the sound of a gentle wind in the trees. There was no one else in sight. *I love the feeling of his arms around me. I wonder what my parents will think of him and where he wants to settle down . . . What if he doesn't really like me? What if he is just interested in a physical relationship?*

Kissing my forehead, he broke the silence. "I can't tell you how much I love spending time with you. I feel like I found the missing puzzle piece in my life."

Well, there is your answer. I smiled contentedly as I looked out at the pond. Strong, physical desire surged through my body as I turned to face him, his lips meeting mine with a kiss. Before I knew what I was doing I had hiked up my white nursing skirt and placed my knees on the inside of his legs.

"Well, hello there, Nurse," he said, as he looked slightly up at me, his face eye-level with my chest. "What treatment are you going to prescribe me?" He put his arms around me, resting them on my back before sliding them down.

"The good news is, you are going to survive," I answered, slowly unbuttoning a few buttons on my uniform. "But, you are going to need a lot of TLC."

"I think I can handle that diagnosis. TLC from you is my favorite kind of medicine."

⟿

September 30, 1946

It's me again. I am really worried about Margaret. I think she is hiding something.

She was late for dinner tonight. I remember asking myself aloud, "Where is she?" Thomas was in the library reading, so he couldn't hear me, and it was nearly six o'clock Margaret knew dinner time was always at 5:30. Thomas and I agreed to wait a bit longer, especially because she'd left so early that morning.

"Go ahead and plate the meal, dear," Thomas said, as he sat down at the table. His tone was flat, and as I looked back at him, I saw his face buried in the paper.

I wish he said "dear" like he used to.

In an attempt to be back in his and Margaret's good graces, I'd made chicken, cabbage steaks, and sweet potatoes. I even baked an apple cobbler for dessert. (As if one homecooked meal would make a difference. I am such a fool.) As I put my plate on the table, I heard the door open. Exhaling with relief, I grabbed Margaret's plate and served her as well.

She apologized for being so late, telling us she grabbed ice cream with a friend after work and lost track of time. She sounded breathless as she talked, and I remember noticing a few details: her uniform looked like it needed pressed, and I was certain I saw a blade of grass in her hair.

Thankfully, Thomas inquired about her friend. I was curious too, but I hated to be the one to ask.

With food in her mouth, she mumbled something like, "One Martha introduced me to. You remember Martha, right?"

While Margaret's story seemed plausible, I could tell she wasn't divulging the whole truth.

Feeling deceived, I felt the compulsion to shame her. Before I could stop myself, I blurted, "You started before Father had the chance to say grace." I regretted the words as soon as they left my mouth, but I also knew there was nothing I could say to smooth them over. Thomas's look told me I was a hypocrite, and after he dutifully recited his regular dinner prayer, we ate in silence. I guess

I am disappointed Margaret has no regard for prayer anymore, but how can I blame her with everything she has been through? And it isn't like I am a shining example of faith. Neither is her father.

Their disappointment in me is palpable. And worse, Margaret lied, at least by omission. I'm praying for divine strength to change. I know if I am actually going to be the mom Margaret needs and the wife Thomas used to boast about, the transformation needs to be from the inside out.

A wandering sheep,
Violet

CHAPTER 6

I dreaded the upcoming holiday season. It was the Saturday before Thanksgiving, and I was off because I was working Thanksgiving Day – one of the drawbacks to being one of the younger, less established nurses. I didn't mind, though; it gave me a distraction. This year would mark the third Thanksgiving and Christmas without Johnny, and his absence still stung. *Why did he have to die, God? Are you even out there? I don't understand how people could treat other human beings that cruelly. If you are the Creator, why would you make the kind of people who would go to war?* Joe had told me earlier in the week it was a good thing I didn't understand how people could torture or kill because then I would think that way and be that way. Valid point.

Oh, Joe . . . Thoughts of him held all the other questions at bay, at least temporarily. I was thankful to have his perspective, and he often balanced me out. I worried; he was carefree. I planned; he flew by the seat of his pants. I was a creature of habit; he encouraged me to try new things. In the past two months, we had spent more and more time together, and I was growing increasingly fond of him. He made me laugh and feel alive – feelings that had been absent in my life in the months before I met him.

The power he wields over you is dangerous, a small voice cautioned, quickly followed by a louder, more domineering one. *When was the last time you felt so full of life?* Brushing off the warning, I focused instead on the question as I lay in bed, annoyed I had to get up to use the bathroom. *Probably before the war. If only Johnny would've made it home. If only the last telegram would've brought joyful news instead of news of his death that December day.* I stopped my thoughts before they trailed any further and remembered what Joe had said. *You can't rewind. While you can take time to remember, don't look in the rearview mirror for too long. You don't want to miss the life you have now – you only live once.* A long kiss followed his sage advice, which I readily gave into.

My thoughts returned to the present. Thanksgiving and Christmas were especially rough on Mama. Last year, she had drunk more and cooked less. I swear Father offered to take on additional shifts to avoid her, which infuriated me because I knew she needed someone, but I also understood why he did it. I certainly didn't want to be around her more than I had to; honestly, I didn't think she wanted to be around me either. I couldn't help but wonder if she would rather have Johnny with her than me. *She has been trying recently, you must admit*, the gentle voice reassured me. *But will it last?*

Another reason I dreaded the holiday season was because of the hypocrisy. People's fakeness angered me. It was like a switch flipped and suddenly everyone's lives had to be picture perfect for six weeks straight, as they assumed a façade of joy, peace, and thankfulness. I hated the fake smiles on the advertisements, the forced laughs in the stores – from the grocery store to the department store – and how everyone's answer to,

"How are you?" was obnoxiously chipper. I wanted to scream, "Why the hell can't you tell the truth!?" But of course, that question and that tone were not acceptable. *You do have Joe now, and he completes you. He said it himself: you are his missing puzzle piece.* I wished I could have seen him on my day off, but he had told me earlier that week he was driving south with his brother to visit family for Thanksgiving.

Unable to ignore Nature's call any longer, I reluctantly threw off the covers and started the day. After a long, hot shower, I made my way to the kitchen to find – much to my surprise – a plateful of freshly baked scones on the table. *Mother made scones?* In recent weeks she had been making an effort to prepare breakfast more often, but I couldn't remember the last time she had made my absolute favorite – raspberry chocolate chip scones.

"Good morning, Margaret," Mother greeted me cheerfully.

I glanced skeptically toward my mother's voice, wondering what she wanted.

"Morning, Mama."

She walked over with a skip in her step, two coffee mugs in hand, and sat down. "I know you have the day off, and your father told me you hadn't made plans, at least as of Wednesday."

I recalled Father's questions; I'd been a little taken aback at his uncharacteristic interest. *So that's why he was curious about my weekend plans . . .*

"I thought we could go to the salon today and then go to Rike's and pick out a few things for you for Christmas. What do you say? Want to make today a lady's day?"

Cautiously optimistic, I agreed to both, keenly aware I should not get my hopes up too high, but also desperate for her to be her old self again – to have my mom back. She had, after all, been noticeably different the last two months. So, after smothering two scones with salted butter and her delicious homemade cream, we finished them with coffee and left.

The day was all around marvelous. It was unusually warm for November, the sun shining in a cloudless sky as we made our way to the salon. Light flooded the entryway, and wafts of hairspray filled my nostrils as we checked in. Hoping I would agree to join her, Mother had already booked appointments. They offered us water, coffee, or mimosas. I tensed, wondering what Mother would choose. "Coffee," she said without hesitation. I asked for the same, relieved she did not opt for the mimosa. While not as long as Rita Hayworth's nails, we had ours painted Cherry Red. My hands looked beautiful, and I felt like a million dollars with red fingertips.

After a light lunch, we went to Rike's department store. I picked out a beautiful festive dress for the Christmas Eve church service, and Mama bought a pair of Wohl black peep-toe pumps. After trying a few on a few of the furs, we gawked at the jewelry counter. I tried on a stunning emerald necklace, admiring the gorgeous green stone nestled in a circle of diamonds lying delicately on my neck.

"It looks perfect on you," Mother exclaimed in unison with the salesclerk.

I smiled; then, after glancing at the price tag, I quickly handed it back to the Rike's employee. We both remarked about the necklace's beauty as we headed for the exit, each of us with a bag in hand.

The drive home was enjoyable, and I could tell Mama was trying to connect with me.

"Are you dating?" she inquired, catching me off guard.

I hated to lie to her, especially with how earnest she had been the last few weeks and the sincere effort she had put into the day. In fact, her recent behavior reminded me of my mother from before the war. I decided to tell the truth. "Yes, actually. I have been since September. His name is Joe, and he is remarkably handsome and quite creative." I hoped she wouldn't ask about employment, religious beliefs, politics, or anything else she deemed highly important.

"Oh, really? Thanks for telling me. I'd like to meet him sometime. I'm sure your father would too. Perhaps we can plan a dinner around Christmastime. I can look at the calendar when we get home if you'd like."

"That sounds perfect, Mama," I heard myself say, with a measure of relief, though the thought of the dinner conversation made my stomach churn.

Thanksgiving came and went without any drama. The hospital was relatively quiet, and our family Thanksgiving meal the Friday after was almost like it had been before the war. Despite the potential triggers of the holiday season, Mother did not revert to drinking; she even politely refused wine. I dared to allow myself to think that maybe she truly had turned a corner. Father was quiet, polite, and reserved, complimenting Mother on the effort she'd put into the meal. He seemed more at ease than I'd seen him in some time, no doubt because of Mother's behavior.

The next morning, as soon as I stepped out of bed, a wave a nausea sent me running to the bathroom. I barely made it to the toilet before vomiting. As I rinsed my face with cold water, I went through all the meals I'd eaten the day before. *Mother didn't make anything unusual for Thanksgiving dinner*, I thought, confused about what could have caused my unsettled stomach.

And then, I panicked.

CHAPTER 7

I feigned sickness the rest of the weekend, and every time I used to toilet, I prayed I would see red swirling in the water.

I counted thirty-five days since my last cycle; seven days late was significant.

All I could think of were the recent occasions Joe had forgotten a condom, and we had thrown caution to the wind.

My mind spun. *What have you done? You should've known from the first night he was bad news. What are your parents going to say? Mama is finally back to her usual self, and you are going to ruin it. How will he take care of you with a gardener's salary? Wait — would he even stick around?*

I needed confirmation, and I knew someone at the hospital who would be able to help and do so discreetly.

December 1, 1946

Dear God,

It's me again. Are you listening? Do you see me, even after all I've done?

I read the Bible every day this past week. My mother and grandmother would be so proud of me for cracking it open. I wonder if they know what a mess I've made in my family life these last few years? They would be so ashamed.

I read in the gospels today. In the passage where Jesus says, "How long should I put up with you?" I can't help but wonder if that sentiment is how you feel about me. I hope not, but I wouldn't blame you. I really have been trying. Later in the passage, though, the father in the story says, "I believe. Help my unbelief." I can't describe the encouragement this man's honesty gave me today. I certainly need help overcoming not just my unbelief, but a whole host of other things. Help me overcome the thirst for drink. Help me overcome the anger. My anger. God, I am still angry about Johnny. I don't want to think about that loss right now though because my recent time with Margaret has been a blessing. The time out with her last Saturday was just marvelous. It felt like I had my daughter back. More, I feel like I'm back and participating in the land of the living again. Oh, how I would love to buy that emerald necklace for her. Thomas and I are certainly not on good enough terms for me to ask to spend that kind of money though, even if it was for her. I hope she had an enjoyable time. She seemed to. Most of all, I hope she trusts me and finds it in her heart to love me again. Maybe even like me some day.

I wonder about this boy she is dating. Her description of him sure was shallow. You would think she would lead with other qualities, if he had them. Regardless, meeting him will tell a lot. Help me to be hospitable and loving, even if he doesn't impress.

Oh, and I pray Margaret feels better, as her stomach has been queasy all weekend. She didn't even want chicken broth when I asked at dinner. At least she was able to eat some toast the last two days . . .

No, it can't be. She wouldn't. I am sure it is just a stomach bug. She works at a hospital, after all. Don't be paranoid, Violet, and invent something else to worry about.

That is all for now. Thomas will retire soon, and I hope he will talk with me again tonight.

Violet

CHAPTER 8

I had to wait a few nerve-wracking weeks before I could even take the test, and then another tormenting week after I gave my urine sample to see if the rabbit died or not. The test was ironic and strange – given the rabbit died if new life was detected – but at least it could be done with privacy. I could not risk seeing my doctor; he knew my parents, after all.

My head felt like it was stuck in a dense cloud, and despite holding a dwindling, counterintuitive hope, I knew the test would only confirm my worst fears. Beyond the morning vomiting and feeling unusually tired no matter how much sleep I got, I did my best to smile and act normal. Although no one said anything, whenever I saw my pallid-looking face in the mirror, I felt like the secret was branded onto my skin.

On a Thursday morning I opened my locker and a white, sealed envelope fell out. I grabbed it quickly and ran into a bathroom stall on wobbly legs. My head felt like a spinning globe, and my hands trembled as I opened it. *Pregnancy confirmed.* I dropped the piece of paper like it was on fire, and if I hadn't already been sitting down, I would've fallen because I lost all feeling and strength in my body. I turned around quickly to vomit, more out of fear than nausea; reality came crashing down, and I wanted to disappear. *No. No. No. This isn't happening. What am I going to do?*

I willed myself to work that day. While I desperately needed a distraction, each time I held a newborn baby in the hospital nursery, my stomach lurched with the cold reality. The infants were utterly helpless and completely dependent, yet they had the power to completely turn lives upside down.

You are not ready for a child, Margaret! half of me screamed. The other part of me whispered it would be okay. *What is done is done. You have to accept it and start taking some necessary steps.* The planner in me won over, and by the end of the day, I reasoned I had to tell Joe first. Ideally, he would agree to meet my parents the following week and ask my father for my hand in marriage, so we could have a wedding before I started to show.

Joe and I had plans that Friday night, and I told Mother I would invite him to dinner for the following Saturday. I rehearsed the conversation in my head many times and concluded Joe would make the principled decision. He had told me countless times how much he loved our time together, how I was "the missing puzzle piece" in his life. Surely, he would do nothing less than the honorable thing. Right?

After work, I dressed in Joe's favorite outfit – a black V-neck patterned dress. It was knee length and moved nicely when I walked. Despite the pregnancy, my stomach still looked flat. I left my coat unbuttoned so he could see I was wearing it, and I gave myself a small pep talk before I stepped out of the locker room. *He will do the right thing.* Despite reassuring myself over and over, I had a sickening feeling he was only in the relationship for shallow reasons; he hadn't, after all, ever said anything about *loving* me. I pushed the doubts aside and forced myself to think positively.

As I walked down the steps from the hospital, I saw Joe waiting by the ice cream parlor, our usual meeting place. It was dark, the air unusually warm, and wispy clouds blacked out the stars. Forcing a smile, I greeted him and took his arm as we began walking to the diner.

"How was your day?" I asked, trying to sound normal and upbeat.

"Well, I was sent home early again today because there wasn't enough work. Landscaping is seasonal and weather dependent; when there is no snow, there isn't much work to do in the winter," he replied, agitated.

"It is bound to snow soon. It is December after all," I responded, trying to sound reassuring. "What did you do for the rest of the day?"

"I shot a few photos by the Miami River. We'll see if any of them turn out. I haven't sold any artwork or prints in two months."

The conversation was not off to a great start. *How will he provide for you and this child? You aren't exactly used to a blue collar salary, and Daddy certainly isn't going to give you a stipend each month.* I shook the thoughts away as we arrived at the crowded restaurant. He perked up once we sat down, had food in front of us, and were talking about current events. The smell of his chicken dinner sent my senses into hyperdrive; even the thought of poultry made my stomach churn. I did all I could to focus on my mashed potatoes, rolls, and bland meatloaf.

"*Life* magazine ran a story on Japan and how the country now loves America. Ha! I don't believe their fake news for one second. I wonder if our group would be interested in hearing an update on it once we resume after the new year. I would mention it this weekend, but it is more of an end-of-year party. You're coming, right?" he asked, chewing while he talked.

I hadn't attended the group since early October, and for once I frankly didn't care what they thought about Japan. I was having a hard enough time focusing on what he was saying.

"I have a few things I wanted to share with you," I practically blurted out.

"You sound serious. What is it?" He shifted his weight in his seat, put his fork down, and reached for his beer.

Smiling, I started with the lighter of the two topics. "Well, first, my parents want to meet you."

"Oh," he managed, clearly not thrilled. "I didn't know they even knew about me. I thought we were keeping this casual," he said, his hand motioning from me to him.

My heart sank. *This? Well, that response was not the "I would love to meet them" you were hoping for, was it?*

"*Casual?*" I looked down at my abdomen and whispered, "Joe, I am pregnant."

He stared at me, and then, without a word, took a bit of his breaded chicken breast. *Did he hear me? He is acting as if I told him something about the weather.* After what felt like an hour, I finally spoke up.

"Joe, did you hear me? I am—"

"I heard you," he spat, cutting me off. "Are you sure? Maybe you're just late. Hell, do you know if it's *my* baby?"

His baby?! I was infuriated, and without regard to being in public, I shouted, "How can you even ask that question? Of course I am sure!"

"Be quiet," he snapped with a voice ten decibels lower. He looked around at all the eyes fixated on us, smiling, as if to say, *everything is okay over here.* "Well, I am not ready to be a father. What are you going to do about it? I am sure you can afford the procedure to fix it."

My head spun. *Does he think I am ready to be a mother?! This is not happening. How is he not the man I hoped he would be?* And then reality slapped me across the face. *He was never more than a good-looking boy who could shave. You just thought you could change him.*

Beyond that loaded statement, Joe had never mentioned my social status or anything about me coming from a wealthy family. I had told him about my father's profession, but to suggest what he was suggesting, especially knowing my role as a delivery nurse, was insulting. In that moment, I finally saw him for who he was: a shallow jackass.

"Joe, I was hoping you would, well, take responsibility," I responded, my resolve weakening.

"You were hoping I would be thrilled, and, what, *marry* you by the new year?" he mockingly said. "I think you should at least consider looking into a way to fix the situation."

"It is a *child*, not a situation, Joe," I retorted, finding some strength in my convictions.

"To you maybe." His gaze was mean and piercing. "I'm not hungry, and I told my brother I would be home early tonight."

"Okay."

No part of me believed he needed to be home early. Anger, fear, and regret pulsated through my body. I crossed my arms, hugging myself in an attempt to calm my spiked blood pressure and racing heartbeat. But although I was livid, all I wanted was for him to wrap his arms around me and comfort me that everything would be okay.

"How about we talk about this later? I am just in shock and responding out of emotion." His tone was kinder, almost reassuring.

He stood up, kissed my forehead, and headed for the door. I sat there alone, hands instinctively falling to my belly. *I guess he left the responsibility of the bill to me?* I sat, composing myself for a few minutes. Then, I paid and left.

CHAPTER 9
2015

"I was a complete fool, and even today, I am ashamed of my lack of judgment regarding Joe. He just had this . . . this unexplainable hold on me," I admitted to the young woman sitting with me, as I spun the pendant on my necklace and locked eyes with my distorted reflection in the coffee mug. "I still remember being incredibly angry at him, and I certainly blamed him. But I was equally at fault. After all, I practically threw myself at him, skirt lifted every time we were together. I wanted so badly for him to love me."

We sat in silence for a minute or two, sipping our lukewarm coffees. I twirled the pendant on my necklace a few more times and confessed, "Or rather, I wanted so badly for someone to love *me*."

My eyes met hers as the words left my lips and I felt the weight of the truth lifting from my aging shoulders. Megan smiled at me with understanding and asked if I wanted to take a break. Part of me wanted to go back to my twelve-by-twelve room and keep the rest of my untold story to myself. But a stronger part of me wanted someone to know me, warts and all, so I continued.

"Girls grow up reading storybooks full of fairy tales with princesses, knights, and the bluest of skies. Somehow, foolishly, I thought I could mold him into my handsome prince charming, and we would live happily ever after."

"The quest for fairy tale endings certainly hasn't changed over the decades," Megan gently interjected.

"I suppose it is what sells."

She looked at me with another soft smile and then down at her electronic device.

I excused myself to the single-stall restroom. Staring at my stooped, withered frame in the mirror, I asked aloud, "Well, should you tell her the entire Joe story or not?"

CHAPTER 10

That following Monday, Joe wasn't standing outside the ice cream parlor like usual.

Maybe he is inside? Or maybe he will be at your car with flowers, apologize for his initial reaction, and tell you he will be at your house for dinner in a few days?

He was not inside the parlor or at my car.

A week went by without contact, and I decided to visit his apartment over lunch on Friday. I had only been there once, and it was just so he could pick up a flash for his camera he'd accidently left behind. His unit was one of many in a plain-looking brick apartment complex, which was not well kept. The pavement was cracked badly, and trash littered the outside of the building.

I walked up the stairs to the second floor and approached 2D. After knocking with no answer, I tried to peer in the dirty window, but the blinds were shut. Luckily, his neighbor came out just as I was about to leave.

"Hi, there. My boyfriend lives in 2D. Did you see him this morning by chance? We were supposed to meet earlier, and I haven't heard from him," I inquired, smiling and hoping he would know something.

"I am pretty sure I saw him loading up a truck yesterday. Sorry," he answered apathetically as he locked his door and started to walk away.

A truck!? A truck for what? I wondered, starting to panic. And then delusional, wishful thinking chimed in. *Maybe he was loading things for work or for his brother.*

I hurriedly made my way back to work and considered my options. *Ask Martha. She knows everything, and you need answers.* It was cold, but I was sweating from a mix of panic and frustration. I found Martha near her locker.

"Martha! Thank God you are here," I gasped, out of breath.

"I don't know if I would be thanking an imaginary being, but good to see you too," she chuckled.

I ignored her attempt at humor. "I need to talk to you. In private."

She eyed me knowingly as we walked down the hall and ducked into a single bathroom. I locked the door and turned around to face her, my eyes practically bulging with emotion.

"Let me guess. You just found out?" she asked, a hint of reluctance in her voice.

"Found out? Found out about *what?*" I questioned, the words spilling out.

"Joe told the group on Sunday that he and his brother were moving to Lexington to be closer to the family they have left. I guess his brother really wanted to go. At least that is what he said."

"How could you have not told me earlier this week?" I demanded harshly, channeling my anger with Joe onto her.

"I figured you would've been the first to know, sister. I didn't want to bring it up because I wasn't sure how upset you were about it," she explained gently, moving over to give me a side hug. I believed her. She was never one for personal conversations anyway. "I am sorry he left without talking to you. I guess he didn't think you two were that serious. Even so, what a low move on his part to not tell you," she added, shrugging her shoulders.

Not that serious? I thought to myself, dejected and feeling abandoned. The tears I'd been fighting suddenly started flowing, and I slid to the floor. I didn't want to tell Martha. I didn't want to tell anyone. I wanted to reverse time.

"Please, just leave me alone," I whispered.

Martha gently placed her hand on my shoulder and stood up. "Let me know if you want to talk later."

I hid in my room after work, hoping my parents would forget I existed. *They are going to kill you. Or worse, disown you. Maybe Joe is right — maybe you could look into making this situation go away.* Then, my conscience chimed in, loud and clear. *Don't you dare. You made your decision, and you have to live with the consequences. It will be hard, but the life inside you is not an item to be disposed of, even if possible.*

I aimlessly walked into my bathroom and turned on the shower. I wanted to scream, but I didn't want to draw Mother's attention. I sat in the shower for a long time, letting the hot water hit my back as I hugged myself and cried. *What have I done? God, are you there?* I tried prayer, desperate. *I am sorry. I am so, so sorry. What am I going to do? They pretty much make unwed women give their babies up for adoption; I have seen the anguish on a mother's face who would never hold their baby again because a married couple was adopting the child. But the alternative —* I shuddered — *I can't do that either.*

God, if you are out there, I need a miracle.

⌇

December 23, 1946

Dear God, what are we going to do?

Without conversation or dinner, Margaret retired to her room after arriving home. For several weeks now, she has been on edge, and since Friday, she has been a raging tempest. I was hoping she would tell me Joe had happily accepted our dinner invitation. In fact, I'd wanted to know the week prior, but when I asked Margaret, she told me he had to "look into something." Her vague answer has bothered me ever since.

When I went to check on her and ask if she planned to eat dinner at home, I heard the shower turn on. I murmured a quick prayer and went to make a mug of her favorite hot cocoa. I understood why she didn't want to talk to me. For too long, I'd selfishly retreated inward, sought comfort in the bottle, and had no regard for her emotions or what she was going through. The shower ran for quite some time, and I decided to check on her. I knocked on the bathroom door, concerned, but hopeful the cocoa would perk her up.

I called out to her, "Margaret, sweetie. Are you okay? I made some hot chocolate — your favorite."

Her voice sounded off . . .

⌇

I froze when Mother asked how I was and if I wanted hot chocolate. *No, I don't want hot chocolate. I need a time machine. I don't want to see the look on your face when you learn I am an unwed pregnant woman and that the baby's father took off.* But reason reminded me she would be suspicious if I didn't join her.

"Sure, Mama. I'll be out soon," I responded as calmly as I could, hoping the running water masked my trembling voice.

. . . and coupled with the unusually long shower, I wondered if Joe had broken it off. Why else would she be so upset? The timer went off, and I returned to the kitchen and gathered two mugs, marshmallows, and cinnamon. When another five minutes passed, I started to worry, but rather than reach for Thomas's Baileys, I read Psalm 3, which my mother always used to recite to me when I was fearful: "But you are a shield around me, O Lord. To the Lord I cry aloud, and He answers me . . . From the Lord comes deliverance."

More than anything, I wanted Margaret to feel calm and able to talk to me like she used to. I turned on the lamp in the living room instead of the overhead table light, made sure tissues were in reach on the kitchen counter, and lit one of my many Christmas scented candles. After what seemed like another hour, she finally joined me.

I am proud of myself for how I handled the news. Honestly, I can't take credit — Lord, you helped me react with love and grace. Thomas, on the other hand, was filled with a different spirit . . .

I turned off the shower shortly after Mother knocked on the door and reached for my pajamas and plush robe. After brushing my teeth and sliding on my slippers, I examined myself in the mirror.

Mascara. You need some mascara and lipstick. You look like you've been crying, I chided myself. *You have been crying. You should tell her the truth. She has been much more loving recently, and she may surprise you. Besides, you can't keep it a secret forever. You are already eight weeks along.*

Confused and scared, I decided to see how the conversation went and go from there.

Mama was far more gracious than I thought possible.

Not long after I sat down and had a sip of hot chocolate, fresh tears came. Her reaction was just what I needed. Quietly, she sat with me and gently squeezed my hand, just like she did when I was a little girl.

Her touch reminded me of the third grade. Richard, the class bully, had been held back a year and towered over everyone in the class. During inside recess, the teacher stepped out just long enough for him to start picking on Charles, a sweet boy who had trouble hearing. Other people were cheering Richard on as he taunted Charles, pushing him up against the wall. Charles stood there helpless, not fighting back. I stepped in.

"Back off, Richard. You don't have to be so mean all the time." I looked up at him, my head barely reaching his chin.

"Well, if it isn't little miss Margaret. Well, I am certainly not going to punch a *girl*," he jeered. "But I can tickle torture you!"

He then picked me up like a rag doll. I kicked and squealed, and when he started tickling me, I squirmed and fought back as hard as I could. Finally, as the teacher walked back into the classroom, I resorted to my last means of defense: I bit him. We were both sent to the principal's office, and while I evaded any real discipline, I was sent home because I needed to change my underpants. Mama had been nothing but gracious and loving that day. I remember her holding my hand and squeezing it when she picked me up, tears of embarrassment streaming down my cheeks. She brought me a change of clothes and took me out for ice cream. Beyond telling me she was proud of me for standing up for Charles, nothing more was said. She knew just what I needed.

This time, however, I couldn't just change my clothes and not be pregnant anymore. I stood up, grabbed the tissue box, and sat back down in the chair.

"I'm pregnant, Mama," I confessed as we sat at the table, hands now interlocked.

She moved her chair over and put her arm around me. Tears of shame, regret, and dread came pouring out. I grabbed tissue after tissue, throwing the used ones on the floor until there was a mountain of white beside my feet. "It is going to be okay, sweetie," she whispered. "We will figure this out together. Thanks for telling me."

". . . And Joe left," I blubbered. "I wasn't his missing puzzle piece after all. He was a manipulative liar." My voice trembled with indignation.

A dark voice sneered to my heart, *He left you. Abandoned you. You weren't special to him, and he never really wanted you. How would anyone want you — damaged goods — now?*

Mama interrupted my thoughts, handing me another tissue. "Do you want to talk some more, or would you rather go to bed? I will stay up all night if you want, but I just wanted to ask."

I opted for bed. Exhausted mentally and physically, I fell into a fitful sleep.

. . . When I first told him, he asked, dumbfounded, "She's what?"

His fists clenched, and his face contorted with outrage. Trying to stay calm and collected, I told him we would eventually need to discuss next steps. I certainly didn't want to that night, but knowing his desire for control, I thought it best to mention the need to plan. I tried to plant the idea of finding a relative to adopt the baby so Margaret could still see the child, but he adamantly was against the idea.

I remember Thomas's response verbatim. "A relative? And let everyone know about the shame she has brought on herself and us? No." He fought to regain his composure, a stoic look replacing the red, emotional face. "Once Margaret starts to show, we will send her to my sister's lake house up in Michigan and tell others Billy needed her help. We will find a family up north, and it will be a closed adoption."

Shame – I know a thing or two about that. Granted, Margaret was in the wrong, but I didn't want to heap burning coals of shame on her head. He voiced his decision as if it were final and nonnegotiable.

I didn't challenge his plan – yet. He needs time to calm down, and hopefully, his heart will soften to the idea of letting Margaret's child, and our first grandchild, stay in the family.

With a heavy heart,

Violet

CHAPTER 11
December 25, 1946

I woke up frantic, with intense back and abdominal pain. Despite the chill in the air, I was soaked in sweat. After I pushed the covers off me and clicked on the lamp beside the bed, I saw my stained nightgown.

Rather than answering my prayer with the requested miracle, God had cursed another December for me; I would forever hate Christmas Day. While the whole world celebrated the birth of their so-called Savior, I mourned the loss of my child.

The doctor told me the D&C procedure would spare me the physical trauma of a natural miscarriage. And even though the pregnancy wasn't planned, the idea of having my baby suctioned from my womb was almost unbearable. I fought the instinctive bond to the life removed from me, and to survive, I retreated to an apathetic, zombie-like state, telling both myself and my mother I was fine.

While my father gave me lip service, likely because Mother told him too, it was obvious he was relieved that his disappointment in me wouldn't leave our house's four walls. At the same time, my relationship with Mother grew complicated. She often asked if I wanted to talk. I didn't want to. She began reading Grandma's well-thumbed blue-leather King James Bible each morning. The sight of the book angered me. All of a sudden, she started to mention prayer outside of mealtimes, talking about Jesus like he was some friend who lived down the street. For me, the thought of talking to a crutch was absurd; if Jesus was real, he was cruel. Mother's newfound faith agitated me, and even though she tried, I continued to reject her invitations to spend time together. The gap between us grew wider.

CHAPTER 12
2015

***

I looked up from my coffee mug, the remaining coffee cold now, and saw tears in Megan's eyes. She reached for her oversized bag and pulled out a small pack of tissues.

"I am so sorry," she whispered. "I can't imagine your heartache or how long it would take to heal from such a loss."

"Thanks. I am over it now," I lied.

As for healing, the gaping wound had gone almost sixty-nine years without treatment. All those decades ago, I'd just wanted to forget and move on. It seemed easier to bury the memories of Joe and the pain of that Christmas morning than to mourn the loss. I lived in a fog of grief for months. To this day, the memory surfaced unwittingly whenever I saw a young babe, but I'd become an expert at quickly brushing the distressing thoughts under the proverbial rug.

"A friend of mine experienced a similar loss, and she always said it was helpful for her to think of herself as a mother to a child with wings," Megan added, reaching for my hand. "She wears a necklace engraved with a mountain top and the words, 'The God on the mountain is the same God in the valley.'"

Her friend's words resonated deeply, and a flicker of hope sparked in my heart. *I am not sure if the God of the mountains wants anything to do with my valleys, but I like the idea of being a mother to a child with wings.*

"You really think the baby would be in a better place?" my voice pleaded.

A brief silence ensued, the sounds of the other café patrons blurring into white noise.

Before she could answer, I added, "Honestly, I've brushed the memories and pain aside since it happened. My father was extremely disappointed and angry with me then, and I felt like a failure in many ways. The thoughts bring too much pain and too much anger," I admitted aloud for the first time, spinning the gold pearl ring.

Megan squeezed my hand. "First off, yes, I believe your unborn child is in heaven. The God I know has a Father's heart, and I cannot imagine any other outcome consistent with His character. And thankfully, grace means that you work *from* acceptance, not toward it."

Grace? Ha. You certainly are past the point of deserving grace . . . I shook my head as if to dismiss the thought.

"Would you be opposed to continuing with your story? If so, I completely understand."

You can do this, sweetie, I heard my mother's voice encourage me. "No, it's okay. I'll continue."

CHAPTER 13
1948

I stared at myself in the full-length mirror. My makeup was perfect, my hair beautiful, and the delicate, two-layered veil framed my face well. Like many other dresses, mine was inspired by Princess Elizabeth's gown from the previous year. I could not pretend to be as beautiful or dignified as she, but the satin dress looked stunning and the breeze that Saturday in May made the sleeves bearable. The veil's applique matched the detailing on the dress, and I knew Mama would soon wrap her saltwater pearls around my neck to finish off the look.

I felt like a hypocrite wearing white. But Edward loved me despite my stained history, and when I'd confessed to him my hesitance to wear white, he told me none of it mattered to him. We'd met the previous summer. My father knew Edward through the hospital, and while he was not a physician, he was Father's new, preferred pharmaceutical representative. To discuss business in a less formal session – but mainly to introduce us – my parents had invited him over for dinner. Edward was a few years older than me, well established, from a wealthy, connected family, and religious. In short, my parents approved

– especially my father. And a part of me wanted to please my dad and be back in his good graces.

In recent months, I'd gone through the proper steps to join the Catholic church for Edward, so we could be married in his family's parish, something extremely important to his mother. In truth, Edward was a prince in those early years, and his family seemed perfect. While I didn't really know his brother, William, because he lived out of state, I adored his younger sister, Shirley. His parents, Robert and Helen, were also delightful; his mother welcomed me like I was her own daughter, and his father was a kind, older man with gray-streaked receding hair, half-rimmed glasses, and deep-rooted convictions on how life should operate. As far as I could tell, his views didn't conflict with any of mine, but I had the feeling not to voice any, should they form.

Although I didn't feel the same burning passion for Edward as I had for Joe, he was handsome enough, sensible, and held a respectable position. And, unlike Joe, he loved me, and his family seemed to also. I would've been a fool to turn down his proposal. Moreover, he helped me pick up the broken pieces in my life and accepted me despite my scarlet letter.

So, as I made my final preparations for my "big day," I was full of hope for the future that lay ahead with Edward.

My mother knocked on the door to the bathroom. "Margaret, dear. Are you okay?"

I opened the door and replied with a smile, "Yes, of course. I was just soaking in the day."

Motioning for me to turn around, Mama held up her pearls. "I love you, dear. You look stunning. I hope today is just perfect for you."

Our relationship since the miscarriage had been cordial at best, despite her attempts to love me. Guilt was my constant companion when I was around her, and although she tried hard to spend time with me, any mention of prayer, blessing or the like annoyed me and made me push away from her. I'd met Edward at the perfect time. He gave me a reason to get out of the house, and I all but fell into Edward's mother's welcoming arms. Helen was a devout Catholic, but she was not super religious like my mother and certainly didn't impose her beliefs on me by bringing it into regular conversation.

After Mother hugged me, she opened the door to welcome Father into the room.

"You look beautiful, Margaret," Father told me, eyes moist.

I couldn't believe he was emotional; perhaps he was remembering me as his little girl. We'd hardly spoken for four months after that Christmas, and when we did, he couldn't mask the disdain in his voice. Despite my repeated apologies, he never extended a hand of forgiveness, and while we were cordial around each other in recent months, our relationship was shallow, our conversations never going any deeper than work or the weather. I was happy to marry Edward, and even more thrilled to move out from under my parents' stifling roof.

"Thanks, Father," I said, forcing a smile. I gave him a side hug and motioned toward the door, as we heard the first few cords of Mendelssohn's "Wedding March."

As part of our wedding gift, Edward's parents funded our honeymoon to Atlantic City, New Jersey, including our stay at the

Marlborough Blenheim. The hotel was grand, and I felt like a celebrity staying there.

Overall, the honeymoon was enjoyable. The city glittered with excitement and grandeur, complemented by pleasant weather and palatable cuisine. We walked along the beaches, and although it was too cold to enjoy the water, I let my toes feel the still-icy Atlantic. We even went to a nightclub one night, at my request. I enjoyed the scene, but Edward was uncomfortable, even with a Jack Daniel's in hand. He tried not to show it for my sake, but I could tell he wanted to retreat to our suite. I, on the other hand, wanted to avoid our suite.

Unlike me, Edward was a good Catholic and waited until our wedding night. I completely captivated him, creating in him a hunger he knew nothing about. He was eager. I pretended to be. He couldn't get enough of me. I had to think of Joe to convince Edward I wanted him in the same way. Regardless if we lacked a spark or not, I had a duty to him, and I would fulfill my role in exchange for his love, financial security, and a new family. I just hoped he would love me if I miscarried again, as I knew he wanted children. I prayed to any god listening that I would conceive without difficulty and carry a child full term.

Two weeks after our wedding, Edward and I returned from Atlantic City and moved into our new, three-bedroom two-story home, complete with an attached one-car garage. Robert and Helen had surprised us before the wedding with a large sum of money, enough to pay in-full for a new house. It came with two conditions. First, we live within a ten-minute walk, and second, we join them every Sunday for lunch. With tears in Helen's and my eyes and hugs between us all, we happily accepted.

Eddy and I fell into a comfortable norm as a married couple. After furnishing and decorating our home, we spent our evenings and the weekends playing Scrabble, listening to the Hallmark Playhouse, going to the movies, or visiting our respective parents' homes. We agreed to visit my parents monthly and joked I would need to have a glass of wine beforehand to calm my nerves.

Upon arrival, Father would attempt to hug me like he used to, to which I either stiffened or returned with a side hug. Conversation with him was either superficial or work related. After exhausting the topics of the weather and current events, he always reverted to medicine. For weeks Father raved about the potential to win the battle against polio, relaying the details of the recent vaccine test a laboratory researcher had performed on himself and his assistant. My mother was hospitable, although she seemed more tired each time we visited. With a twinge of guilt, I wondered if it was because of the strain in our relationship.

Thankfully, outside of a prayer before supper, God was rarely a topic of conversation. Still, I was certain she was judging me whenever she mentioned church attendance or her involvement in a ladies' Bible study. Aware of my sensitivity to the topic, Edward would graciously pivot to a new topic whenever Mother mentioned anything religious.

Needless to say, I much preferred our time with Robert, Helen, and Shirley. With them, I finally felt like I belonged to a normal family. Conversation flowed easily and was always lighthearted. Robert and Edward's Sunday drinking habits, however, were a painful reminder of my mother, even though they remained in control, at least for the most part, and they were not drinking to drown out their sorrow. While Edward was sensible in most ways, he often had one too many whiskeys with his father when they talked business. His tongue loosened, his language became more colorful, and he sometimes showed a mean streak that surprised me. Perhaps that is why one of the two house-buying conditions involved being within walking distance! Regardless, the time together was fun, Shirley and I grew close, and the meals were always delicious. Helen was a wonderful cook, and I longed for a relationship like Shirley had with her. It was the kind of mother–daughter connection I hadn't had my entire adult life; Helen could answer Shirley without her even finishing the question, they read each other's facial expressions with ease, and they could gossip about anything because their lives were so interconnected. I wanted nothing more than to win Helen's favor and earn her love.

August 14, 1948

Hi. It has been quite some time since I opened this notebook. So much has happened.

Margaret and Edward visited today and a whole host of memories flooded back. And — to make things worse — while Thomas talked easily with Edward, I knew they only accepted my invitation because she felt obligated. I don't blame her; I know Margaret is still angry over Thomas's reaction to her pregnancy. It all but severed their relationship, and while I loved her through the trauma, the miscarriage broke her. It pains me to be reminded of the past, when she rejected every invitation to talk or spend time together, rolled her eyes when I told her I would pray for her, and how her countenance noticeably changed whenever she saw my mother's Bible or if I even mentioned a lady friend from church.

And while I am thankful she found someone, I still just don't know about Edward. After she met him, I rarely saw her, and while polite, he was painfully superficial – and he still is. More, I am disappointed she joined the Catholic church just to please him . . . or perhaps Helen . . . I am not 100 percent sure who cares more. I would bet Helen. Regardless, faith – the Catholic faith included – means nothing to her; how do they not see that? Perhaps they don't really care as long as she goes through the proper steps?

I know Thomas was initially thrilled with their relationship. After all, Edward was – and still is – well established, stable, and religious. In recent months, however, Thomas's heart softened, and it was as if scales fell from his eyes because even he sees it now. In regard to our daughter, he is concerned Edward's demeanor is more prideful than confident. However, the damage done to their relationship makes it impossible for him to tell Margaret – or rather, it makes it improbable she would listen.

And now, here I am weeping again for my darling daughter; she is like an injured bird who refuses help. I suppose I can't blame her for that either. In less than four years, Margaret has lost her brother to the sea, her mother – me – to the bottle – at least for a period of time – the relationship she had with her father to a relationship she regretted, and a baby. And soon I will have to add even more sorrow to the mix when I tell her that she will lose me to the cancer my drinking habit has likely caused.

Since her wedding, we've tried to make each visit as welcoming as we could, but Margaret's responses to any question have been, well, curt. Edward does a nice job of engaging in small talk, and so we often talk about work, sports, the weather or some major event. Any attempt to talk about what we were learning at church is politely, but immediately, shut down. For heaven's sake, Margaret visibly squirms if my truthful answer to any question includes the words "church" or "Bible study."

After they left, I asked Thomas again when we should tell Margaret and Edward about my diagnosis. I started off strong in my resolve to reach a decision on the "when," but that strength is certainly not deep-rooted. Every time I feel a shred of confidence or faith, worry, discouragement and despair fight viciously to control my thoughts. Like now.

I have cancer. There it is, in black and white.

Thomas had suspected something was wrong before the wedding, but we didn't want to bring any clouds over Margaret's big day. She deserved to have a smooth, joy-filled, perfect wedding. And, while Thomas wanted me to be seen, even he hadn't anticipated the diagnosis. After a variety of tests performed while the newlyweds were in New Jersey, doctors confirmed our worst fears. And here we are in August, and I can't continue to ignore my deteriorating physical health or live in a state of denial.

To my question, Thomas put an arm around me and lovingly answered: "I want you to undergo a few more tests and get a second opinion. We want to give her an accurate diagnosis and timeline. Regardless of the results, perhaps we should wait till after Labor Day. You know how much Margaret is looking forward to that weekend."

While my prayers for him to soften were answered before the wedding, the cancer, ironically, was the catalyst that changed our marriage for the better. We received the initial test results on a Wednesday, and at first, Thomas treated me like a patient or business partner. I didn't want to be treated so stoically, but I held my tongue and tried to see the situation from his eyes. The following Sunday, I heard him screaming. I hurried outside, and by the time I reached him, he was on his knees, head in his hands, weeping. I knelt down beside him and placed my hand on his back. We sat in silence for a long time, until I finally asked if he wanted anything to eat, and he nodded yes. As we walked toward the ranch house we called home, he grabbed my hand. The conversation that followed was raw, difficult, humbling, and much needed. It was the first of many, with each one healing our relationship a little more.

I desperately want to have an authentic conversation with Margaret. Ashamedly, I have yet to apologize to her fully . . . although part of the reason is because she refuses to meet with me one-on-one. When we finally do talk, I pray my confession breathes life into our relationship for my remaining time on earth.

Oh goodness. Lord, I need help. Give me strength for another day.

Violet

CHAPTER 14

Labor Day weekend finally arrived. I was so grateful Edward and I had the weekend off; I'd offered to work Independence Day, affording us the Labor Day weekend holiday. Our green Ford station wagon with wood side paneling was packed to the brim. While I would likely only wear half of what I'd packed, I wanted options. Edward just smiled as he loaded them.

"You're just excited about seeing me in my new strapless swimsuit!" I said in jest, gently pushing his shoulder as he lifted the suitcase off the hardwood floor and headed out to the car.

"You better believe it! We do have about twenty minutes if you want to try it on for me again," he teased with a wink.

Our marriage strengthened that summer more than I thought possible. At some point, I finally understood that the desire Joe and I shared had been only lust. Nothing more. Accepting that truth was freeing, allowing me to embrace Edward for the man he was – hardworking, fun, and attentive. The summer was also educational. Edward liked to sleep on the side of the bed closest to the bedroom door, which was something I had to adjust to, as I preferred being on the side closest to the bathroom. Edward was an early riser, while I preferred to sleep in; his never-failing morning gas, however, made me quickly retreat to the kitchen to start the coffee pot! He also had quite a temper, a characteristic I hadn't seen much of while dating, and alcohol certainly fueled the flame. Unlike my father, who probably believed me naive, Edward never physically harmed me. He did, however, have a harsh tongue and considered himself infallible. After any argument or thoughtless comment, he would act like nothing had happened. Accustomed to such a pattern of behavior, I essentially held the rug up for him to brush things under – just as my mother always had. *Until recently. She now wants to talk . . . if you would just give her a chance, that is.* I pushed the thought aside. "There is nothing to talk about," I mumbled under my breath, reassuring myself it was best not to resurrect uncomfortable, although festering, topics. Instead, I focused on the highly anticipated weekend ahead with my new family.

"Did you grab all the snacks for the drive? I could really use some peanuts. I told Mom we would meet them at ten o'clock," Edward called down the stairs, using the bathroom one last time.

"Yes, dear. I am ready," I replied, as I put on my white-framed sunglasses and wide-brimmed hat.

"Wonderful! Let's go!" he said, opening up the front door for me.

The drive to Torch Lake House was smooth and enjoyable. I was thankful for the extended one-on-one time together, and with Robert and Helen's car ahead of us, we didn't have to worry about directions once we left the boulevard. I had joined the family the previous summer, which is when I'd met his brother and a few extended family members. William was handsome, humorous, and, unintentionally, a magnet for attention because of his skill in telling stories. The weekend had also included an annual drinking contest between Edward and William, boating, and relaxation. It truly had been a memorable, merry time. I especially enjoyed the mornings with Helen, when we would casually sip our coffee and talk about the latest family or neighborhood gossip. She made me feel like a cherished daughter, something that had been largely absent at various points during my adult years.

"I am excited for some cinnamon bread and jalapeno poppers! And some daytime drinking on the boat," Edward interrupted my trip down memory lane.

"Same." I was most excited to soak in a little more sun and have the extended family time.

"Oh, did I tell you William is bringing a lady friend?"

"Your mother mentioned it a few days ago." I inwardly rolled my eyes. Helen was so eager to meet the girl, but I selfishly hoped the new guest wouldn't take away from my time with her.

"I have to win the shot competition tonight. William's won it the last three years. It is my turn!" He hit the steering wheel, smiling but serious.

Ever since the family had been going to the lake, the first night had always included a competition to see who could take the most shots before sitting down, with the winner taking fifty dollars from the loser's wallet. Beyond accomplishing his goal to drink William under the table, I asked him to hold off at least till four o'clock the rest of the weekend. He laughed and agreed, although I doubted his sincerity.

We pulled into the shaded gravel driveway shortly before dinnertime. Helen hurried into the house to begin preparing the meal. Despite my offer to help, she told me to rest and unpack. While Edward said he liked my cooking, it was nothing compared to Helen's, and I think she still considered me more of a hindrance than a help in the kitchen.

Shirley and I opened all the windows, organized our respective closets for the long weekend stay, and rushed outside to tan in the day's waning sun. Edward and Robert joined us outside, sat down in the shade, and lit cigars.

After the pork chop dinner, a few family members and local friends arrived with desserts to share, filling the kitchen counter with everything from bread pudding, molasses cookies, and pecan pie to pineapple upside-down cakes and chiffon cake. While I wanted to try a bite of everything, I only indulged in one molasses cookie. I wanted to feel amazing in my new two-piece swimsuit the next day.

Nibbling on my cookie, I heard William's distinct laugh and introductions being made. I quickly finished my dessert, slightly annoyed that I didn't get to really enjoy the last half of it, and walked out to the back porch to meet his girlfriend.

"Shirley, meet Ruth. Ruth, Shirley," I heard William say.

I felt Edward's arm slink around my shoulders. "She seems sweet. Did you meet her yet?" he asked.

I noticed the shot glasses in his hand, and then met his eyes and answered him. "No, I just came out." She was easy to spot in the crowd, with her simple but striking beauty. Her blue eyes were level with mine, her skin golden from the summer sun, and a thin white headband held back her short, curly, blonde hair. A modest, knee-length white and pink checkered dress with a Peter Pan collar hugged her slim figure.

"Hi, I'm Ruth. You must be Margaret," she said with a perfect smile.

"Yes, nice to meet you," I responded, starting to extend my hand when she hugged me and told me how nice it was to meet me too.

I was slightly taken aback. I didn't like strangers hugging me, and she was just a little too bubbly for my liking. She reminded me of . . . *me*, from before. Before Johnny died. Before Mama drank. Before Joe. Before the miscarriage.

"Ruth, dear, would you like some dessert?" Helen asked excitedly, gesturing toward the kitchen.

"I would love to try one of each!" Ruth responded, and after saying a quick goodbye, she practically skipped to the kitchen.

One of each? Well, at least I will look better in a swimsuit tomorrow, I thought, not sure why I suddenly felt the need to compare. *Helen called her "dear" already? Uh oh.* I hoped my expression didn't give away my agitation.

The aromas of cinnamon bread and freshly brewed coffee wafted through our open window the following morning. As newlyweds, Edward and I received the nicest bedroom in the house. It was painted a soft blue, had ornate rugs covering the dark hardwood floors, and two twin beds were pushed together.

The clock read ten till seven. I rolled onto my back and reached my legs and arms toward the ends of the bed to get a good stretch. Lying next to me, facing the wall, Edward's soft, steady breathing signaled he was not yet stirring. I gently touched his back, and he rolled over.

"Good morning. How did you sleep?" I asked, brushing some hair out of my face and pulling the sheet up to my shoulders. After meeting Ruth, I'd spent a brief amount of time with Shirley and Aunt Marty before calling it an early night; I was sick of hearing how great Ruth was and how she fit William perfectly. Eddy was talking to a cousin when I found him, so I just kissed him and told him goodnight.

"Fine," he responded, not his usual morning self.

"What's wrong? Do you have a headache from too many drinks last night?" I smirked.

Not answering my question, Eddy responded, "I don't get why William wouldn't take shots with me. I mean, he just hugged me, handed me a fifty, and said, 'Not this year, brother.'"

"I'm not sure. Maybe he was tired from the drive?" I sat up and rolled my head from one side to the other. "I am going to get some coffee. Want to join?"

"You go and hang out with Mom. I know you loved your morning time with her last year. As for William, I don't know. He seemed different somehow. Anyway, just because he didn't drink with me doesn't mean I didn't have one too many! Bring me up some coffee when you're done with your uptown gossip."

"Will do, dear."

After giving him a quick kiss and putting on my robe, I made my way downstairs. Much to my chagrin, Helen and Ruth were already halfway through a thick piece of cinnamon bread.

"Good morning, Margaret!" Ruth greeted me with an overly chipper voice for this early hour.

I waved and feigned a yawn.

"Well, good morning, Maggie dear," Helen said. "There is cinnamon bread on the counter, fresh brewed coffee, and Ruth made brioche, which should be ready soon. Come sit with us."

Of course she bakes, I thought to myself.

"I actually told Edward I would bring him up a piece of bread and some coffee," I lied. "Thanks though."

Pangs of jealousy pierced my heart. *Morning time was sacred last year. How could Helen spend it with Ruth?* As I approached our bedroom door, I forced myself to think differently. *Don't be a child. She is the shiny new thing in the family. The attention will fade.*

I quietly stepped into the room and closed the door. Edward had fallen back asleep already and was snoring, so I sat alone at the small table and chairs in front of the window. The view was beautiful. I would've enjoyed it immensely, coupled with my warm coffee and bread, if not for the nagging question in my head: *are you sure that attention will fade?*

I removed my robe and slid back in bed. I needed something else to think about, and I knew Edward wouldn't be distracted by anything else in the world after I woke him and he realized I was lying naked next to him.

The drive back to Dayton that Monday was long. Edward focused on the road as rain pelted the windshield and windows; he hated talking when driving during any sort of inclement weather, and I was sure he had a headache from the whiskey consumption the night before.

My thoughts replayed the events of the weekend. For the most part, it had been enjoyable. The weather was beautiful and the time on the boat with Edward was perfect. On the last full day, the gentlemen enjoyed a round of golf while all the ladies – except Helen and Ruth – went horseback riding. Helen and Ruth decided to stay back to prepare the final dinner. I pushed aside the slight irritation and used the time to bond with Shirley.

Thankfully, on both Sunday and Monday morning, Ruth sat outside reading a book, allowing Helen and I our precious one-on-on time. Shirley even woke up early on Sunday and spent it with us. Much to my annoyance, they both gushed about how wonderful Ruth was, and I tried discreetly to redirect the conversation whenever her name surfaced.

As we continued motoring down the boulevard, I could tell Edward was still irked. *Is it because of William?* I wondered. Besides a drink at dinner and one in the evening, William had drunk only water. He was still as fun and comical as ever, but Edward seemed to feel a pang of rejection every time William denied his offers of whiskey. In the evenings, to calm Edward's irritation and soften his language toward me, I invited him to bed, which he always accepted.

The rain slowed as we neared home, and much to my surprise, Edward started talking. "Does he think he is better than me now?" he asked. Before I could reply, he continued, "I mean, he wouldn't take shots with me. He stayed sober the whole time, and when I would hand him another drink, he would just smile and say no. I swear that when I would just put the glass in his hand, it ended up in one of the bushes." He shook his head.

"I am not sure," I started. "Did you ever ask him why?"

"I finally did on the back nine," he practically growled, agitated.

"And?"

"He's turned into a religious quack!" Edward answered, throwing his arms into the air and off the thin black steering wheel for a moment.

I sat there pondering his explanation. *Well, we attend mass regularly, and I wouldn't call us "religious quacks."*

"He stopped going to a Catholic church too. Why? Because of his girlfriend. Her family is Protestant, and I guess he now attends with *them.*"

A smug sense of victory washed over me. *Well, Helen isn't going to like William attending a Protestant church, is she? Ruth may not be a saint after all . . .*

"Give it some time. The relationship may not even last," I said softly, reaching out and resting my hand gently on his thigh.

"We are almost home." His wanting eyes locked with mine, and he reached out his finger and placed it on my lips. "Hold that thought."

I actually was not thinking about that, I thought, even though I smiled back at him. My mind snapped back to the revelation about Ruth and William. *Perfect! Once Helen knows that Ruth is to blame for William's rejection of the Catholic church, her opinion of "dear" Ruth will certainly change. And . . . I guess it wouldn't hurt if we could get pregnant.* I smiled, earnestly this time, as we pulled into our driveway.

CHAPTER 15

Mother invited us over the next Saturday, but we postponed till the following weekend because I had to work. As the clock's arms passed four o'clock, a familiar sense of dread set in. Each meeting with them seemed more strained than the one before. I hated being in the same room as Father, and while my relationship with Mother was amicable, I increasingly felt like Helen was more of a mother than my own. *That comparison is harsh, don't you think? You have to let go of your anger toward her. How many times has she apologized? She only wants to talk because she cares about you. And shouldn't you be happy for her faith? It has transformed her for the better. Who knows? Maybe that faith of hers has something to it.* I knew those thoughts held a grain of truth, but my mind's tune quickly changed. *You have good reason to still be angry at both her and Father. She messed up. She always favored Johnny anyway, so of course she wasn't going to care about you when he died. As for her recent change, it won't last. And Father, even if he seems a little different, he was ready to send you packing when you needed him most.*

"Are you ready to leave?" Edward asked, interrupting my internal chatter.

"I guess."

"Come on. It has been a few weeks, and at least it's a dinner you don't have to cook," he coaxed.

"True. And for that reason alone, I will go," I replied, taking his arm.

We drove the few miles to their house and arrived promptly at five o'clock. I would help Mother with any last-minute needs, Father would offer Edward a drink and start talking about the latest medical news, and dinner would be served at five thirty, just like it always had been growing up.

As soon as we got out of the car, however, something felt off. The garden was slightly overgrown, there were more weeds creeping up the pathway than I could count, and Mother's seasonal door decor was not hanging on the walnut double-front doors. *Unusual.* The living room was also not put together like normal and there were no fresh cut flowers on the table. *I wonder if Mama wasn't feeling good this past week? She didn't mention anything when we talked on Thursday.* And then, as soon as we entered the living room, I saw both Father and Mother already seated, holding hands, waiting for us. *Okay, what is going on?*

"Good evening, you two. Please sit down. There is something we want to tell you before we have dinner," Father said. His voice was thick but gentle.

We sat.

"Your mother and I have something very difficult to tell you both," he said, looking at my mother, his eyes starting to moisten.

"I have cancer, sweetie," Mother said, looking straight at me, her eyes filling up with tears.

I stared at her. Then at my father, and then back at her. Edward reached for my hand. *No. The universe cannot be so cruel to one person. This is a nightmare, and I just need to wake up.*

Father started talking again, this time about the type of cancer, and I felt like I was listening to him underwater. He continued on about the variety of tests she had undergone, and how they both decided to forgo any existing treatments because the time she had left was short, and she didn't want to spend her last months in a hospital. And then it clicked: they had known for weeks, maybe months, and hadn't told me.

"You've already gone through all those tests? How long have you known?" I asked. My angry tone shocked even me.

"Well, dear, we didn't want to ruin your last summer or . . ." Father started to reply.

"How long have you known?" I screamed, hitting the table with my fist. A wave of pain pulsed through me, but I didn't care.

"We realized something was wrong in May, but we didn't want to darken your wedding day. We found out it was cancer while you were on your honeymoon, and we received the results from the last set of tests four weeks ago. We decided to wait till after your Labor Day plans to tell you," Mother said calmly. She was noticeably sad, but her demeanor demonstrated a strange peace.

"And you thought it was a good idea to delay telling us what was going on?" I shot back, my voice still raised.

"We wanted . . ." Father started.

"I don't care what you wanted, Father," I said flatly, never breaking eye contact with Mama. The temperature of my anger reached boiling point. *If it wasn't for you, Father, we would've spent more time together over the last year.* As if reading my thoughts, Edward placed a consoling hand on my shoulder.

"Darling, our decision was from a place of love. We wanted to be sure about my diagnosis before we told you. I understand why you are angry now, but hopefully you can understand our timing," she said, standing and starting to walk toward me.

I collapsed in her arms. Her body was noticeably frail, but she held me tightly. She gently combed through my hair with her fingers, and like she did when I was scared as a child, she started reciting Psalm 23. "The Lord is my Shepherd . . ."

September 18, 1948

We told Margaret and Edward tonight. I wanted to transfer strength to her and somehow absorb her sorrow and pain. While I've made peace with my poor choices after Johnny died, regret sure has a way of rearing its ugly head, reminding me of the lost time with my precious daughter and the irreparable damage it has had on our relationship.

Edward and Margaret left without eating. I sent them home with food, hoping it would at least be reheated the next day. The night couldn't have gone any better, I suppose. I just pray Margaret eventually releases her anger, forgives me, and reaches a point of acceptance without self-sabotage.

After they left, I reiterated to Thomas the need for him to forgive Margaret fully, and I practically pleaded with him to also seek her forgiveness for how he treated her. Oh Lord, if he doesn't, he will lose her after I am gone. He won't admit it, but I know he still harbors bitterness toward Margaret . . . if he doesn't rid himself of it and offer heartfelt forgiveness, I just know she will never allow herself to get close to him again.

His response was at least encouraging: "I will do my best, and I will do it for you, my beautiful Violet."

While the cancer is killing my body, I am grateful it has breathed new life into our marriage. Since finding out, we have worked through years of unaddressed anger, bitterness, hurt, and resentment. Many conversations have ended in tears, but my have they been a healing balm to our still-open wounds. And, while he still rejects it personally, I'm thankful we have at least been able to talk about faith without him shutting the topic down.

I pray for his heart, oh Lord, and I pray I am able to have the same open conversations with Margaret.

Violet

I was in a daze after hearing Mama's news. Edward and I drove home in silence. When he asked if I wanted anything to drink, I simply shook my head. I retreated to our bedroom and curled up in a fetal position on top of the embroidered bedspread.

How could you be so cruel? I asked God. *She even has been living a "life of faith," or whatever she calls it.* I increasingly doubted the existence of a supposedly all-loving God who cared about His children. *How could he care about you after everything you've done?* I thought to myself, tears starting to dampen my pillowcase. *Please, don't take Mama. I know she wasn't perfect, but please don't punish her like this.* I sobbed for all I had lost over the years.

Edward joined me a while later. He gently touched my shoulder and asked if I wanted to change or at least lie under the covers. While I didn't want to get up, I needed to use the restroom, and it would feel good to slip into my nightgown. And there it was: evidence of another failed month. Three months, and no news to share.

"Well, this day can't get any worse," I mumbled to myself, as I searched for a sanitary napkin.

My puffy eyes couldn't cry anymore. *What is wrong with me? I certainly hope I have the chance to tell Mama I am pregnant before she's gone*, I thought as I left the bathroom and climbed into bed with a desperate desire to conceive.

CHAPTER 16

2015

"For years, I blamed my father for my choice to not spend time with my mother." I averted my eyes, embarrassed at the admission.

"I am sure anyone would look for someone else to blame under those tragic circumstances."

I winced at the painful reminder of my past and stared blankly out the window. In the reflection, I saw my younger, attractive self. Nicely dressed, hair immaculate, married to a respectable, handsome man with a good income. Any onlooker would've believed my life was perfect. But I buried the truth under a carefully cultivated rainbow version of my life and held on desperately to a victim mentality. *It wasn't just your father you blamed for family dysfunction*, a prosecuting voice reminded me.

"It wasn't his fault," I admitted. "I certainly didn't want to be around him at the time, but I don't know how many times I told her 'no' because I just didn't want to broach any difficult subjects or hear about her faith. Honestly, she never pushed it down my throat. I just perceived it that way because it always magnified my guilt."

I heard Megan apologize again, as if she were somehow responsible for the series of unfortunate events in my life. I knew now, of course, that there was only one person to hold responsible – me.

"Were you able to spend more time with your mother? What ended up happening?" I heard her ask. Curiosity must have gotten the best of her.

"For that, I think I am going to need something a bit stronger than regular coffee." I reached into my handbag and discreetly pulled out a small bottle of Bailey's Irish Creme. "Would you be a dear and get me a refill?"

CHAPTER 17
1948

After the news, I spent as much time as I could with Mama. While I still didn't want to see Father, I brushed those feelings aside for the time being. Helen was gracious and included my parents every Sunday, insisting they bring nothing but themselves.

The value of Mama's limited, precious time was incalculable, and the two of us spoke freely to one another. The keen awareness of Mama's terminal disease peeled away my defenses, replacing them with regret for wasting the time I could have had with her. Both words and tears flowed from parts of our hearts we had not let the light shine on since the war. I accepted her apologies, and while I wanted nothing to do with her God, I even listened to her faith speech without interrupting. I hated myself for not doing both earlier. I also couldn't help but confess to her what had happened with Joe, the anger I felt toward God about Johnny and the baby, and how Labor Day weekend really went.

"Oh, sweetie, you cannot let jealousy in your heart or it will consume you," Mama cautioned.

"I am not jealous of Ruth," I defended.

"Perhaps I heard wrong, but it does sound like there is a seed of it," she gently responded, reaching for my hand. As my posture deflated, she continued. "For your own sake, you need to rid yourself of that seed or it will take root and damage a relationship, or prevent a beautiful one from forming."

I squeezed her hand and nodded slightly, then redirected the conversation back to Johnny; I didn't want to talk about that bubbly blonde anymore. "Do you still have any old letters from Johnny?"

Mother smiled, and although it took a concerted amount of energy, she stood up. "I will be right back."

"Mama, I can get them. Just tell me where to look."

"No, no. I may be sick, but I am still capable of fetching my box of memories."

She returned with a box brimming with old photos and letters. Some of the photos I hadn't seen in years. My favorite was the one of Johnny, about three years old, in an adorable sailor outfit, and me, almost one year old, in a frilly white gown. Even at age three, he wore the same closed-mouth smile I remember him having when he left for the war.

When Mama showed me a few of Johnny's letters, a familiar hatred toward the Japanese bubbled up in my heart. I tried my best to brush it aside and let his words wash over me, willing myself to hear his voice as I read them. Gradually, as Mama and I laughed and cried over his letters, I felt all the pent-up sorrow and regret begin to lift, replaced by a feeling of closure, as we wept over his final pieces of correspondence.

November 26, 1943

Dear Mother,

I am taking some time this morning down at camp to write this letter to you. I was shifted from Fabrica to Magallon last Monday right after I wrote you my weekly letter. It seems that the Col. didn't like my attitude so he brought me back to Magallon where I could repent of my sins.

I really appreciate getting a letter from you and Margaret each week. It is really nice to hear from you. About all I do is wait for your letters, as there isn't really much to do these weeks.

On the weekends, I usually go into Bacolod, which is the capital of this province. It's not a very big town, about the size of Tipp City, but it is the largest on the island. The hotel where we stay does have indoor plumbing, although no hot water. I look forward to returning home. I miss you all as well as hot water, newspapers and shows that are not over a year old.

Take good care of Joan. Tell Margaret not to wreck her and to be easy on the clutch! Remember she has to last me when I get back, which will probably be in two more years. Treat her like she is a child. Don't forget she took me a long time to earn. But, I do hope you like how she drives as much as I do. Sure wish I had her over here, but the conditions of the roads and the excessive moisture would not be good for her.

The weather out here is really hot. It is awfully hard to get used to the fact that on November 26 it is 98 degrees in the shade, that is, if you can find the shade. There are so few trees in this godforsaken hole that the dogs almost go wild. But a breeze has started up now so it isn't really so bad. Sure would like to see some of that snow you talked about, and some of those lonely females. The women situation is horrible; they are just lacking. (A familiar Filipino phrase.)

Tell Margaret I really appreciate her letters every week, and I will try to write her an entire letter sometime. That is all for now. To your question — I don't know what you can send me for Xmas. By the time you read this letter, it will probably be too late anyway. We are only getting about two boats a month, food has gone up, American food that is, and everything is taking on a much grimmer hue. I will write you again next week.

Love,

Johnny

P.S. Did you ever get the piña cloth dollies?

We laughed about Johnny's concern about his car and his comment about the "lonely females" in the states, who were only lonely because most men were off at war. Before handing it to me, Mama asked if I wanted to see the last postcard, noting that he specifically mentioned me. I nodded my head and held out my hand.

Imperial Japanese Army
1. *I am interned at <u>Philippine Military Prison</u>*
2. *My health is — excellent; <u>good</u>; fair; poor*
3. *I am — injured; sick in hospital; under treatment; <u>not under treatment</u>*
4. *I am — improving; not improving; better; <u>well</u>*
5. *(Re: Family); hope that all is well, everybody in good spirits, everything is fine*
6. *Please give my best regards to <u>Joan and Margaret, always and forever</u>*

The last comment was loaded with meaning. He was so proud when he'd saved up enough to purchase that 1940

DeSoto Custom, and his parting words to me before he left were, "You better treat her like a sister." I smiled at the memory. Johnny must have suspected he would not return home, and my parents decided it was his way of telling them to give me his car. That car was his most prized earthly possession, and I still cherished it like it was a child, as he said to. While Edward and I had purchased our own car in recent years, Joan still sat in my parents' garage as it had for almost four years. Now, after reading his last words to us, I knew I could never sell it.

Thanksgiving came quickly that year, and while Mama was still with us and had a peace about her, she was increasingly frail and easily tired. Knowing Mom's diagnosis, my coworkers were graciously flexible with holiday time. We spent the holiday together at Robert and Helen's house, arriving just before noon, with lunchtime set for one o'clock. William and Ruth were expected to arrive a little before we ate, hence the later lunch. Their attendance was last minute, and despite my attempts to heed my mother's words about harboring jealousy, I was annoyed they were coming. *I wish Ruth wasn't coming. Why couldn't they have spent it with her family?* I wondered, breathing out a sigh of frustration as I closed the car door and went to help Mama out of the car.

The house smelled heavenly as we let ourselves in. I heard music playing in the living room, and both Robert and Shirley greeted us with hugs. Shirley helped Mama remove her coat, and Robert started hanging them up in the closet.

"Happy Thanksgiving, dears!" Helen called cheerfully from the kitchen. Father and Edward joined Robert and Shirley in the living room, while I walked slowly with Mother to the kitchen to greet the cook. Helen had renovated much of their first floor in the last month, and she pointed out the changes as she stirred the gravy. The kitchen cabinets were now a mint green and the patterned linoleum floor matched perfectly. Apparently, it was the next big color. They also added a home bar in the living room and a new upholstered red couch. Lastly, the first-floor bathroom showed off turquoise tiles with pink accents.

"The kitchen looks lovely," I complimented Helen, "and Edward said the couch is quite comfortable."

"Oh, I am glad you like it! You will have to tell Ruthie you think the kitchen is lovely. She helped me pick the color scheme out. She is a marvelous decorator," Helen boasted, as she set the cheese tray out on the counter.

Ruthie? I wondered in disgust. Before I could respond, the front door opened, and William's voice boomed a loud, warm, "Happy Thanksgiving!" Immediately, Helen set down the wooden spoon and rushed out to join the group. *She didn't set down anything for you. And Ruth is now Ruthie? She only gives nicknames when she really likes someone. She told you that herself.* I stopped myself. *Put on a smile, Margaret. Remember what Mama said.*

"We are going to be sisters!" Shirley squealed.

Oh wonderful. They aren't going to break up after all. Looks like Ruth managed to hijack Thanksgiving. All we are going to talk about now is the proposal and wedding. And, with that, I gave in to the gnawing feelings of jealousy, retreating to the bathroom to delay seeing the happy couple.

Before I made it to the restroom, Mama stopped me, leveling her gaze. "Darling, where are you going?"

"I have to use the restroom," I answered curtly.

"Remember what we talked about, sweetie," she gently said as I walked out of the kitchen.

When everyone finally settled down and Helen realized it was past lunchtime, we made our way to the dining room. Each place setting's placemat had Helen's favorite china plate, china teacup, and silver flatware all properly laid out. Helen and I carried out the food to line the table, and for a moment, all I could think about was the delicious meal.

Robert and Helen were at opposite ends of the table, with William and Ruth closest to Helen. Shirley flanked Ruth's one side. While I sat next to both Shirley and Mother, I made every concerted effort to focus on Mother during the meal and stay out of the wedding conversation. Edward sat across from me, next to William and Father. As Edward lifted a forkful of turkey to his mouth, William asked if he could say grace.

"With all the excitement, I completely forgot," Robert said, seemingly embarrassed to have not offered to pray before a holiday meal.

"Father, if you would prefer to . . ." William began.

"No, please, you pray. You and Ruth have so much to be thankful for; it seems only right for you to lead us," Robert insisted.

Edward and I exchanged eye-rolls as everyone else either closed their eyes or stared at their food reverentially. After William had finished his fairly casual prayer, we could finally eat. Dishes out of reach were passed around clockwise and the buzz of excited chatter filled the room. Sure enough, William's proposal, Ruth's engagement ring, and wedding plans dominated the conversation. *A diamond engagement ring? Seems a little showy to me*, I thought to myself, as I glanced at my modest, plain wedding band.

"It is just beautiful!" Shirley gasped.

"Thank you. William picked it out at De Beers. I have them and their 'A Diamond is Forever' slogan to thank," she beamed, and then smiled at William with every muscle in her face.

Despite my earnest attempt to ignore any mention of wedding plans, I learned the wedding would be in February. *Three months away! Why so soon?* I wondered.

"I've always wanted a winter wedding, and we hated to wait another year to marry," Ruth said, followed by nuptial details she'd already ironed out.

I tried to steer the conversation at my end of the table to other news, successfully baiting Eddy with subjects guaranteed to get him talking – his love for Gordie Howe and his annoyance with Dewey's vagueness, which Eddy claimed had cost him the election. Then, Robert spoke up.

"Ruth, did I hear you won't be getting married here, in William's hometown? What is the name of the parish you will be married in? Perhaps I can concelebrate alongside your priest since I am a deacon."

Oh, you are not going to be so favored now! I thought, as I shifted in my seat, inwardly bursting with joy that the topic of church had come up.

William answered. "Ruth and I will be married at the Protestant church we have been attending since we started dating," he began.

"Wait," Helen interjected, her fork frozen halfway between her plate and mouth. "You won't be getting married in a Catholic parish?" Her face paled.

"No. We can talk more about this subject after lunch," William answered definitively, looking both at Helen and then at Robert. "So, Eddy, what is new with you?" William asked rather abruptly.

His attempt to change the subject worked, but not before I noticed the disconcerting looks exchanged between Helen and Robert. I smiled smugly. *So, dear "Ruthie" will not be the perfect, favored daughter-in-law after all, will she?*

As William and Eddy chatted, I stood up to help Helen take dirty dishes to the kitchen and get ready for dessert. As soon as the bomb had dropped, I felt much more relaxed, and the rest of the afternoon passed pleasantly – if more subdued – with delicious desserts, small talk, and card games. As much as I wanted to stay and hear the conversation between William, Ruth, and my in-laws, by early evening Mother was tired so we headed home.

Immediately after we dropped Father and Mama off, I turned to Edward. "Well, what do you think about the location of William and Ruth's marriage ceremony?"

"Mother certainly wasn't thrilled. I couldn't care less. We only got married in a Catholic church because it was expected. Hell, I think Mother only cares because of what others will think," he added with a shrug.

We pulled into the drive and after making our way into the house, I offered to take Edward's trench coat. I hung it up and then slid off my new teal box coat. Father had bought it for me a few weeks before, at Mother's request no doubt. I adjusted my blouse, and, giddy as a schoolgirl, I decided to channel my mood to show Edward just how thankful I was for him. *The timing for a pregnancy announcement couldn't be more perfect . . .*

Mother collapsed the day after Thanksgiving.

And equally concerning, she did not fight when the doctor and Father urged her to stay in bed and rest. In my heart, I knew we didn't have much time, but in my head, I refused to believe it was over. I didn't leave her house the weekend after Thanksgiving, and while she still had a calm peace, her spunk was noticeably absent.

That Saturday, I fixated on decorating for Christmas. Just like Mama years ago, I thought the season had a magic to it, and I was convinced the Christmas spirit would cheer her up and improve her health. And, I was hellbent on distracting her and myself from a month that was otherwise emotionally heavy for us all. While most people looked forward to Santa and his large bag of toys, for us, December brought a different kind of baggage – the painful reminder of Johnny's death and the miscarriage.

"Let's go buy Mama and Father a tree."

"This early?" Edward asked, yawning, as he turned onto Whipp Road returning from our donut run.

"She may not have much time," I snapped.

"I meant this early in the morning, dear."

We pulled into my parents' driveway, and Eddy reached for my hand. "We are going to get through this. Your mom is a strong woman."

With the car in park and Eddy holding my limp hand, I stared out the window, desperate for a task to focus on. I resolved not to cry. "Advent Tree Farm may not be open, but we can start decorating *that* tree." The large spruce in the front yard was clearly visible from both my parents' bedroom window and the bay window in the living room. *She will be able to see the tree lit up, and it will remind her to fight this disease.*

Edward didn't dare argue. "I will find the ladder. You go see if the McCrays are available to help."

After an hour and several cups of hot cocoa, Father, Edward, the three McCray boys, and I stood back and smiled at our handiwork. The colored lights around the beautiful spruce truly were a joyous sight, and I was certain Mama would love it.

"I don't see your mother looking out the window. It is safe to assume she is napping," Father said after we waved goodbye to our helpers.

"Then we have time to cut down a tree." I was on a roll and wanted to continue decorating for the season, putting unfounded faith in the magic of Christmas. Halfway to the car, I yelled back, "We will be back soon with a tree! Edward, come on."

With it being the first day of the season, Advent was packed. Despite the heavy crowd, we grabbed a sled and an axe and headed for the countless rows of trees, scrupulously choosing one that I deemed would be the perfect one for Mother. After waiting thirty minutes to pay, we were finally headed back to my parent's house.

Mama was awake when we returned. Her plush robe did its best to hide her thin frame. Despite her deteriorating body, Mama's spirit was encouraging. With lips tinted by her favorite red lipstick, she greeted us each with a kiss on the cheek.

"Welcome back. Thank you kindly for decorating the spruce outside. It looks immaculate. And a tree for inside too? I have so much to be thankful for."

Internally, my heart leaped. *She is going to get through this. I just know it.*

With Sinatra's Christmas music filling the room, we decorated the tree with multi-colored bulbs, garland, and tinsel, and placed the bottle brush trees on the mantel. In unison, we took a step back to assess.

"It's perfect. Thanks, everyone." Mama's voice was sincere but lacked enthusiasm. "I think I am going to retire to our room and rest," Mama added, her eyes now drooping with exhaustion.

Father helped her to their room, and by the time he returned, we were ready to leave.

"Thank you, Mags. Mama thinks the tree outside is, in her words, marvelous. And the Christmas tree inside sure adds joy to the home."

I considered the day a success. Other than that, the business of the hospital helped to keep me distracted, and Edward and I spent every weekend with Mama. Despite her frail body and obvious lack of physical strength, she was her usual self on Christmas Day. When we celebrated New Year's Day with sauerkraut sundaes, I'd even convinced myself that she could be stronger than her cancer.

Then, later on New Year's Day, as Edward and I were enjoying a cup of coffee, the phone rang. I answered with a cheerful, "Happy New Year!" But when I heard Father's voice, my insides crumbled and my knees buckled.

CHAPTER 18

January 7, 1949

I stood outside, the ground blanketed in a fresh sheet of snow, and watched each exhalation fade into the crisp winter air. While the brilliant sun gave the illusion of warmer temperatures, the bitter cold chilled me to the bone, numbing my ears and fingers.

The numbness reached far beneath my outer extremities.

I stared off into the distance at the leafless, bare-branched trees. *Those trees will come back to life in just a few months*, I thought.

"Sweetie, everyone has gone back to the house, and it is very cold. Please, come to the car with me," Edward pleaded.

I didn't respond. I heard him say something, but my head was in an invisible fog and my ears felt plugged, as if I were underwater.

"Margaret? Did you hear me?" he gently asked again, reaching for my arm. He followed my gaze to the trees and added, "This season is a shitty one, but just like those trees, you will feel life again soon."

I glanced at Edward, down at Mama's fresh grave, and then to my snow-covered black shoes as my legs robotically carried me to the car.

Apathetic to my loss, time moved on. After a few weeks, everyone in my circle tried to help me re-establish a sense of normalcy. Edward asked if I was ready to start helping around the house again, our Sundays at Robert and Helen's home resumed, and I was put back on the normal rotation at the hospital.

The weekend after the funeral, Father came by with a box Mama wanted me to have. Edward took it to our bedroom, and as he carried it away, Father attempted an apology for how he'd treated me after the miscarriage. "I'm sorry you felt hurt," he said. But his apology lacked sincerity, his phrasing chosen carefully to somehow shift the blame onto *me* for how I felt. Later, after talking to Edward, I accepted it was the best "apology" I would ever receive from someone incapable of humility and admitting fault, and I knew then that our relationship would never be anything like it was before. How could it, after all he'd said and didn't say? How could it when he refused to acknowledge his wrong? And how could it when the glue that held our family of three together – Mama – was gone?

To add insult to injury, I still wasn't with child.

"Are you ready to go?" Edward asked.

"Go? Go where?" I responded, my voice stoic.

"It's Sunday. I told Mom we would be there today," he responded, reaching for his coat.

Without answering him, I stood up and started walking to our restroom.

"Margaret, come on. I think it would do you good to get out of the house and be around people who love you. Besides, we still haven't heard the whole story about Ruth and William's wedding plans yet," he teased.

"True," I answered flatly. With all that went on with Mama in December, we hadn't heard how the church conversation went between Helen, Robert, William, and Ruth. "We can go after I use the restroom and powder my nose."

During the short drive to Robert and Helen's, Edward brought up the wedding. "Mom and Dad want to leave the Friday before the wedding. I went ahead and told the hospital you needed that weekend off."

"Okay," I responded apathetically. I'd resumed my regular schedule of working one weekend a month, and it would've been a perfect excuse to not attend the wedding. My hand instinctively reached for my necklace as I absentmindedly fingered the diamond-encircled emerald pendant around the gold chain, a new habit I'd formed since Mama's death. It was the same one Mama and I had seen together years ago at Rike's. She had surprised me with it on Christmas Day – her last gift to me.

I dreaded the upcoming nuptials. Despite Mama's advice, I wished William would've picked someone else. Someone less cheerful, inviting, authentic. Someone who didn't share Helen's love of cooking. Someone less pious. Someone who didn't remind me of my old self. I thought back to our wedding, when Edward tried to set him up with one of my friends from the hospital. William was polite and took her on one date, but when we asked about it after the honeymoon, he simply shrugged and said she wasn't right for him.

Helen was waiting at the door for us. As soon as I stepped in, she hugged me. I teared up in her embrace.

She loosened her arms, smiled slightly, and looked me in the eyes. "Let's shed no more tears tonight, Maggie."

"Okay," I responded with a half-smile. I knew that Helen sincerely cared about me, and now, with Mama gone, she filled that void in my heart.

"Drinks all around!" Robert called from the living room, and we all went in to join him.

After casual conversation, Edward poured another drink and switched topics. "The wedding is a few weeks away now. I assume we are carpooling?"

Helen uncrossed and then recrossed her legs and took a drink. The temperature of the room changed slightly, and I noticed the tension in Robert's face as he stood up to refill his only half-empty glass.

"Yes, February fifth is less than two weeks away," Helen answered, an artificial smile on her face.

"Are they still not getting married in a Catholic church?" Edward asked.

I smiled slyly. *Good job, honey.* Anything that helped tear down Ruth's reputation built up my spirits.

"No, they are not. We talked about it after Thanksgiving, if you remember, and a few times since then, actually. We are content with their decision," Helen replied with a seemingly sincere tone.

"You mean, 'We have no other choice but to be content with their decision,'" Robert added, with some derision in his voice.

Helen shot Robert a stern look. "Like I said, we are content. We are thrilled with Ruthie and how she fits in so well with our family. They are only a few hours away too, and we want to be in their lives as much as we are a part of yours – to the extent possible, of course. Hence, we must be happy for them and accept William's decision to marry someone outside of the Catholic faith. I suppose some religion is better than none, even if it is Protestantism." Helen's resolved tone communicated more than her words. *Ruthie? Helen is still calling her Ruthie, despite her marrying her son in a Protestant church?* My mind raced, already in overdrive from Mother's death and another failed month of trying to conceive.

The fire in my eyes revealed the anger in my heart as Helen continued. "And, I highly doubt they will wait long to have kids. After Thanksgiving, Ruth mentioned she has always dreamed of having a large family and staying home with her kids. Especially with being a state away, I won't get to see William or those babies if I burn a bridge with my soon-to-be daughter-in-law!" Helen said with a mix of joy and seriousness in her voice.

Knowing your luck, Ruth will conceive the first month she tries, and then you, well, you will take a backseat to the child-bearing daughter-in-law.

"William should call off the wedding," I blurted out without giving any thought to the potential long-term consequences.

Three pairs of eyes fixed their gaze on me. *Now is your chance to ruin her. Speak now or be prepared to be replaced,* the inner voice taunted. *You already lost your mom. Are you going to lose your place in Helen's heart too? Remember, the second Ruth gets pregnant, you will be tossed aside like a rag doll.*

"I didn't know if I should tell you all or not," I continued. Edward cocked his head slightly, his brow furrowed in confusion, obviously wondering why I hadn't told him what-ever I was about to voice. "I hated to upset you all, and with everything going on with my mother . . ." My voice trailed off.

Don't weave this web, Margaret, a different voice whispered to my soul. I brushed the plea aside.

"After the Thanksgiving meal, Ruth and I talked. Mother had encouraged me to try to be her friend, probably knowing I would need friends soon. I was trying to get to know her more, so I opened up. I shared a few things about my past – before Edward and you all brightened up my life – and I also told her we hoped to have children in the future." The words came so easily, I could almost convince myself they were truthful.

Helen's whole demeanor seemed to light up at the mention of children. Although she'd never asked me about it, I knew she was desperate for a grandchild – and that knowledge cut deep into my heart, fueling my tongue. Edward stared at me, clearly dumbfounded I hadn't told him about this one-on-one conversation I had with Ruth.

"Anyway, when I told her about wanting to get pregnant, she said something incredibly hurtful. I don't know though . . . The last thing I want to do is put a dark cloud over their wed-ding day or upset anyone," I said, fidgeting now with my skirt.

Stop! the second voice whispered again, but not strong enough to sway me.

"What did she say to you?" Edward and Helen asked si-multaneously, eyebrows raised in alarm. Helen added, "Please, tell us. It may be something William really needs to know."

And then I said it – spoke the lie that would haunt me for the rest of my days; words that would forever stain Ruth's reputation and seal mine as the unwitting victim of her cruel tongue. "Ruth told me I hadn't conceived yet because of all the sin in my life. She told me God is likely punishing me for not being religious enough."

For a split second, I could've heard a pin drop on the entryway's linoleum floor. Helen's eyes widened, Robert shook his head in disgust and mumbled something under his breath, and smoke could've come out of Edward's ears.

"That *bitch* said what?" Edward broke the silence, standing up.

"Eddy, you must tell William before he marries her," Helen said to Edward, a look of desperation on her face. And then, shaking her head, she said softly, "I was so, so wrong about her."

"Hopefully William has the sense to listen to you, Edward," Robert stated flatly and lit a cigar. "Maggie, dear, thank you for telling us. With everything going on with your dear mother, I am sorry that woman said those hateful words to you. Don't you listen to her, you hear?"

I nodded and wiped a tear from my cheek, my body language committed to the lie. I was relieved that they appeared to believe the tale without question and didn't seem the slightest bit concerned with seeking Ruth's side. *That was too easy!* I applauded myself for my theatrics.

"Robert is entirely correct. Pay her no mind. I am just glad you had the courage to tell us the truth. Who knows? Maybe it will save William from making a life-altering mistake," Helen added sharply.

"And what if he doesn't call off the wedding?" Edward asked, venom in his voice. "I, for one, wouldn't want to go."

The tension in the room was thick and uncomfortable. After a long pause, Helen took a deep breath and spoke. "Let's just see what William says. I will let you handle it, Eddy, and if we don't hear word of it being called off, I suppose we will still go." Helen looked from Eddy to Robert, both with the same cross expression on their face. "However, how I can look his fiancée in the eye after what she said to you, Maggie, I just don't know." She reached out, embracing me in a hug.

A few days passed, and, to my knowledge, Edward still hadn't picked up our Western Electric to dial William. The topic hadn't surfaced between us, either. When Sunday rolled around again, I decided I needed to ask if he was going to call. Helen had cancelled our regular Sunday Fun-day in anticipation of the following weekend, and as I browned the ground beef, I considered how best to bring up the topic.

After setting the table with a spoon, sour cream, crackers, cheese and water, I ladled each of us a healthy serving of chili. *Mama loved chili. Thank goodness she left you her recipe.* It was one of many things that I'd found in the box Father had brought me.

"Your Mama worked on that box for months and called it 'complete' on New Year's Eve. She called it your 'box of memories,'" Father had told me when he dropped it off. Unable to bring myself to open it, I had let the box sit in the empty bedroom for a week. When I finally had the courage to look inside, I smiled at the box's thoughtful packaging. It was lined with a blanket, which was gathered and tied together with a burlap ribbon. Within the burlap ribbon's knot was a thin pink ribbon holding a tag on the priceless gift. It read, *To: My Darling Daughter, Forever yours, Mama.*

Her scent wafted from the blanket, and I buried my face in it, pretending I was in her embrace. After untying the ribbon, I carefully removed a few of the contents – a photo album, a brown woven box with countless recipes, her favorite handkerchief, and her go-to coffee mug. I chuckled when I saw my pink baby blanket and Raggedy Ann doll, but a flicker of anger quickly replaced my smile after I pulled them out. There, at the bottom of the box, was her blue King James and a few notebooks. *Those notebooks are full of prayers for me to change, no doubt.* Agitated, I put the items back in and pushed the blanket into the box, hoping to preserve her scent.

I rolled my eyes as I thought back to the Bible and notebooks. *Some good her faith did her.* "Dinner is ready!" I called to Eddy and focused on the task at hand: finding out about the call.

But when I asked, rather than answer my question, he responded, "You should get the suitcase out tonight and start packing. We have a busy week ahead, and I don't want to forget something."

I decided it best not to ask any more questions, and simply replied, "Okay, I will."

"Remember, we are leaving Friday. Dad and Mom want to leave a little later than originally planned though to limit the time with William's fiancée. We will just say something came up with work so all we have to deal with is dinner," he added brusquely.

Maybe he did call after all, and William didn't care or believe him? I retrieved the suitcase and began laying out clothing to take. *It doesn't matter what William says. Helen, Robert, and Edward all believe you 100 percent,* I reassured myself. With that, I focused on packing. Edward would wear his best black suit, and I decided to pack the dress I wore to Mama's funeral. *You just had it laundered anyway.* In addition to clothing, I made sure to tuck away a bottle of Jack Daniel's and a silk nightgown.

CHAPTER 19

The drive to Carmel, Indiana, was painfully boring, seeming to take days instead of hours. An agricultural community, Carmel had a population of less than a thousand; without the train, I was sure they wouldn't have access to the modern world. I rolled my eyes when we passed Clay Center School. *What a drab-looking building.*

After driving through miles of empty, featureless landscape, we turned into a large driveway, passing gardens and grounds I could tell – even in the winter months – were carefully manicured. *Where are we?* The brick house was enormous. The main home, flanked by two smaller buildings, was three stories tall, with a two-story front porch supported by white pillars. When I stepped out of the car, I saw smoke coming from both chimneys, and while I was busy trying to not look impressed, a well-dressed gentleman asked if he could unload our car.

"You will be staying in the east guest house," he informed us, closing my car door. "I can take your bags to your room. Dinner will be served in twenty-eight minutes." He was in the middle of describing the location of the dining room when Ruth opened the front door and stood atop the flight of stairs.

"Thank you, John. I will escort them. Hello, everyone! We are thrilled you've arrived!" I could hear her smile before I saw it.

I felt my skin turning green. Her trendy royal blue dress was stunning, with a cinched-in waist that made her look like a model. *Must be Christian Dior*, I thought, grateful I had worn my Bar Suit. I had chosen it carefully; it was hard to miss, with its white tailored jacket and full, pleated black skirt. While tired from the drive and agitated about the weekend's event, I was now sick with envy. *I didn't know she came from such money. What the hell does her father do?* I asked myself, then bottled my emotions, resolved to play my role in the story I had crafted.

"Please come in. It is dreadfully chilly outside. I can't wait to introduce you to my parents, Sherman and Susan, and my brothers, Matthias and Mark," Ruth added, William joining her in greeting us. He brought with him her coat, and as they approached our cars, I was positive it was mink. *Of course it is. Well, she won't be chipper for long.*

"Margaret, that skirt looks perfect on you!" Ruth exclaimed.

"Oh, this thing? Thank you." I was instantly annoyed she'd noticed, and when I refused to reciprocate her compliment, I was even more irked that she didn't seem to care.

They eagerly greeted Robert, Helen, and Shirley, clearly unaware of the seed I had planted. I was pleased to see the smile on Ruth's face quickly fade as Helen greeted her coolly, addressing her as "Ruth" rather than her nickname, and then curtly excused herself to go to her room before dinner.

I slinked away and joined Helen so I wouldn't have to speak to either of them further, nodding to Edward to follow.

"Eddy, brother. Hi!" William called out as we began walking to the east house, his tone noticeably bewildered.

Edward slightly turned, and without eye contact, he called over his shoulder, "We are going to freshen up. See you at dinner."

Oh, how I wished I could have turned around to see his and Ruth's expressions! *Keep your eyes forward. Remember, act aloof this entire weekend and ask nothing about this giant estate.* I smiled slyly, pleased with the web of deception I'd woven.

Robert, Helen, Shirley, Edward, and I walked together to the grand house, our collective disapproval almost tangible. To escape the raw, blustery wind, we hurried past a garden and toward a side entrance, as directed. The square garden was pruned, with an elaborate fountain in the center. It had been turned off for the season, but I heard Helen mention how beautiful it must be in the warmer months, to which Robert made a colorful comment about how unnecessary it all was.

The inside of the house was as ostentatious as the outside. A grand, sweeping staircase led to the second floor; its walnut railing, stained a rich coffee color, was wide, and the oriental stair carpet, eye-catching. The middle of the home was hollow, and I could see a painting on the top of the ceiling three stories up. A black railing encircled each level, with the family crest emblazoned at regular intervals. *How humble.* Was a small part of me envious? Of course, though I would never have admitted it at the time. I thought that I'd come from a family that was well off, but I'd never been in a house of such luxury before. As we made our way to the formal dining room, my heels clicking on the skinny wooden planks, I took in the rich furnishings, dustless surfaces, fresh flowers in elegant vases. Right outside the room, a tuxedoed man who I assumed was part of the household staff, asked us to sign in. Underneath a greenery wall with "Mr. & Mrs." wired into the center, a table displayed a canvas book and several quill pens. The open book indicated a place to sign our names and write a piece of advice for the couple. Taking the pen from Helen, I bent slightly to sign my name along with Edward's. Helen's advice read, "Apologize and have a good relationship with your mother-in-law." *Ha. How perfect.* On one level it sounded innocent enough, but I could read through the lines. I added our names to the book. Nothing else.

Edward whispered, "You think I should draw a man with a ball and chains around his ankle?"

I gently hit Edward's shoulder and chuckled, but my laugh was drowned out as we entered the dining room. The walls stretched high, with the bottom fourth covered in wainscot paneling and the rest in floral wallpaper. The china cabinet spanned several wall panels, sconce lighting framed a giant mirror above the marble fireplace, and an ornate gold chandelier hung from the ceiling's center. One long table filled the room, with Ruth's parents at one end and seats for us at the opposite end. Robert's and Sherman's chairs matched, with large, royal backs. The fire behind Ruth's father crackled as it warmed the room.

Before dinner, Ruth's father prayed, blessing the meal and the engaged couple. Especially given the occasion, his prayer was overly familiar, as if chatting casually with a friend, just as William's had been at Thanksgiving. It seemed almost irreverent to me, especially since I'd joined the Catholic church and had seen the solemn, sacred way in which priests conducted the mass. I could tell Helen was bothered, and I made sure to roll my eyes in agreement when she glanced my way. We were soon distracted, however, by servers offering every kind of beverage imaginable, from champagne in fine-stemmed flutes to beer in traditional steins. In tandem with the drink offerings, we were served the first of three courses, plated on elegant porcelain, hand-painted plates. With a smirk I reached for one of the three fancy forks laid out in front of me and leaned over to Shirley.

"Did you know William was marrying the princess of Indiana?" I whispered.

We both laughed quietly.

Based on the traditional menu, a copy of which had been artfully laid at each place setting, I gathered Ruth's family was of German descent. The menu listed the traditional name for each dish, followed by a description. As much as I didn't want to like any of it, I couldn't deny that each of the three courses was nothing short of delicious. We were first served *Herzoginkartoffeln*, a mashed potato dish baked in individual ramekins. Next, servers brought out large plates filled with *Maultaschen*, a German ravioli, *Grießklöße*, a dumpling, and *Leipziger Allerlei*, a vegetable dish mixed with crab meat and a rich crab butter. Halfway through the main course, Sherman raised a silencing hand. With everyone's attention, he shared an old tale about the *Maultaschen* and how monks created the dish in an attempt to hide meat from God during Lent. He tied the legend to marriage and the importance of truth and honor before signaling for a toast, and while I could've done without the proverb, I had to admit that he was a gifted storyteller. The same joy Ruth had radiated from him, and for a split second, I envied her for having a father so much warmer than my own.

During the meal, I kept my eyes fixed on our end of the table while my ears focused on the opposite end, where Sherman was relaying the history of the property.

"Well, in the late 1800s, my parents discovered black gold on their property," Sherman began, giving thanks to God and crediting his parents with the wisdom to use the money wisely. "I just manage the property now alongside my bride." He smiled and reached for his wife Susan's hand. "Mother dreamed of having a quiver full of arrows, but the good Lord only gave her me. He must have known I would be a handful!"

Sherman continued talking, telling stories of his rambunctious youth, and how he pretended to be Huck Finn, Babe Ruth, or a soldier going off to fight in the Great War. Then, abruptly, he signaled for another toast.

"Forgive me, everyone, but I want to raise my glass one more time." After he had everyone's attention, he continued. "Some of you may know Mother worked hard to convince Pop to build this large estate, and as you can tell, once she started, she went all out. Tonight, though, I want to share why. First, she reasoned if the Lord wasn't going to fill her home with children of her own, she wanted to have ample space to welcome others. And boy did she, come the Great Depression! Thanks to her generosity, I consider half of this town my family! And two, something I myself am so grateful for now, she was planning for future generations. So, hint, hint, Ruthie and Will!" His voice was a mix of jest and sincerity. "I can't believe my baby girl turns twenty-five this year. Susan and I wondered if you would ever marry, dear, but now we understand why no one else was good enough. You hadn't met William yet. To the happy couple."

Everyone lifted their flutes to toast the couple. I half-heartedly lifted mine, ready to retreat to the room. *I feel a headache coming on*, I told myself.

The meal concluded with *Germknödel*, a sweet vanilla dumpling stuffed with homemade *Pflaumenmus* and topped with a decadent vanilla sauce. Just like the rest of the meal, it was delicious, but instead of licking my plate clean, I leaned over to Edward and commented about the consistency of the plum jam stuffed inside.

"What a strange dessert filling. And why couldn't they just leave off the fancy German names? Half of their guests – including the husband-to-be – won't have a clue what any of it means."

Edward shrugged his shoulders and took the last bite of his dessert. "I'll finish yours if you don't like it."

Irritated, I pushed my plate in front of him and crossed my arms. Soon after he finished half of the dessert I would've preferred to have eaten myself, I told Edward I had a headache and wanted to retreat to our room early. He raised his eyebrows in understanding, then nodded toward Robert and Helen.

"Margaret has a headache, so we are going to retire to our room," Edward told his parents quietly. I could tell by their knowing looks that they saw my supposed headache for what it was: an excuse to slip out early. We left without saying a word to William and Ruth.

Once in the room and in my nightgown, I unveiled the surprise. We both indulged, drinking more than normal, and after our clothes were on the floor, Edward, his libido satisfied, quickly fell asleep. I, however, could not stop questions from assaulting my mind. *What if you can't get pregnant now that you actually want to? What if Helen presses and finds out you are a liar? What would your mother think of you?* After trying and failing to redirect my thoughts, I finally stood up, grabbed the whiskey bottle next to the bed, and went to the bathroom. I stared at myself in the mirror and took a swig. With both hands on the counter, I began my internal pep-talk. *You will get pregnant; you are well aware it can take time to conceive. Helen will not question you; you have been in the family longer, you live only minutes away, and she will do nothing to jeopardize her relationship with Edward and you. Besides, she has always favored Edward for staying close to her. As for your mother, let it go. She isn't here anymore, and even if she was, would you really want to risk Ruth taking your place in Helen's heart? Absolutely not. Stick to your story.*

I tilted my head back one more time, finishing off the bottle, and lay back in bed.

The next morning, February 5, was obnoxiously beautiful. Light, fluffy snow blanketed the ground, and while the air still held a chill, it wasn't a bitter cold like the night before. The sun shone brightly, with a few wispy clouds adorning the blue sky, and the blustery wind was gone. The wedding was scheduled for half past eleven in the morning, with lunch to follow.

I looked at the clock. A quarter till ten! *We slept in way too late!* I thought as my head fell back heavily on the pillow. It felt like a bowling ball. I rolled over to my side and let one leg dangle over the bed to help slow the dizziness. I pushed Edward's shoulder and mumbled something about needing to get up. A few minutes later, Edward hurried out of bed and threw up in the bathroom.

After hearing the shower turn on, I willed myself to get up and lay out our clothes for the occasion. I needed food to settle my churning stomach, but I knew that we'd missed the scheduled breakfast. We rushed to get ready, managing to meet Robert, Helen, and Shirley at the vehicle only five minutes late. I smiled inwardly as I took in the sight of the four of us, dressed head to toe in black, as though we were going to a funeral. *I wonder if Ruth will notice?* Shirley was the only one wearing a different color, dark purple.

"Well, you look like hell," Robert commented when he first saw Edward, handing us both a biscuit. "You missed another extravagant meal. Two extra coffees are in the car along with blueberry muffins."

Edward responded with a sarcastic smile and climbed in the driver's seat. On the way to the church, we drove past fields and two farmhouses, complete with barns and grain silos. The snow glittered and glistened in the sun, blinding in its beauty. After a ten-minute drive, we pulled up to a small white church – the same one artistically depicted on the back of our invitations. The steeple reached high into the sky with a cross on top. The double doors were a dark-stained wood, each adorned with a wreath hung with a crimson red ribbon. When we had first received the invitation, I scoffed at the ostentatious calligraphy and the hand-sketched map from Ruth's parents' house to the church. I looked at the invitation again, crumpling it slightly, and wondered how much they'd paid to have them printed.

We walked in, a little past eleven o'clock.

"Good morning, everyone! Welcome!" William greeted us warmly. As he reached to shake his dad's hand, Robert shook back limply, mumbling "Good morning" under his breath. Helen gave William a side hug, her universal hug of disappointment, and Edward just waved as he simultaneously excused himself to go to the restroom. I tried to read Shirley's face for a sign showing that Helen had relayed the fake news, but it was inconclusive. From her attitude yesterday, I was fairly certain she knew, but I hadn't had a chance to speak with her myself to confirm.

William's face dropped, and his eyes seemed to plead, "What is wrong with you guys?"

Did Edward actually call? William seems clueless, I wondered.

"Mom, Margaret, Shirley – would you like to go see Ruth before she comes down the aisle?" William offered, most assuredly an invitation passed on from Ruth herself.

Helen's response confirmed her desire to avoid any interaction. "I would prefer to be surprised like everyone else," she answered politely.

Her response was plausible, and after Shirley and I added similar sentiment, William smiled, excused himself, and left.

The interior of the church was plain but elegant, the gentle play of the light cast through the stained-glass windows illuminating the building in an angelic way. Both hymnals and Bibles were placed on the pews, which were overflowing with guests wearing their best dresses and suits. If a pew had not been reserved for us, we would've been hard pressed to find a seat. As we took our seats, a man in a black suit made his way to the chancel, which was decorated with white ribbon-adorned hellebore bouquets. William followed, smiling, gaze locked on the door where Ruth and her father would enter. A string quartet began playing the well-known "Wedding March," and the doors opened. While I didn't want to, I stood up with the rest of the crowd and looked back. Ruth, of course, looked stunning, and I hated her all the more for it. Annoyed, I turned away to see William lift a handkerchief to his face and brush away a tear. *Wow. Is he crying?* I asked myself, as I remembered my own wedding day. While Edward had been excited to marry me, he certainly was not emotional when I walked down the aisle.

"Who gives this woman to be married to this man?" the pastor asked.

"Her mother and I do," Ruth's father answered. Sherman turned toward Ruth, smiled at her lovingly, and then unveiled her glowing face. Ruth beamed with joy. He extended his arms, and after she gave him a child-like hug, Sherman placed her hand in William's.

The heavy-set man up front introduced himself as Pastor Mike. He was in his fifties, had peppered gray hair, and was about William's height. With a deep, booming voice, he began his prayer, "Dearly Heavenly Father . . ." He followed the prayer with a short scripture reading and something about God's intention for marriage, and then William and Ruth lit a unity candle and prayed together. After the traditional vows and kiss, the service was over. *That's it? How strange.*

William and Ruth walked out of the sanctuary, the guests trailing behind them. Church staff directed the crowd into an auditorium set for lunch. A table for two was along one of the walls, and the rest of the room was filled with large round tables, each set for ten people. The tables were covered with white tablecloths, decorated with greenery and candles in the center.

Once we sat down, Edward was the first to speak. "Want to know one good thing about a non-Catholic wedding? It was short!"

The three of us smiled at him and gave half-hearted laughs as we watched the catering staff bring food to the buffet table. Chatter filled the room. The guests sitting at the table behind me chatted about the soon-to-open Carmel Theatre, President Truman's recent Four Point Program, and the newlyweds' honeymoon destination – Boyne Mountain.

"Willie told me the first chairlift in the Midwest was built there last year. He and Ruthie initially talked about traveling out to Aspen but decided to postpone their trip to next year so they can witness the FIS World Championships," I overheard the well-dressed man behind me tell his table.

They are going skiing? Who, in their right mind, would choose to spend time out in the cold? I asked myself. Two other family members and Ruth's parents joined us at the table, making eavesdropping impossible, and began talking about the upcoming meal. Then, the room erupted in clapping and whistling as the newlyweds entered, William giving Ruth a playful spin as they made their way to the front. William kissed his new bride and began to speak.

"On behalf of Ruth and myself, I'd like to thank everyone for coming today. I'd also like to extend a big thank you to Ruth's parents," he opened and then continued, looking directly at Sherman and Susan, "Thank you for everything you did to make this day possible, and for raising such a beautiful, intelligent, God-fearing daughter. You have taken me in as your own son, and I am grateful for the love and guidance you have given both of us during our courtship." He shifted his attention and said, "And to my own parents: thank you for bringing up such a talented, good-looking, successful, and incredible man." William smiled, and the crowd laughed.

He continued, "Now, to the most important person in my life – Ruth, my wife. Ruth is the most kind, beautiful, charming, intelligent, hard-working, and trustworthy person I have ever met. While her outer beauty takes my breath away, it is her inner beauty that captivates me. She does everything for me, including editing this speech, and she is an excellent judge of character." He paused, letting the audience chuckle, and then turned to Ruth. "You look perfect, and I am blessed to be your husband. To expand some on what Pastor Mike said earlier, marriage to me is what we promised today – to be faithful, devoted, and true. To display the love of Jesus to one another and to cleave to one another. You mean the world to me. Thank you for being my wife. I am honored, and I am excited to grow old with you. You certainly are my perfect fit, handpicked by our creator." After a pause, he turned and canvassed the audience. "Lastly, to you all, thank you for your kind words, sage advice, generous gifts, and loving support. Now, let's celebrate! Cheers!" William added, raising his glass.

Everyone went up to the buffet line shortly after the speech, and I was thankful to see bread and mashed potatoes. Besides those carbs, I added salad, roast beef, and a seasonal fruit mix. Edward, Shirley, and I caught up with one of Helen's siblings and his spouse during lunch, while Susan tried to hold a conversation with Helen and Robert. I could tell Helen was not in a chatty mood; normally a social butterfly, she simply answered Susan's questions and did not ask any in return.

Finally, it was time for cake. Adorned with white roses and crowned with a bride and groom topper, it was undeniably beautiful. Brush strokes of white icing covered the three-tiered cake, with a pearl border piped perfectly around the bottom of each layer. Greenery and red petals delicately encircled the cake's base. Thankful to have a break in conversation, we all watched the newlyweds cut the cake. *It is almost over*, I encouraged myself.

After William and Ruth sat down with their dessert, the guests grabbed a piece of the cake, socialized, or said their good-byes. Ruth's parents were among those who promptly went for cake, joining their two sons, Ruth's younger brothers, in line. Both young men were handsome, one with dark brown, almost black, hair and the other with a head full of amber-colored hair. They looked earnestly joyful for their sister. I clenched my teeth when I saw them. *How nice to still have brothers . . .* As Helen was about to stand, Edward asked his parents about leaving. "Margaret and I were wondering if you would want to leave tonight instead of tomorrow morning."

"That plan is appealing," Robert replied quickly.

"We were supposed to have breakfast tomorrow with Ruth's parents," Helen answered hesitantly.

"I, for one, don't think Ruth's mother could possibly have any more questions to ask after today's lunch," Robert responded sarcastically.

Helen shot him a look.

"What? You aren't interested in getting to know that woman any more than I want to interact with her father. After what William's *wife* said to Maggie, I have no interest in meeting more of her kind." Robert's definitive tone and caustic inflection of the word "wife" left no room for negotiation.

Helen fidgeted with her hands, twirling her thumbs around and around.

"If it matters, I would like to return home," Shirley added to the conversation.

I decided to speak up. "Edward and I will go get some cake for all of us." I grabbed Edward's hand and gently pulled him in the direction of the cake. The line had dwindled by the time we each took a few pieces. I scanned the room, pretending to look aloof, and noticed William and Ruth chatting with some friends. When Ruth looked up and noticed us getting cake, I looked down at the cake, as if I was inspecting every granule of sugar in the icing, and then quickly walked toward our table. If I could help it, I would go the entire day without speaking one word to her.

As we sat down to eat our cake, Robert gave us an answer. "We will leave tonight. After all, Margaret, you were fighting a headache yesterday, and Helen is awfully tired."

"Thank you, Father," Edward responded.

And with that victory, I savored every bite of the cake. Something about knowing they'd chosen us made it even more delicious.

The drive home was quiet. While tired, my mind was active. *I would call today a win!* I told myself, applauding my idea to use Ruth's religion against her. *I made it the entire day without saying one word to Ruth, Helen and Robert clearly believe me and even skipped breakfast with Ruth's parents, and I don't think Helen or Shirley even spoke to Ruth today. Bravo!*

Still, my heart ached. *What if I can't get pregnant? Would Helen still love me if I was barren? And . . . what if she found out the truth?*

CHAPTER 20
2015

"A small part of me noticed the absence of any remorse that night when we drove back to Ohio. It was as if I had silenced a voice inside by knowingly lying with the intent to damage the relationships between William and Ruth and the rest of the family. I also hated to think about my mother after that weekend because I knew she would be disappointed in me. But, at the time, I brushed those thoughts aside and relished the fact that my plan had worked," I admitted shamefully.

Megan stared blankly at the pen she idly twirled in her hand.

She hates you, you know? How could she not? a dark voice said flatly.

Feeling a sudden need to defend myself, I added, "Truly, I never thought it would go on so long. In my head, I thought it would damage the relationship, but not damn it for eternity. You have to understand: Helen was like a mother to me. Besides, while Ruth never actually said anything to me, her faith lived loudly within," I reasoned, trying to convince myself and my audience I was partially justified.

"Thanks for sharing how you were feeling," Megan began, speaking slowly as if choosing her words carefully. "It is good to begin to understand the other side of the story. So, what happened next?"

CHAPTER 21
Ruth

Weeks after the wedding, William made a special trip to see his parents and ask why they had treated us so poorly on our wedding day. After all, a wedding is supposed to be remembered as one of the happiest moments of someone's life. While we enjoyed the ceremony and celebration, his family's lack of support and love certainly left a stain on the day. I was especially hurt because no one in William's family spoke to me the entire time. Ever since Thanksgiving, it seemed that Robert, Helen, and Shirley – not to mention Edward and Margaret – were shunning us, as if we'd done something wrong. It just didn't make sense. William wanted to know why.

I never could have imagined what William would discover.

William arrived home late on Saturday. *He didn't even spend the night? Oh dear.* As he sat down at the kitchen table, I quickly grabbed two wine glasses, thinking that wine might help relax William's noticeably strung nerves. I joined him at the table, gave a small toast for him returning home safely, and then steeled myself to listen. As he told me about the dialogue with his parents, my mind spun. Apparently, even Shirley sang a similar tune and walked away when William started to defend me, claiming she didn't care what he had to say.

"*What?*" I exclaimed, after hearing the lie Margaret had told the family about me. "William, dear, I have never even had a one-on-one conversation with Margaret! And for heaven's sake, we even had Matthias and Mark sit somewhere else at the reception because I wanted to be sensitive to her feelings!"

"I am fully aware, and I said that," William said, defeat in his eyes. "It doesn't matter what you or I say though. They believe her, no questions asked. And they see nothing wrong with how they treated us at the wedding."

"That is utterly ridiculous!" My voice's volume increased as I went on. "Is this all because you left the Catholic church? Or is it because we don't live down the street?"

"Could be both, actually. My parents don't like confrontation, and they remained defensive the entire time, so the conversation wasn't remotely productive. All my mom wanted to do was resume packing," William said, shrugging his shoulders. "I wonder if the root of it is jealousy. After all, my mom and Shirley took to you immediately, and especially with her mother's death, maybe Margaret felt you threatened her relationship with my mom."

"William, we would see your parents only a few times a year. She would have your mom ninety-five percent of the time! How in the world would I be threatening?" I asked, my voice now laced with frustration. I was angry. Angry that Margaret lied. I was even more upset that his parents and sister chose to believe the accusation without question and then let it dictate how they treated us. *No wonder God spoke against lies and partiality and warned His followers that their faith would cause division.*

"And packing? I don't remember them mentioning a trip? Or maybe we aren't privy to that information either," I asked, circling back to what he first said.

"I shouldn't have mentioned it."

"Mentioned what?" I asked, insistent.

William rested his head on his palms for a few seconds and then rubbed his temples. He grew despondent as he told me about the "girls' trip" that Helen, Shirley, and Margaret had planned along with a few other family members.

"And they didn't think to invite *me*?" I said as I slumped back in my seat.

"I asked. My dad responded and justified their decision. Apparently, they didn't think you would have enough vacation time."

"Nonsense."

We both sat in silence, finishing off the rest of our wine. My head throbbed, and my heart hurt. *It is not supposed to be like this. I was supposed to have gained sisters, a mother, a father*, I told myself, as I thought of a friend from church whose mother-in-law refers to her as "daughter-in-love." *Too bad I'm stuck with Helen*, I thought, envious now of my friend and not yet aware of the bitterness taking root in my heart.

"Well, how did you leave it before you came home?" I asked, reaching for William's hand, trying to be supportive but certain my tone reflected my emotions.

William looked at his glass, empty. He grabbed the bottle from the table, refilled both our glasses, and then told me his parents advised him to "reconsider his decision," as Edward supposedly had advised before the wedding. I stared at him in shock. *Reconsider your decision to marry me?* The question reverberated in my mind. I wanted to scream, but I was suddenly out of breath; I felt like I had been punched in the chest, and fear assaulted my heart.

William continued as my eyes darted from my wine glass to him and then back again, fighting tears. "Edward never called. He must have lied too," William said, taking a large gulp of red wine, practically finishing his second glass. "I told them we loved them and would have open arms if and when they had a change in heart, but I could not have a relationship with them if they were going to stand against our marriage. I told them I would choose you a million times over if they were going to make me choose."

After a few minutes of silence, he seemed to read my thoughts amidst his own pain. "My bride, nothing will change my mind about you. God placed you in my life to be my wife, I made a promise to Him and you, and I will always guard our marriage. Remember, you are my world," he softly whispered, reaching to the depths of my heart. He then gently kissed my quivering lips before excusing himself to take a shower.

I waited for him for what felt like an hour. When I asked if he wanted to talk anymore, he simply said, "No." Then, he lay down in bed and just held me.

CHAPTER 22

April showers brought May flowers early that year. Helen enjoyed gardening, so I decided it wouldn't hurt to show some interest. Mother had always liked gardening anyway, and while the time spent in the dirt was bittersweet, I envisioned Mama being proud of me for learning about perennials, annuals, pruning, and how to grow rhubarb, tomatoes, and basil.

More, I knew Helen hadn't heard from or seen William since February, and I wanted to try to cheer her up. In fact, Edward found out from Shirley that Robert and Helen hadn't invited William and his wife for Shirley's high school graduation or the celebration afterwards, nor did they send Ruth a birthday gift. In sharp contrast, for my birthday, Robert and Helen bought me platinum hoop earrings, and Helen made a cherry chocolate cake that was deliciously moist and beautifully decorated. I cherished their affection, and while I was thankful to not share it with another daughter-in-law, I sometimes still felt a twinge of guilt for lying. *The lack of communication won't last too much longer. They will eventually get over what happened, and when we all move on, you will still be securely in first place in the family's eyes*, I told myself, rationalizing the lie.

Edward and I celebrated our first anniversary with a trip to Holden Beach, North Carolina. Our cottage was a quaint place, characterful and within walking distance to the beach and pier. Holden Beach was serene, the wind soothing, and as I stood, toes buried in the wet sand, gazing at the horizon, all my worries seemed to retreat with the ebbing tide. Edward especially enjoyed the fishing and shrimping activities, and he got it in his mind to keep an eye on the future of Ocean Isle Beach, a sliver of an island recently purchased by the state's legislature and named by him and his wife, Virginia. In fact, to show support for the changes in Brunswick County, the cottage we were staying in had been named Virginia's Inn.

While we had a marvelous time, I was annoyed that William's name surfaced, not just once, but several times.

"William would love this place, and I am sure he would've been interested in buying property on Ocean Isle. How could he marry that woman? She completely changed him," Edward brought up, for the second time in four days.

"I know, Eddy dear," I said, as I sat down on one of the cottage's comfortable living room chairs. I swirled my just-refilled Riesling around in the glass before taking another sip, desperately wanting to switch topics.

"That woman caused all this shit. I hope he comes to his senses and divorces her," he continued, pouring himself a third glass of whiskey.

I had hoped the night would be a romantic one, and I wanted even more for it to be fruitful – so much so that, before we pulled out glasses, I'd slipped off my undergarments and was only wearing my robe. A full twelve months had passed without a pregnancy announcement, and I hoped the vacation would relax us both.

I decided it was time to stop talking about William and stop thinking about Ruth, so I stood up and started rubbing Edward's shoulders. He continued talking until I slid my hands down his chest. Then, I moved in front of him, opened up the top part of my robe, grabbed his hands and positioned them, and kissed him. Dazed, he didn't object when I stood up to walk toward the bedroom, my robe pooling at my feet on the way.

I took a sip of water and decided it was time to finish packing for our Labor Day weekend getaway. This trip would be different than previous years for several reasons. First, I was three months along in the pregnancy and still felt nauseous on a daily basis. Second, while no formal invitations had ever been sent, I knew that no one had asked William if he and his wife were coming. In fact, the family had not spoken with him for almost six months.

I hope you can make it the whole drive without vomiting. While the symptoms were not intrinsically enjoyable, I had never been so thankful to feel sick. In a way, I felt like my life now had real purpose. Yet, despite being joyfully pregnant, my mind tended to spin in even more circles from wishful or negative thinking to positive thinking and then back again. And, whenever I thought of Mama, the guilt from lying about Ruth always seemed to follow. *I wish Mama were here. She would know what to do to help the nausea. She would've been so excited,* I started. *Margaret, stop looking back. Focus on the positives. You are finally pregnant. Labor Day weekend will be enjoyable and remember: you won't have to share Helen and Shirley with anyone,* I told myself before hearing a condemning voice. *Yes, you won't have to share your mother-in-law or sister-in-law because you are a liar. Just think how disappointed Mama would be.*

"Margaret?" I heard Edward calling from the kitchen.

Thankful to get out of my own head, I called out, "Coming, dear." I started my way toward him and then said, "I was laying out clothes for Labor Day. I can't believe it's next weekend!"

"It will be the last holiday weekend as just us two," he said, hugging me and kissing my head. I smelled bourbon on his breath. "You just glow with joy, my beautiful, pregnant wife. How are you feeling?"

"Thanks, love. I am okay. I haven't vomited yet, but I still feel like I could. I hope it improves in the next week so we can enjoy the weekend more."

"I agree!" Edward responded, giving my hips a squeeze. "I miss our time under the sheets," he teased. "And, Mom told me we can have the same room this year since my asshole brother isn't coming. I guess there is a perk to his wife screwing things up."

William's and Ruth's names were rarely mentioned anymore, especially by Edward. When alcohol was involved, he always replaced their given names with colorful terms. And, if they happened to come up in conversation without alcohol, he commonly used the terms "brother" and "his wife," as if to distance himself from them.

I smiled, kissed him quickly, and then said, "I am going to go finish packing before I start dinner."

Labor Day weekend came and went. The days spent in the sun and on the boat were enjoyable, but despite her attempts to be her normal self, everyone felt the weight of Helen's heavy heart. Over dinner on Saturday, Edward, attempting to cheer her up, asked, "Mom, what do you want to do tonight? It is your turn to decide." With a solemn shake of her head, Helen simply answered, "It just isn't the same without him." She then quickly stood up and started busying herself in the kitchen.

Beyond that exchange, Robert and Helen said nothing else that weekend about William and Ruth. It was as if they didn't exist, especially for Robert. Liquor, however, loosened Edward's tongue, but even then, Robert shot the topic down, leaving me to be the sounding board once we retreated to our room.

"How could he put that woman over his family?" Edward said harshly, throwing his dirty shirt in the suitcase, anger radiating from his body. "I should call him and tell him what a coward he is for not facing the truth about his wife." I stayed calm during his tirade, adding appropriate "uh-huh" and "I know, babe" responses when necessary. *Perhaps you should've taken your Mama's advice after all. Was your selfish need to be number one worth it?* I asked myself. A shard of shame pierced my heart, and my inner lawyer was quick to defend, dismissing the question. *This anger and hurt will pass. Just give it time. Besides, confessing would only ruin the family relationships you have left — and you can't afford to do that with a baby on the way.*

"Margaret, are you listening to me?" Edward said, now naked on the other side of the bed, visibly ready for me. Luckily, I was feeling better that night. I told myself he wanted me, but Edward's passion felt more fueled by anger than desire.

He crawled across the two twin beds pushed together, pulled me onto the bed, and ripped my dress open, sending buttons everywhere. I wondered then about Mama and how many times she had told herself Father wanted her when he really just wanted an outlet.

Summer turned to fall as my belly rounded out. Our baby's first kick happened on October 20, and it was the most wonderful sensation I had ever felt. While I wasn't due until February 21, we dreamed about whether it was a boy or a girl, envisioned what he or she would be like, and tossed around name ideas. Best of all, I no longer struggled with nausea in the second trimester, my energy returned, and beyond my legs feeling restless near the end of the day, I felt like my normal self. My co-workers were all excited for me, Helen started planning a small gathering to celebrate the pregnancy, and Edward and I began to talk about the nursery.

As an additional benefit, Helen gradually returned to her usual self as she dedicated more and more time to the baby. In turn, I spent less time wondering about William and Ruth and worrying what would happen if the truth came out. As Thanksgiving approached, Robert and Helen surprised us with a new crib, changing table, and rocker, and, with each passing Sunday, I caught a glimpse of the most recent blanket, outfit, hat or bootie she was knitting for the baby.

If I ever wanted, Shirley provided me with what she called a "WAR update," the name derived from their initials, "W and R" – and from seeing Ruth as an enemy.

"Hey," I said, sitting down on the porch swing. "Any 'WAR update'?" I asked her before a Sunday Fun-day family dinner. The November air was chilly, but with a warm mug of tea in hand, we didn't mind sitting on the porch. Since graduation, she had moved into a one-bedroom apartment nearby and taken a job as a secretary for a law firm. Similar to Eddy and me, she came to Robert and Helen's house each Sunday for a home-cooked meal.

"Nothing to report again, actually. I thought Mom would be more upset around Thanksgiving since it's the holiday she made William promise she would see him each year. I think she is just consumed with you and the baby." She smiled, her gaze fixed on my increasingly round middle. After a few minutes in silence and a few sips of tea, she added some more details of the last in-person conversation. "I doubt they will reach out to William, and I doubt they will hear anything either. Last I heard, they told him they didn't know who he was anymore and suggested he reconsider his decision. That's a major thing for Mom to suggest, considering what the Catholic church believes about it and all. Not that I didn't agree with her." She gave an abrupt laugh and continued after we made eye contact. "He was firm in his position that Ruth was innocent." She paused.

Is she hoping I admit something? Does she suspect? My mind darted, as fear gripped my heart. *Don't give any reason for her to doubt you.*

"Anyway," Shirley's voice filled the silence, "Dad and Mom defended you, telling him, 'Well, that is what Margaret said.' From what I can tell, they are at an impasse." She shrugged her shoulders and took another sip of tea. "William was set on working things out, to which they said there was nothing to work out. It felt like a 'choose us or her' conversation."

"Time will tell," I responded, not knowing what else to say.

The whole pregnancy experience was surreal, and I loved every day of it – that is, until mid-December. It started off with an itching sensation on my chest. I applied lotion before bed, but I woke up in the wee hours of the morning scratching my ever-growing belly. Unable to fall back asleep, I took a shower and tried to distract myself from the itch. As soon as the doctor's office opened, I called and scheduled an appointment around lunch. Counting down the minutes till I saw the doctor, I applied ice packs at work to numb the sensation.

"Well, Margaret, you have a rash known as Nurse's late onset prurigo," Dr. Wood explained.

"What?" I said knowingly, trying to remember the details about the rash I'd learned in school. "Remind me, how long does it last?"

"While rare, especially for a woman of your stature, some women develop this rash in the third trimester. It should go away within two weeks of delivery," he explained in a scholarly fashion.

"I will have this rash the rest of the pregnancy? That's almost twelve weeks away!" I exclaimed, desperate.

"I will prescribe a cream to help with the itch. You can also apply unscented lotion as needed. Unfortunately, there isn't much else you can do," he replied, more sincerely this time. "If it is any consolation, the rash hints at the baby's sex, as this rash is more common when the mother is carrying a boy than a girl."

I left the office incredibly discouraged. *How am I going to deal with this itch? Of course this is happening to me, of all people. What is Edward going to think? Our sex life was basically non-existent in the first trimester, and he was clearly frustrated then*, I complained to myself as I slid into the car. *I can't even rub my belly to communicate with my baby.* And with that last thought, I cried.

CHAPTER 23
February 1950

"Good morning, baby Mama!" Martha called me one dreary February morning. "Slight change of plans. I know we agreed on one o'clock for lunch today, but something's come up and I need to move our lunch date to eleven. Is that okay?" she asked hurriedly.

"Hmm, let me check my busy calendar," I replied in jest. With my due date around the corner, my doctor had advised me to limit my activities. And – with my belly itch – I wasn't interested in leaving the house often anyway. "Yes, I think I can squeeze you in this morning."

"Grand! I've got to go. See you at Culp's in a few hours!"

Martha was outside pacing anxiously when I arrived at the café, and she quickly took my hand and led me through the door. A chorus of well wishes erupted as I walked in and saw my hospital colleagues gathered with big smiles on their faces. Tears of happiness welled in my eyes, as I'd never anticipated the surprise baby shower. It was a bittersweet occasion. They all knew I wouldn't be returning after the baby came, but their excitement reassured me that I would be a good mom *and* that I wouldn't miss the hospital as much as I thought I would.

A part of me wished my plans hadn't shifted, that I would've been out of the house all afternoon as originally planned – that I would've continued my life in blissful ignorance.

When I pulled up to the house at around one thirty, I was surprised to see Edward's car. *He is home awfully early*, I thought and wondered why. Mainly because of the rash, but partially because I was simply uncomfortable, we had not been intimate since the weekend after Thanksgiving. I tried to sympathize with him, but he regularly told me he was okay. I learned that afternoon why.

When I went inside, the first thing I saw was a pair of red heels by the front door. My stomach churned. Hardly breathing, I listened and heard noise coming from upstairs. I tiptoed up the stairs, avoiding the areas that creaked, and saw clothes strewn along the hallway leading to our bedroom. Adrenaline surging, I walked toward the moaning and stood in the door frame for what felt like an eternity before Edward noticed me standing there, watching. He frantically pushed the woman off him and began to sit up. That's when I made eye contact with her. Long dark hair framed her plain face. I'd expected a gorgeous, young girl with large breasts and a perfect body. Instead, she looked painfully normal. She quickly covered her bare chest with the sheets Edward had bought me for Christmas a few weeks earlier, and her eyes widened when she noticed my pregnant belly.

I walked down the hall, descended the stairs, and vomited in the first-floor toilet. Before Edward could stop me, I drove away with no particular destination in mind. After about twenty minutes of aimless driving, it started to snow and my car's gas tank neared empty. Before I even realized where I was headed, I pulled into my father's driveway and parked on the far side of the garage. If Edward came looking for me, I didn't want him to readily see my car. Still having a key, I unlocked the door on the side of the garage and took in the sight of Johnny's DeSoto Custom. *Why did you have to die?* Overwhelmed with a sickening cocktail of emotions, I crumpled to the cold, concrete floor. A layer of ice hardened my heart that afternoon, and I decided if I could not find intimacy and security in Edward, I would focus all my attention and devotion to the child in my womb. *Could it be a son? If so, I hope you are nothing like your father.*

"You alone are my purpose, little one," I whispered to my large belly.

When my back began to ache from the concrete floor, I let myself into the house and put some water in the teapot. "Father?" I called tentatively, hoping he wasn't home. There was no reply, so I assumed he was out for his daily walk. Though I hadn't seen him much, he had surprised us with a large sum of cash to begin a savings account for the baby, and I did my best to sound sincere as I expressed my gratitude; I knew gift giving was important to him. While our relationship would likely never mend, at least in my mind, his apology on the anniversary of Mama's death had seemed heartfelt. I had visited him alone that afternoon. Edward encouraged me to spend time with Father that day, but now I wondered, bitterly, if he was just trying to get me out of the house for a few hours. *Who was under my sheets that day?*

That afternoon, Daddy served tea in the formal dining room with Mama's favorite English Bone China tea set.

"Margaret, dear. I know I have not been the perfect father," he began, handing me the Rose Filigree sugar bowl so I could add a cube into my matching cup.

"Father, please. It is fine."

"No, let me finish."

"Okay," I answered, waving my hand, inviting him to proceed. I crossed my legs and spun the pendant on my necklace.

For a few minutes, as my dad spoke candidly about his wrongdoings, asking my forgiveness, I wondered who the aging man was in front of me. Was this the same father who wanted to ship me off to an aunt's house when I was pregnant with Joe's baby, to preserve the family name? At first, I suspected he had an ulterior motive, but his tone, posture, and humility seemed entirely genuine.

When I asked what had changed, he simply answered, "I met Jesus."

I rolled my eyes at the revelation. *I have never seen him this vulnerable,* I remember thinking before my internal thoughts shifted tunes. *Why couldn't he come to the realization he was a jackass on his own? What kind of man needs a crutch to get through life? A weak one.*

"Daddy, if you need the crutch of Mama's faith to make it through living without her, then so be it. Either way, thank you for what you said," I managed to say, although my voice was harsher than I intended it to be.

"Can you forgive me? I understand it may take time. Or is there anything else I did to hurt you that I need to apologize for?"

"Sure, Daddy. I forgive you." And with that, I hugged him.

I believed him; I *needed* to believe him. *At least one man in your life is — or is at least trying to be — dependable.*

So, as I stood in the kitchen on that cold February day, I tried to comfort myself with the thought that at least one man in my life cared about his relationship with me. As my body temperature increased, my belly itch returned. So, rather than a mug, I reached for Daddy's black Hoppalong Cassidy Thermos and walked around back. I sat on the wrought-iron bench by the massive red oak tree, its branches blanketed in snow, looking striking against the blue sky. To distract myself I replayed happy childhood memories, and while my mind was years in the past, the itch of my skin receded.

Sometime later, I heard Father call from the backdoor. "Margaret? What are you doing outside?"

"The cold helps my belly."

"How about I make you an ice pack instead? Please, come inside."

Not in the mood to argue, I stood up and made my way into the house. "Tell me you didn't call Edward," I half said, half asked.

"No, I haven't. Why? What is wrong?"

While I had vowed to myself to never share anything negative about my husband with anyone, especially my parents, Edward also had vowed to be loyal to me. So, defenseless and vulnerable, I sat down on the familiar couch and told Daddy everything. I felt like a child, weeping and in desperate need of unconditional love, something I had never really experienced. All the people in my life who were supposed to love me wholly had failed me. *What is wrong with me? Why am I not enough for anyone?* I asked myself.

A dark voice answered, *Why would anyone love you for who you are? You are broken. Damaged goods. A liar.*

Father sat next to me and put his arm over my shoulder. He didn't speak, and I was glad. What could he have said, anyway?

—

The following Sunday, I returned to the house I used to call home. I wasn't sure if I could ever call it home again, nor did I plan to sleep in the bed he had defiled. Edward must have been watching for me, because as soon as I pulled in the drive, he was at the door full of apologies and cliché statements.

"You are full of bullshit, Edward James," I answered him, calm and collected. I felt numb, and while I was angrier than a hornet on the inside, I was resolved to keep my feelings bottled and respond with cold indifference.

"It was a one-time moment of weakness," he answered me, arms raised in the air.

"You expect me to believe it was a *one-time* thing?" My voice was thick with cynicism. *He isn't genuinely remorseful. He is just upset he got caught.*

"Well . . . with her," he answered, hands finding his pockets.

"Finally, some honesty," I shot back. "Who is she? How many have you brought to our bed?" I asked, not sure I wanted to know the answers.

"She is just a girl I met. She means nothing." He twiddled his thumbs, just like his mother did during an uncomfortable situation.

"How many?" I pushed.

"There were two others," he finally answered after a few moments of silence.

I stared at him in disgust, shook my head, and walked away. Thankful to have an extra bed in the guest room, I started moving my things into it. I would not be sharing a room with Edward for the foreseeable future. While divorce had crossed my mind, I knew it wasn't really an option. Too much was at stake, not least my reputation and the family I cherished. The only family I had.

⸺

After twenty-one long hours of arduous labor, James Michael was born on February 23, 1950 at 8:11 p.m., weighing eight pounds, eight ounces and measuring twenty-two inches long. The hours leading up to his first cry made me swear off conceiving again. At some point during my labor, James turned, and while head down, the doctor said he was facing the wrong way. The back pain was excruciating, and I grew panicky when I watched the nurses and doctor step aside to speak. Finally, I was fully dilated and ready to push. The minutes crept, and while the hospital staff was encouraging, after forty-five minutes I had no strength left in me. Holding my hand, Mary, one of my nurses, leaned in close and said, "You are so close. Give this last push everything you got." While very real, I immediately forgot about the pain when I held my son. His eyes were a mosaic of blues, a color I knew would change over the next few months, and his hair tinted red, like his father's. He was perfect, and I knew I hadn't understood love or my life's purpose until his birth.

Edward was at the hospital waiting to meet his child. Although a gaping divide still separated us, we were both able to enjoy the first few days of our son's life together.

Once home, where I would be spending all of my time now, Edward went back to work and Helen began visiting daily. She cooked and cleaned and helped in any way I needed her. She was an absolute angel. From what I could discern, she didn't know about Edward's unfaithfulness, although she did ask about my sleeping arrangements one afternoon. James was finally napping without being held, and we were sitting at our new blonde wood dining room table. The sleek dining set, a recent purchase from Edward in an attempt to buy back my favor, blended with our beamed ceiling, contrasted nicely with the stone fireplace, and set up an appealing neutral base for the chair's plum upholstery.

"I noticed you moved a lot of your things out of your bedroom. Why are you staying in the guest room?" she asked innocently.

"It is just that much closer to the nursery," I said quickly, keeping my voice level. "I don't want to wake Edward in the middle of the night."

"You are just the perfect wife for my son. Eddy is so lucky to have you. James is too, along with any other child you bring into this world," she said adoringly and smiled.

I smiled back weakly. "Do you mind if I rest while James is napping?"

"Of course, dear. Please rest, and I will start dinner." After a hug, Helen headed for the kitchen.

I went into the guest bedroom and shut the door. While exhausted, I couldn't sleep, my mind in overdrive, replaying the events of that fateful day when I'd walked in on Edward. I felt utterly alone and defeated, and while I wanted to cry, no tears would come. It was as if something had broken inside when I saw Edward with that woman. To make matters worse, I already felt the pressure to have another child, Helen's words ringing in my ears – "along with any other child you bring into this world." *Yeah, right*, I thought to myself. I couldn't believe women had multiple children! The pain from delivery was terrible; I certainly never wanted to go through it again. Moreover, I didn't recognize my body. I knew my stomach would go down and my boobs would not always throb, but nothing would ever be the same.

Edward isn't interested in your body anyway, a voice heckled. *Be prepared for him to cheat again, especially with the way you look now.*

Overwhelmed, I laid my head on the pillow. I longed for my younger years, yet chided myself for doing so. After all, I was mother to a beautiful baby boy. With an unused tissue in hand, I succumbed to exhaustion and fell into a dreamless sleep.

CHAPTER 24
1954

"Edward, did you pick up the cake?" I called from the bathroom when I heard the back door close. While long potty trained, James still needed supervision if I hoped for him to wash his hands properly.

"Yes, and I picked up some ice cream to go with it," he responded.

"Daddy!" James said, as he ran out of the bathroom, hands dripping.

"Hey, sport!" Edward said. He picked up James and spun him around before he threw him over his shoulder, asking, "Did you see where the birthday boy went?"

James flailed his arms and legs around and screamed, "I am right *here*, Daddy!"

Holding the atomic-patterned towel intended to dry James's hands, I watched the interaction and smiled. While I could not call Edward even a decent husband, I couldn't deny that he was a wonderful father – when he was around at least. Despite his long hours, Edward did carve out time for just the two of them on the weekends, be it taking James to the park to introduce him to fishing, challenging him to wrestling matches, or telling him a bedtime story. I did wish, however, he was around more during the week, for James's sake.

Edward sat James down for his afternoon snack – a sliced Honeycrisp apple with peanut butter – and I returned the hand towel to the bathroom. Staring at my weathered skin in the mirror, I tucked my hair behind my ears and adjusted a bobby pin. I was turning thirty in a few months, and while I didn't feel different from one day to the next, the few gray hairs reminded me I was aging. I locked eyes with my reflection, my mind drifting back over the last four years. While Edward never showed remorse for his indiscretions, he was a gentleman toward me around James and others, and we had reached a tolerable place in our marriage since James's birth.

For a while, I believed we could repair the damage and come out stronger for it. Shortly after James was born, I decided to push aside my anger and hurt and to try to be who Edward wanted. I did everything I could think of to please him. I assumed every household chore, I tried hard to improve my cooking, and I initiated sex often. While he readily accepted every invitation to bed, I often felt like his mind was somewhere else, and our conversations were superficial, focused on calendaring, finances, sports, or the weather. Still, despite no meaningful intimacy, I persisted – for a time, at least.

Edward had received a promotion in late 1951, climbing up another rung on the administrative ladder, and from that point, his identity revolved even more around work. With the leadership role came late nights, supervisees, and a secretary to keep his calendar and be at his beck and call. Shortly after he had started his new job, I made the mistake of visiting the office unannounced.

"Have a good day at work," I said as he left that Friday morning.

"Thanks. Today is a light day, and we actually have our office Christmas party over lunch," he said to me, adding, "I will be home a little early so I can spend time with James before poker." He then turned to James, almost two at the time, and said, "Bye-bye, buddy. Be good today." After kissing James's forehead and giving me the obligatory peck on the cheek, he walked out the door.

James incessantly asked for "Daddy" that morning. He hadn't spent any meaningful time with his father since Sunday, and I asked Helen if we could all go Christmas shopping instead of our regular visit at her house. That way, we could stop by Edward's office on the way so James could say hi over lunch. And, as part of my desperate plan to please Edward in every way, I hoped for a few minutes of alone time to add a little sugar and spice to our visit.

Helen, James, and I entered the building and found an older receptionist sitting behind a desk in the lobby. She was polite, and after playing a few rounds of peek-a-boo, told me where to find both the room for the luncheon and Edward's office. Leaving James with Helen in the lobby, I went alone to ask Edward if he had a moment to visit or if he wanted to introduce James to his colleagues. As I walked around the fifth floor, I found the expected group of people in a conference room for the Christmas party. I didn't see him, however, so I proceeded down the hallway toward another corner of the building. Finding his name on a door, I reapplied my red lipstick, unbuttoned one of my dress's buttons, and adjusted the girls. *Hopefully adding a little spontaneity will help our marriage.* I then gave the door a quick two-knock tap and started pushing it open, peeking my head in before opening it all the way. The picture I had envisioned of us in his office was shattered when I saw his pants on the ground and his hands around the waist of some young thing sitting on the edge of his desk.

We made eye contact, but I shut the door before Edward could say a word. I tried to gain my composure as I walked to the lobby.

"James, Daddy is busy right now, but you will see him at supper time," I told my son as calmly as I could, all the while thinking, *I hope he is nothing like his father.*

No doubt noticing my barely restrained fury, Helen gave me a questioning look but said nothing. We continued on and shopped until James's nap. All the while I desperately tried to act as if the day hadn't been cataclysmic to my heart, hoping small talk would be a suitable distraction. I talked about how cold the weekend was expected to be, the shopping craze, and how excited James would be for the Little People fire engine and figurines that we'd bought him.

Edward kept to his word and was home early, acting as if nothing untoward had happened. We ate as a family of three, and after supper, he played trains with James until reading him his favorite bedtime story, *If I Ran the Zoo.* Before leaving for poker night, he simply and impassively instructed me to "Call before stopping by the office again."

Since that December day, I'd stopped trying to be what he wanted. I still felt a stab every time a new young, beautiful secretary sat outside his office. In the past twenty-seven months, I had met – at least briefly – three when I dropped something forgotten off or, if time permitted, Edward took James to a nearby park or bought him an ice cream cone. While I could not confirm if he had been intimate with them, his previous infidelities left me with little doubt that his unfaithfulness was as much a part of our marriage as I was.

However, I tried to remind myself that I still had much to be thankful for. I had a precious son turning four, in-laws who adored me, and a full bank account to do with as I pleased. We stayed married for the benefit of James, our family relations, and our reputations. I certainly did not want to share James, lose Helen, or forfeit the financial security I had gained from being married to Edward and into his family. And although we'd never spoken about it, I knew that Edward would never want to disappoint his mother, hurt James, or have his professional career impacted, as it was best for him to maintain a positive family reputation to climb the ladder. Besides telling Daddy that cold day in 1950, I never told another soul, as I didn't want anyone else knowing our picture-perfect family was just that – only perfect in family photographs. Within our home, we were cordial roommates. While I moved back into our bedroom for appearance's sake, the twin beds remained pulled apart. Our relationship was symbiotic, our conversation shallow and formal, and I learned to accept that I would never again be enough for Edward.

"Margaret, did you hear me? What time is everyone coming over?" Edward asked.

I blinked my eyes a few times, bringing my head out of my mind's cobwebs, and called, "At four o'clock." Entering into the kitchen, I looked at the GE ceramic clock on the wall. "Birthday boy, it is time for a nap," I said, body lowered, hands on my knees.

"I don't want to take a nap," James whined.

"Well, you at least need some quiet time. You can play on your own or read a book if you can't fall asleep. But, if you do take a nap, you can stay up a little later than normal," I responded, hoping the appeal of a later bedtime would win him over. Shirley was coming over early, and I wanted some time with her.

I walked up the stairs with James and tucked him in after he jumped in bed. "I will see you in a little bit, my big boy," I whispered, kissing him on the forehead.

In the kitchen again, I stirred the chili and started working on the cornbread. *What does Shirley have to share?* I wondered. *She mentioned she had an important WAR update, but she wouldn't divulge any further details.* It had been years since we heard from William and Ruth, and I was certain Robert and Helen had never reached out.

"I am going to head out and see if I can find the Blinky Fire Truck for James," Edward said, interrupting my thoughts.

"Good luck," I responded, not looking up from the mixing bowl.

I wish things were different, the whispers of my discontented heart roared. *Why couldn't he have been stronger? Why couldn't I have been enough? I used to be. Hell, I was out of his league when we met, and now I am just his roommate with a wedding ring.* I laughed out loud, rolled my eyes, and looked at my left hand to divert my thinking away from self-pity. *At least he upgraded it at Christmas*, I reasoned, smiling. But then a dark voice mocked, *He just did it to keep up the mirage of a happy marriage for his parents.*

While Robert, Helen, and Shirley had likely noticed a distance between us or wondered why we never had another child, as far as I know they never found out about Edward's affairs. Raising challenging topics was not their style, which I appreciated. However, sometimes I wondered what it would be like to have a friend whom I could be transparent with.

"Mags, you there? Can I come in?" I heard Shirley call from outside the back door.

"Of course!" I replied, but she had already turned the handle.

Shirley threw her leopard print coat over one of the kitchen chairs and sat down. "Are you at a good stopping point?" she asked, clearly wanting my full attention.

"Just two seconds," I answered, turning around and noticing her attire. "I like your sweater dress," I added.

"Oh, thanks. Charles is taking me out tonight after dinner, so I thought I would dress up some. He wants to talk about the wedding and honeymoon," she said, a smile painting her long, thin face. Her nose was also thin and long, but proportional, and her wavy blonde hair made her look more lively than the dark color she had earlier that year.

Charles and Shirley had met two years ago, and he proposed on Christmas Eve. Spending the night at Robert and Helen's had become a tradition since James had been born, and that night, after he went to bed, we all gathered around the Christmas tree to open one gift. With Robert and Helen in on the plan, Robert assigned Charles the role of Santa, allowing him to pick what gift to give each person. Being the youngest, Shirley opened her gift last. Charles placed a large box in her hands, and much to her surprise, she found a small box on the inside of the larger box, and when she looked up, Charles was on one knee.

Charles was a bit of an enigma. Behind the permanent grin painted on his face, I could never tell what he was thinking or gauge his thoughts on a topic, simple or complex. And, being with Shirley, he hardly had room to speak his opinion if he had one, as she often spoke for them both. At first, I was surprised Robert and Helen approved of the relationship due to his heritage. His mother was from Venezuela, and while he grew up in America, his darker skin and short, dark, spiky hair left no question that he was not of European descent. Regardless of his conversion to the Catholic faith, I concluded Helen didn't want to rock the boat with another child over a relationship, especially her only daughter. Charles entertained Edward in whatever conversation topic he chose, picked up Robert's fishing hobby, and followed Shirley's lead. Without knowing her birth order, one would think Shirley was the oldest child. She was demonstrative, and while I thought a man with a stronger personality would've suited her well, I believed she wanted one who would follow her lead rather than the other way around.

"How fun! Only a few more months now!" I squealed with an exaggerated smile on my face, walking over to the table to sit down, cornbread baking in the oven.

"Yes, I know. That's not why I came over early, though. Dad and Mom received a letter on Thursday," Shirley began, hitting both palms on the table and leaning in slightly. "From

William and Ruth. I mean, William signed it for them, but it doesn't sound anything like him, so I think Ruth wrote it," she added with a sigh.

"When did you see it? What did it say?" I asked, trying to sound interested in the letter, but not too interested.

"I saw it yesterday when I stopped by after work. Mom didn't answer me when I first walked in, and when I turned the corner I saw her sitting down, letter in hand. It said something about how they were hurt, wanted reconciliation, wanted the letter between just them." Shirley dramatically rolled her eyes before concluding the description with, "Blah, blah, blah."

I forced a laugh, and with my hands under the table, counted with my fingers. "Has it really been almost five years?"

"Time certainly goes quickly. I don't know why they can't just forget the past and move on. William, or Ruth rather, wrote something like, 'pretending to be at peace never resolved a conflict,' or some jargon like that. Whatever. But the meat of the letter was to inform Dad and Mom they had another baby!" Shirley hit the kitchen table with both hands. "Another one!" she practically yelled.

"Oh wow. I didn't realize they had one child, let alone two," I almost whispered, conflicting emotions beginning to battle inside. *What will Edward think? Before the impasse, he talked about wanting to have our kids and William's children grow up together. That dream will certainly never happen now.*

"Precisely what I said." Leaning back into the chair, Shirley crossed her arms. "William has done nothing but hurt our family, and for what? For a snake of a wife? He made the wrong choice, that's for sure," Shirley added, her voice thick with annoyance and frustration.

"What do you think Mom and Dad will do?" I asked, referring to Robert and Helen.

"Dad wants nothing to do with them. Honestly, I think he is a little bitter, but don't repeat those words. I can't blame him. As for Mom, she started writing a response, but I don't know if she will send it because Father won't support it."

"Did you see her letter?"

"I didn't see the whole thing. Something about wanting to just move on and not look back, which is incredibly generous given what happened. Besides, who wants to spend time talking about the past?" she answered flatly and shrugged her shoulders.

We sat in silence for a moment, but in my head, I told myself, *Regardless of the amount of time that has passed, I hardly think things will simply be brushed under the rug. And, I am certain the letters Edward penned and mailed over the years were anything but harmonizing. Rather than time healing all wounds, it has likely caused them to fester.*

"Maybe it is time to forget what Ruth said and offer a blanket apology," I started to add, twiddling my thumbs, the nervous habit I'd adopted from my mother-in-law.

"A *blanket apology*? For what? None of us did anything wrong," Shirley snapped back. "You certainly are an angel, Margaret," she added, kinder this time, taking my hand. "Now, what can I do to help prepare for the party?"

James's party was full of laughs, delicious food, and big smiles from our four-year-old. I wanted to bottle up that smile of his so I could remember it whenever I needed a pick-me-up.

Once James was in bed, an hour after his normal bedtime, and Shirley off on her date, Edward and I spent time with Robert, Helen, and Father. What I hoped would be a relaxing night with family turned into an emotion-filled evening when Robert brought up the letter.

"Your brother has two kids now," Robert started off as he poured what I thought was his third Jack Daniel's.

"Robert," Helen shot in his direction with a hushed, scolding tone and wide eyes.

"Who gives a damn, Helen? Besides, you expect me to believe you didn't already tell Shirley?" Robert retorted. With that, Helen looked at her hands, her thumbs beginning to circle.

He continued. "We received a letter. He wrote about us talking, his *second* kid . . . and not telling you because they want to focus on starting things off with just Helen and me. Well, we are a package deal, so I don't give a damn about telling you."

Edward was noticeably upset. Typically, Edward pretended it didn't bother him, and while he was good at compartmentalizing, when the topic arose, his language and temper worsened. The conversation continued for a short while, with the emotional temperature in the room becoming increasingly heated. Finally, Helen stood up and informed everyone she was tired and wanted to leave. She was never one for uncomfortable conversations, her default being to flee the situation. I, however, was thankful the topic was over, especially for the sake of my father, who observed quietly while sipping decaffeinated coffee.

As they were walking out, I thought I heard Edward ask his father to pass on the return address, but I didn't want to pry. It was best to leave Edward alone when angry.

I quietly said to my own father when I hugged him good-bye, "Sorry the evening didn't go as planned. I will stop by this week to see you."

"Sounds good, Mags. I will pray for the situation," Daddy replied, squeezing my hand. His words made my stomach churn. I didn't want or need his prayer.

The house was finally quiet. After cleaning up the kitchen and putting all the new toys in the downstairs oak toy box, I got ready for bed. I tried to escape to the guest room, but Edward cornered me coming out of the bathroom.

"I pushed our beds together," he informed me, whiskey fresh on his breath. He was down to his underwear and his arm blocked me from sliding to the left toward my room.

"Edward, you are drunk." I tried to slide my way under his arm, but he wouldn't permit me to pass.

"True, but today is a day of celebration. Our son turned four, and my brother had a baby. No, let me rephrase – he and that bitch had *another* baby," he slurred, then leaned in to kiss my neck as his hands groped my chest.

"Please, stop," I pleaded. Nothing in me wanted him, drunk or sober.

Ignoring me, Edward removed his remaining garment and started pulling up my full-length nightgown. There was no use fighting him. I didn't want him to raise his voice and wake James, so, once again, I just let him have his way.

CHAPTER 25
2015

"I am sorry the men in your life treated you so poorly," Megan spoke into the dead space after I stopped talking for a few minutes.

"My father turned around after Mama died," I defended.

"I am glad. Would you like something to eat? A scone perhaps?"

"That would be nice, thank you."

Megan excused herself and stood in line for a few moments until the male cashier asked what she would like. I could hear his British accent from my chair, despite my old ears.

She is untainted. Innocent. How you should've been. How you would've been if Johnny hadn't died. If Mama hadn't lost herself to the bottle. If Father wouldn't have felt the need to set you up, my mind began, as I looked at Megan's curls and youth with envy. As she waited for the scones, she smiled at me from across the shop and waved. A softer voice whispered, *She is not your enemy, nor was Ruth. Maybe it is time to accept the consequences of the actions you have ignored for so long now.*

"Here you go. I bought you two, a plain scone and a raisin one," she almost sang. "And here is the jam and cream. Scones are my favorite mid-morning snack. They take time to make, but they are well worth it!"

"Thank you." While not raspberry chocolate chip, they did look delicious.

"Did Edward do anything with the return address?" Megan asked, although I had a suspicion she already knew the answer.

CHAPTER 26
Ruth

March 1, 1954

Son,

We received your letter. You have two daughters now? How wonderful. Congratulations! I am sure they are beautiful children. How could they not be with you as their father? I do hope to meet them soon. We also hope you are able to have a boy in the future, as Edward does, to carry on the family name.

Your Father and I prefer to just move on. Enough time has passed, and we are willing to forgive and forget what was said and done. We don't want you to miss out on anything more in Ohio, and we miss having our youngest son in our lives.

Always & forever,
Mom

Dumbfounded, I read the letter many times over before tossing it on the kitchen table. It was a far cry from what I had hoped for. Hurt and bitterness smoldered in my heart. I thought I had forgiven them completely, but their response ignited the anger all over again, and I wished we wouldn't have invited the trouble into our lives.

"They forgive what was said and done? What exactly are they referring to?" I asked William, asking both questions in rapid fire. "And, it is insulting they addressed it to only *you*."

"Yes, I noticed it was addressed to just me." William said flatly, clearly not thrilled.

"And our children are beautiful because they have *you* as a father? And they hope *you* have a boy in the future!" My voice grew in volume and agitation.

"I am glad both girls look more like you, dear," he managed to say before I kept talking.

"And they miss having their youngest? To them, I am just the woman who carried the babies they want to meet and the one who hasn't given you a boy." I rested my head in my hands, beyond disappointed the response didn't include a different message.

"Ruth, stop. Calm down, please," William coaxed.

"William, you know I don't like it when you address me by my name, like I am a child, or tell me to calm down. You are not helping," I shot back, tears brimming in my eyes. "They blame me. Still. Time and prayer have changed nothing."

William was silent for a moment. No matter what the storm, his sail never was blown by emotion like mine was. His rudder stayed steady and firm, while I swore my spiritual gift was freaking out. Feeling the weight of their rejection, I slumped into the chair and lay my head on the table in my crossed arms.

"You are right. I don't know what else to say," William said, taking my left hand, thumb running over my wedding band. "I love you."

"Are you sure you don't regret choosing me? Your life would've been less stressful and had less heartache if you would've stayed in Ohio and married someone your family liked," I managed to say, removing my hand from his, reaching for a tissue in the center of the table.

"Don't say that, my dear. Please, look at me," he said softly, willing me to make eye contact with him. We locked eyes and his gaze looked past my hazel irises to my heart. "I wouldn't change anything if it meant not having you as my bride. Just as I said on our wedding day, you are my world, and nothing will change that truth."

"We can work on a reply I guess," I mumbled, sniffling.

"Let's give it a few days." William opened his arms up, inviting me in for a hug.

While we were drafting a reply for his parents, we received a second letter, but this time from William's brother. Similar to the previous messages he mailed to my parents' address, it was filled with pride and an underlying tone of contempt toward me.

Hey there, brother. In case you forgot, you have a brother. What happened to loving your family? You have treated your parents and siblings like garbage since you married that woman. We still don't know why. We did nothing wrong. Your wife is the one who can't see eye to eye with us and who started all this strife. Did you forget I have a kid now too? Remember when we talked about having our kids grow up together? I guess she ruined that too.

It would be great to reconnect if you are actually willing to put your family first.

"I guess your parents shared our letter with your siblings." Despite practicing breathing techniques to calm down and praying for a soft heart toward him, I was practically shaking.

"I know," William responded with a stoic tone. "He blames you, when really his wife started it all. He should've listened to Shirley," William replied, almost to himself.

"What do you mean?"

"Didn't I tell you? Years ago, when Edward and Margaret were engaged, Shirley wrote Edward a note cautioning him against marrying Margaret. She was concerned about Margaret's intentions, mostly, but she also questioned the relationship in general. I remember Shirley saying to me before she gave it to Eddy, 'I can't even name what is bothering me about her. Call it intuition.' Regardless, Edward proceeded and married her. And on the flip side, she wanted me to marry you." William recalled memories that seemed to be from a former life.

I thought back to when Shirley was excited to call me sister, and I felt a pit in my stomach. I longed for what could have been before she had tossed me aside like a ragdoll.

"We will hold off responding to my parents. I am glad we haven't mailed anything yet," William stated, interrupting my thoughts.

I blurted out two more questions. "How long do you want to wait this time? How can they live with themselves?" I wanted to shake Helen and scream, "What is wrong with you? How can you treat your son like this?"

"Ruth, dear, I seriously don't know. Let's just give it some time."

William was noticeably agitated. I didn't mean to upset him more than the letter already had. I knew his brother's letter wasn't his fault. And just like William did, I wished things were different. I hardly remembered anymore what it was like to have his family enjoy my company.

As time marched on, the topic of responding surfaced less and less. And when I did ask, each time his answer was the same: not right now. Finally, in late May, I told him I would not bring up the subject again, but instead wait for him.

The summer months came and went, and I knew he wouldn't want to entertain the idea around Labor Day. *I wonder if they still all spend the weekend together?* I thought as I packed for our own Labor Day vacation to Fort Myers Beach, a tradition we'd started in 1951. And although it was hurricane season, we prayed for good weather, and I especially hoped to find sea turtles hatching and making their perilous journey from their nest to the Gulf of Mexico. While we enjoyed Fort Myers, we had our eyes set on the two sanctuary islands off the mainland, Captiva and Sanibel. Our goal was to buy property on one of the islands when development – we were certain would come – started.

I treasured our first trip to Sanibel, even though it was only a day trip during our 1951 Fort Myers vacation. The sun was brilliant as we embarked for the half-hour ferry ride, the gentle sting of sea-spray a salve for our bruised hearts, the steady breeze blowing away every barnacle of worry. Our souls relaxed just a little more when our toes stepped on the warm, firm island sand, and our minds slowed to listen to the beach's symphony: the delicate notes of the waves shuffling the shells backward and forward, the sharp crescendos of birdsong, and the rhythmic whoosh of the breeze. William fell in love with the gentle lap of the water and the way it stretched onto the Sanibel beaches, and he seemed one with his Maker when he fished, knee deep in the glittering sea and a cigar in his mouth. As for me, the sun's warmth penetrated through my skin and seemed to reach my innermost parts. One foot slowly in front of the other, I searched for both shells and intimate time with my God. The island time offered much needed divine healing.

Including our wedding day, our young marriage had gone through hell since 1949. For a time, all I could do was cling to the foundation we had, despite being pelted with rejection, loss, and overwhelming sorrow. Beyond the hurt from William's family on our wedding day, the conversation with his parents afterward was jarring. Then, a few short months after the conversation, came a letter; Edward may have penned it, but the devil inspired it. While I knew William felt the sting, the family rift weighed heavier on my heart, and I envied William's ability to control his mind. To add to the maddening season, I miscarried that summer. We couldn't help but wonder if my anxiety levels had caused it.

While William and I eventually reached a place of forgiveness toward his family and peace about the miscarriage, he decided it was best to not invite the level of stress they brought into our lives as we tried to conceive again. Our hearts leaped for joy the following spring when we conceived. Trying to control external factors the best he could, William made it crystal clear we would not be welcoming any negativity into our lives during the pregnancy. As my belly expanded in a perfect round shape, we planned the baby's nursery, picked out names for each gender, and envisioned our lives as a family of three. As we neared January, the fears of losing another baby faded away.

Our dreams were shattered on January 8 when I delivered a stillborn child, the umbilical cord wrapped around her neck. I felt like I was going to die from the weight of sadness and pain.

They didn't even give me the chance to hold the baby girl I'd felt kick just that morning.

My breasts were full of milk with no baby to feed.

I had a post-pregnancy belly with no baby to show for it.

I loved a lifeless daughter who, instead of being placed in my arms, was delivered straight into the arms of God.

God.

I felt like Job from the Bible, and I began to curse the day I was born. And through my sobs, I hurled questions at the one I called God. I didn't care who was in the hospital room.

The nurse finally let William in, and he wrapped his arms around me, still completely hysterical. The inward pain trumped any outward pain my body just experienced.

As the weeks went by, I felt numb. I refused to entertain any activity related to faith, and my dry soul impacted every facet of life. Be it the devil or the burden of my own sorrow, I even started considering taking my own life. I was convinced I would never be a mother or provide William with a child, and I began believing William would leave me for someone else – a woman who could have his children and who his family would accept. Dark thoughts filled my mind, and as the poison spread throughout my body, I felt like I was dying inside.

Finally, one Thursday morning in March, I knew I was at a crossroads. I had called off from work again, something the department store had truly been patient with, and before he left for work William said something about me having a choice. While my response was a defiant glare, his words managed to crack my icy wall of defense. Once alone, the fury and rage and sorrow I'd been bottling up boiled over into gut-wrenching screams that brought me to my knees, forcing me to face an uncomfortable truth: I could either walk in the faith I claimed or reject it. A soft voice gently whispered my name, and I surrendered to it, silencing the dark voice that had held me captive for months.

When I tested positive for another pregnancy a few weeks later, I was crippled with fear. I simply could not handle another loss. My mind was an epic battlefield from the time I learned I was pregnant until we visited Fort Myers and the sanctuary islands that summer. William surprised me with the week-long vacation, and the time spent in the Florida sun brought vibrant hope and new life to our marriage. And from that week until January 23, 1952, when I heard our daughter's first cry, I miraculously walked with a sense of peace.

Our lives changed for the better, and our goals shifted to equipping our daughter for the world emotionally, physically, and spiritually. We prayerfully decided to send a baby announcement to William's parents when Abigail was three months old. To our disappointment, we received no response. We considered reaching out when she was almost one, but after receiving yet another hateful correspondence from Edward, we decided against the idea. To make matters worse, Edward used plural pronouns and even signed everyone's names, suggesting the message was from everyone. Before long, we were pregnant again, and welcomed another daughter in October 1953.

Thankfully, both girls were sleeping through the night by that December, and one night, after they were both in bed, I asked William about reaching out to his parents. Through hardship and heartache, we had both grown and been refined, and while the subject was still difficult, I believed it was the right time. And, truth be told, I sincerely thought they would be remorseful and apologetic, and I dreamed we could visit them by Memorial Day the following year. The letter included the announcement of Esther and a heartfelt note expressing the desire to reconcile. I earnestly hoped the news of another child would soften their hearts. William hesitantly agreed. And then reality slapped me in the face. First, his parents indirectly insulted me and wanted to pretend nothing had happened, and then, Edward's letter. Sorrow flooded my mind, and I relived the years of interwoven painful memories in a matter of minutes.

I finished packing our suitcase for our family's Labor Day vacation and moved on to the girls' suitcase. *We haven't heard anything since March. Wouldn't it be a miracle to receive a letter reflecting a heart change?* I thought, praying one would come. *Hell will freeze over first*, another part of me retorted. The mental tug-a-war between having faith God could change the situation and believing they wouldn't change was exhausting. I knew God could change the situation, but I also knew the miracle may be within me. And, despite the negative booming voices reminding me of the rejection and miscarriage, I told myself I needed to forgive. *You said everything you needed to. Reconciliation is twofold, and you have done your part to live at peace. Remember, you are not called to be a peacekeeper, but a peacemaker. You cannot force them to reconcile if they are not interested.* Most of the words were from our pastor's wife; she had become a true mentor over the last four years. While my parents were wonderful through it all, they were too emotionally involved to provide unbiased feedback related to William's family, and they suggested we seek out another couple to give us advice on what to do. Hence, we reached out to our pastor and his wife.

And with that reminder, I reluctantly accepted our continued state of impasse and zipped up the girls' suitcase.

CHAPTER 27

In my youth, celebrating the beginning of a new year always energized me, my reflections on the past twelve months and the anticipation of what the next twelve had in store filling me with hope. For the last decade, however, reflecting on the past only brought pain, anger, shame, emptiness, or a strangling combination. And, while I found purpose in being James's mother, I dreaded the upcoming year because he would start school in the fall. *What are you going to do with your time?* I asked myself as I stared outside at the snowflakes settling on the lawn. It was New Year's Eve, and I wasn't sure if Edward would be home before James went to bed. While his new job allowed him to be home for supper consistently, he had abruptly told me early that morning he would be taking a day trip and wouldn't be back till late, shutting the door before I could ask any questions. While no longer napping, James had one hour of independent play time each afternoon, and I was spending it sipping tea, my mind tightly knotted by worry. *You should start dinner. Edward may not be home for supper, but you and James need to eat*, I reminded myself, desperate to focus my energies on a task to escape my thoughts.

Shortly before Christmas, Edward had accepted a new administrative role at the hospital and was now home every night for supper. My father called in a favor, hoping the new environment would please me, especially because it was a male-dominated department and there were no secretaries. While Robert and Helen remained unaware, or at least pretended to be, my father knew our marriage had never recovered from Edward's infidelity. Although the last five years as his wife were far from what I envisioned marriage to be, the desire to leave the home afforded me the opportunity to spend more time with Father. Daddy rearranged his work schedule to spend every Monday with James and me. The mornings included waffles for breakfast and time spent playing doctor; by age three, James knew the names of more body parts and organs than most adults. The days also included bonding time for Daddy and me. Early on, once James was down for a nap, we would play a game or listen to the radio. As we became more comfortable in each other's company, he began to address the emotional baggage between us. I resisted for a time, but he persisted, and gradually the wall I'd built up to keep my father out started to crumble. By James's fourth birthday, my father was "Daddy" to me again, something I never thought possible.

That New Year's Eve evening, James and I enjoyed an easy dinner of spaghetti and meat sauce followed by playing with the Western Clothing set Father had bought James for Christmas. James dressed up in the sheriff's outfit and gave me a bandana to wear on my face.

"Stop right there! Hands up!" James yelled for the tenth time.

This time, however, instead of putting my hands up, I reached for the toy gun. Before I could aim, James shouted out, "Pow, pow!"

"You got me, Sheriff," I said, feigning an injury as I fell to my knees and then prostrate on the floor. Once resting on the rich oriental rug, even for just a moment, exhaustion hit me hard and kept me pinned to the carpet.

"Mommy, are you okay?" James finally asked after a few seconds.

"Yes, dear, I am. It is time to get ready for bed though. Let's go upstairs, and I will start the bath," I responded wearily.

I guess Edward will not be home early enough to see James. Where did he go? I wondered as we climbed the stairs together.

Ruth

Our New Year's Eve unfolded like a scene from one of my worst nightmares.

William took the day off, and he was playing dolls with Esther and Abigail in the living room. While Esther was only fourteen months, she enjoyed sitting with Abigail, almost three, and holding on to her little babydoll. I smiled when I overheard Abigail telling Daddy how to hold the bottle to feed her baby; I could already see her blossoming, nurturing spirit.

I was in the kitchen, my favorite room in the house, preparing a feast for supper. The walls were painted an optimistic yellow and the cabinets a bright, clean white. I was in my element as I stood at my electric range, something William had spoiled me with a few years back, along with the built-in refrigerator and dishwasher. My pots were organized perfectly on the wall above the range, and a porcelain cookie jar duck was nestled in one of the corners – a gift Abigail had picked out the previous Christmas when ducks were her favorite animal.

William and I decided New Year's Eve would be a day of family traditions, at least up until dinner to allow the girls freedom when they grew older. So far, the day had included eating homemade Belgian waffles while still wearing pajamas, building a snowman family of four in the front yard, and making chocolate chip cookies to enjoy after dinner. William and I were especially excited about the Belgian waffles, as the pearl sugar mixed in right before we cooked the dough gave them a delightful crunch. The dense waffles were so full of flavor they didn't even require butter and maple syrup! After cleaning up from the chocolate chip cookie bake, I started making a Shepherd's pie during the girls' nap times, which were beautifully coordinated now, and as I placed the rolls in the oven, I thought of all the other fun traditions we could do when the girls were a little older.

"Supper smells amazing, dear!" William called from the other room. Shepherd's pie was one of his favorite meals.

It was nearing five o'clock, and as I put the deviled eggs down on the table set for four, I heard a car door slam. *Roger shut his door awfully forcefully*, I thought to myself and went to the refrigerator to take out the butter and homemade strawberry jam. I chided myself for forgetting to take out the butter dish earlier. William liked butter soft, and while he would only be teasing if he said anything at all, I still felt a twinge of guilt. He'd bought me the dish just a week ago as a Christmas gift. After I opened the present and gave him a look communicating,

"Seriously?" he answered before laughing, "Perhaps this beautiful dish will help you remember to take the butter out early." The memory made me smile, silencing the start of a self-deprecating monologue. *I will make it a New Year's resolution to remember to take the butter out earlier*, I promised as I laughed quietly, rolling my eyes at myself.

Suddenly, a fist pounded on the door with such force I felt the butter dish leave the palm of my hand as fear surged through my body. Esther immediately started crying, and I heard William's alarmed voice call my name while simultaneously watching the butter dish shatter into a million pieces.

Without hesitation, I ran into the living room. William was peering through the window, his brow furrowed in alarm.

Abigail's arms clung to William's leg, and as I picked up Esther, William whispered to me, "Take the girls out the back and go to your parents. Hurry."

I stared at him, frozen, unsure of what was going on. I wanted to answer, but fear made me mute. The would-be intruder wiggled the locked door handle and pounded again, shaking both my heart and the foyer light.

Noticing my deer-in-headlights look, he added a statement that chilled me to the bone. "Ruth, I need you to focus. Take the girls out the back and drive to your parents. Edward is here."

Adrenaline conquered fear, and after I peeled Abigail off William, balancing her on my other hip, I headed to the kitchen. I had the sense to turn off the oven, but besides slipping on my house slippers by the backdoor, I left the house without even putting the girls' coats on.

Edward finally returned home on New Year's Day during James's quiet hour, wearing the same clothes as the day before, and mad as a hornet. After he threw open the back door, he haphazardly tossed his coat and keys toward the kitchen table, both ending up on the floor, and then stormed up the stairs with his winter boots still on, leaving a trail of slush and reeking of alcohol. *Was he drinking while driving or did he come from a bar?* I asked myself.

He completely ignored both my salutation and questions about where he was and what was wrong. *What a wonderful way to start off the year – an angry husband and a dirty floor*, I thought to myself, irritated at the mess he'd carelessly made throughout the house, as I'd spent my New Year's Eve night cleaning up the entire first floor. *You better follow him. You told Helen you would be at her house for sauerkraut by five o'clock.* I quietly walked up the stairs, checking first at James's door. Thankfully, I could hear the reassuring sound of him sucking his thumb. *Thank God he is asleep*, I thought as I walked down the hall to peer into our bedroom. With no regard for the clean room, Edward was lying on his bed, hands behind his head, legs crossed, and boots still on. My eyes locked onto his feet, and I felt my blood pressure rise because I had just replaced the Christmas-themed bed quilts with white, snowflake-themed chenille ones. *Calm down. Ten, nine, eight, seven . . .* I started counting down. *He will not tell you anything if you harp on him over his boots. He won't care anyway.*

"Edward, dear," I started after I finished counting down to one. Before I could ask any questions or mention our dinner plans, he responded.

"I drove to William's," he slurred, exasperated. "It was a complete waste of gas. He is nothing but a milksop, completely brainwashed by that wife of his. I tried to talk some sense into him, reminded him we did nothing wrong, and even said we would all welcome him back if he would just come home."

He did what? I shook my head slightly, as if I had water in my ears and didn't hear him correctly. *I wonder if he saw Ruth or their kids. Oh, for Christ's sake, I hope he didn't get into a fight.*

Not taking his eyes off the ceiling, Edward continued, "William just stood there, listening to me until I had nothing else to say to him. His response was nonsense. He said he didn't see how we could move on together with my attitude toward everything, especially Ruth," he scoffed and sat up. "I have done nothing wrong. We did nothing wrong. Hell, I am the one who drove to see him!"

"So what happened?" I asked tentatively.

"He asked if I wanted to sit down and some horse shit about calming down, feelings, and working things out. I told him how I felt about him missing out on our kid's birth, Shirley's graduation and wedding, and how James would grow up knowing who ruined the family dynamic," he answered, blood pressure likely too high. His speech was faster now, sweat beads covered his forehead, and he lifted his arms up to emphasize almost every sentence.

"And you know what he did? He just closed his eyes and shook his head, as if he was disappointed. When he looked back up at me, I swear the sissy was going to cry. When he started to defend his *bitch*, I punched him."

"You *punched* him?" I asked.

"I told him I never wanted to see him again and then walked out," he added, and fell back onto the bed. After a few minutes of silence, he asked, "Well, are you going to say anything?"

My head spinning, I tried to calm myself by taking a deep breath. I sat next to him, resting my hand on his knee. "I am glad you tried to fix the relationship between you two, and I am sorry it didn't go well," I said, hoping he didn't notice the tremor in my voice. In the coming weeks, when Edward retold the story to Helen and then Shirley, they would express the same shock and halfhearted sentiment. Robert went as far as to say he never wanted to speak to William again – a statement which made Helen squirm, but not argue with. Sometimes I wondered if they actually believed Edward's intention was to fix the problem or if any part of them questioned what William's side of the story was. *Eddy's intention was certainly not to fix anything.* I rolled my eyes as I gazed in the direction of my oak dresser. *And William is a fool to think we will come together in the end via apologies and sing kum ba yah.*

I made eye contact with myself in the mirror above my dresser and wondered, in a twisted way, if this ever-deepening rift could help bring Edward and me together somehow. I decided to give it a try, physically at least, and then turned toward my husband and ran my hand along his thigh. He glanced at me, and at first I wondered if he was in the mood or not.

"We don't have to," I said quietly, and then added with a smile, "James will be up soon, and I thought it would take your mind off what happened."

Edward took off his shirt and pulled me in for a kiss.

Ruth

Almost two hours later, I finally saw William's car driving up my parents' driveway.

Mama gave me a tight squeeze. "Let him lead the conversation, dear. And take care of those feet of yours. I'll redress both in the morning when you pick up the girls."

"I will, Mama." Running on adrenaline, I'd stepped on pieces of the broken butter dish when rushing out the door. If I hadn't been carrying the girls, I may have spared my second foot, but I couldn't risk falling with them. I didn't realize how bad they were bleeding until I reached my childhood home.

Earlier that night, I sped up their driveway and parked at an angle by the side door. After telling Abigail to walk quickly to the door and knock, I grabbed Esther and followed. Mama opened the door just as I was about to add volume to Abigail's knocking.

Mama's cheerful, surprised tone wavered when she saw my facial expression.

"Alrighty, my dears, how about you go find Papa and your two uncles! Papa is likely napping by now, so let's go wake him up."

Papa was famous for his cat naps. Regardless of the noise around him, if he was resting on a chair, sofa or floor, he could fall asleep at the drop of a hat, even if the nap was only five minutes. William especially envied the skill. Midway through the mudroom, Mama reached for Esther and then gasped when she looked over my appearance. Her eyes darted from my eyes to my feet, and when my gaze followed hers, I saw the source of her shock. The white fur around my new Kerrybrookes was now speckled red.

"What's wong, Gigi?" Abigail asked in her sweet, child-like voice. Her inability to pronounce the letter "r" was still endearing.

"Nothing in the slightest, my darling. I am just so excited you all are here!"

Accepting her answer and focused on the task at hand, Abigail went off in search of her favorite person in the world – my youngest brother, Matthias.

"Now, you, my dear, what happened?" Mama whispered. "You stay right here. I will fetch a water basin and hand Esther to your father."

Once the girls were out of earshot, Mama returned with a basin, towels, a medical kit, and a blanket.

"Ruth, what in God's good name is going on?" She got down on her knees and gently lifted both my feet into the water. With the rush gone, I was fully aware of the pain radiating all the way up to my ankles.

Hunched over in a kitchen chair, I watched the blood spin in circles until the water was a bright shade of red.

Chilled to the bone, I started to shake. Without a word, she offered the blanket she'd brought into the room. As she lifted my left foot up and carefully removed a few shards of glass, I winced and flatly stated, "My slippers are ruined."

"I will buy you another pair. Now, what is going on? Where is William?"

Still in shock, I heard myself answer, "The Devil is at our house. I saw our neighbor Roger outside and yelled to him to phone the police before I pulled out."

Mama knew my nicknames for William's brother included "Satan," "spawn of Satan," and "the Devil." Most of the time she gave me a look communicating, "Forgive," but no such look painted her face now.

Kneeling as she tended my feet, Mama started humming her favorite hymn, "Turn Your Eyes Upon Jesus," no doubt trying to calm her own mind as well as mine. The fog started to lift from my eyes and was replaced with a clear sky and blazing red sun. "He knocked on the door so damn hard I jumped and dropped the new butter dish William bought me for Christmas. It shattered and I stepped all over it rushing out the door with the girls."

"Oh dear," was all Mama could mutter.

To others, Edward likely came across as amiable. He was fairly handsome, although nowhere near as attractive as his brother. He was intelligent, good with a fishing pole, and from what I remembered from my one positive weekend in his presence, Edward was engaging in conversation. I doubted, however, anyone knew how he treated his brother, how he spoke about me and to me, and how he hated us so intensely in his heart. Even if they did, from what William had told me, it would be brushed away with, "That is just how Edward is." Since his youth, Robert and Helen apparently accepted his folly and quick temper as personality characteristics rather than temperament flaws in need of attention.

Feet bandaged, we slowly walked to join the others. The handmade wooden cuckoo clock signaled the hour mark, and Abigail, dressed in her buffalo check nighttime jammies, ran to the corner of the dining room, her arms raised to signal she wanted to be picked up. She clapped and hummed along to the little tune, and then rested her head on Gigi's shoulder and sucked her thumb.

She is so innocent and blissfully unaware of the drama our year is indelibly marked by.

As if a spectator, I stood there observing, watching my mother care for my little angels. I had a momentary flashback of my own youth. Most everyone called Abigail my "mini me."

She was boisterous, always desperate to please, and a spitting image of me at her age. Papa was holding Esther, who was arching back, her signature move communicating her desire to be laid down so she could sleep. I kissed them both goodnight and collapsed into the couch as my parents put my sweet babes to sleep.

"Want a glass of wine?" Matthias offered.

"Please."

While my brother Mark and I had a good relationship, I was closest to Matthias. He was nine years younger than I was, and I'd always had an inherent drive to care for and be protective of him. Growing up, I often watched him for Mama, and to this day he would call me "Mom" when he was angry at me. I loved him dearly, and I hoped he would settle nearby after finishing his engineering degree at Purdue.

"You just missed Mark and Lauren. They were visiting the Zimmermans before calling it a night. Lauren said she was getting tired."

"Well, that happens when you're that far along. Want to bet on the baby's gender?"

Mark and Lauren had married two years back and were expecting their first child soon. I was excited to have a little niece or nephew and for my children to grow up with a cousin close in age. Mark and Lauren met at the University of Chicago. He was there studying law, and she, English literature. A transplant from Denver and not particularly fond of her egotistical father, Lauren eventually decided to move back to Indiana rather than return to Denver, a decision heavily influenced by Mark, no doubt. She was kind, a lover of nature, gifted with a paintbrush – and an atheist. We were all shocked when Mark told us, but given the lessons learned from Helen and William, Mama didn't dare do anything but love on Lauren, for she loved Mark too much to make him choose.

Sitting up, I sipped the Cabernet, tasting the plum and black cherry with a hint of licorice. Dad and Mom never drank growing up – or if they did, they certainly kept it a secret. It wasn't until Matty turned twenty-one that they allowed any amount of alcohol in the house regularly. That, and it seemed to ease Daddy's sciatic nerve pain and help him sleep at night.

"I bet it will be a boy," Matthias offered.

"I was going to wager on a boy as well, actually."

"Do you want to talk about what is going on?" he asked, clearly unable to ignore the elephant in the room any longer.

"No," I said sharply. "Tell me about you. How is school going? How is Jessica?" I answered, wanting a distraction and to talk to my baby brother without parents around. I knew Abigail would receive special attention with bedtime stories and extra snuggles.

Matthias shared about his classes, from the professors who only cared about tenure to the classmates who bonded over Dynamics. If I had a say in the matter, I would not have picked Jessica out for him. She was pretty and exotic in a way, but her bland personality did not fit with Matthias's vibrancy and passion. She hardly said a word in a large group setting and seemed aloof the few times she'd joined us for a family gathering. So, I tried to hide my excitement when Matthias told me he planned to end the relationship.

"The spark is gone. And, I've thought about the questions you and William raised a while back. I cannot imagine myself wed to her," he explained.

"Thanks for telling me," I told him. We both reached for our drinks, the creak of the wooden stairs signaling Dad and Mom's approach.

For another hour, we played euchre, ladies versus gentlemen. Dad and Matthias were fiercely competitive and declared themselves winners when the match ended at the sound of William entering the side door.

"William, dear!" Mama started, but then her voice fell flat, not sure what to say.

"Want a beer?" Matthias asked.

"I'll pass for tonight. But thank you for offering," William answered.

"How about we keep the girls for a sleepover?" Mama offered.

William and I exchanged glances. "That would be lovely, Mama. Thank you."

I stood to hug her but then sat back down quickly, wincing. For a moment I forgot about my lame feet. In fact, during cards, I had been so wrapped up in the game that I had momentarily forgotten about the reason I was back under my parents' roof.

We bid my parents farewell, and like a child, William carried me to the car. Once home and sitting at the kitchen table, I noticed the glass had been cleaned up.

"I am sorry I dropped the butter dish," I began, as William put away the broom in the back entry closet.

"Don't apologize," William retorted, rolling his eyes and shutting the door louder than necessary.

Taking blame and apologizing for unnecessary things was a default of mine; a habit I was trying to break, especially now that Abigail was picking it up. Perhaps it was because I was quick to apologize – and apologize profusely when I was undoubtedly at fault – that it bothered me all the more when others, like his family, could not do the same.

"What happened?" I finally asked into the deafening silence.

A few more moments passed. My eyes widened and my hands motioned, asking the question again without uttering a word.

Reaching for my hand, William helped me into the living room. He sat down on our new, burnt orange upholstered couch and buried his face in his hands. I joined him, sitting down and carefully resting my bandaged feet on the gray, patterned carpet. I leaned up against him and crossed my legs. Staring at the coffee table, I noticed the girls' small Bibles, crayons, pens, and paper on top. We had planned to read a story after dinner and write down or draw out – whatever Abigail preferred – what we hoped to do in the new year. And, once alone, William and I wanted to write out lessons learned from the year and agree on our goals for 1955. Instead, I had a mess in the kitchen, a ruined dinner in the trash, and upsetting memories to add to the collection of those around William's family.

After what felt like an hour of silence, I finally nudged again, "William, dear?"

He looked at me and reached for my hand. "It was awful. Edward still blames you because of your 'inability to see eye-to-eye' with everyone," William added with air quotes. "He even said something about you calling my mom a crybaby – a word which isn't in your vernacular. He was just pulling at straws. I told him his attitude would not help salvage the relationship."

I narrowed in on the accusation. "William, I never said that to your mother," I stated, likely more defensive than necessary.

"I know," William responded. "I asked him if he would sit down and talk about the situation in a civilized way. I guess I thought if we walked through what happened, and he heard my side of the story, we could get past this mess. I was a fool to think that idea would work. Edward would have none of it; instead, he started yelling about his son, Shirley's wedding, and . . ."

William stopped, as if he didn't want to remember what had happened next. He pushed his fingertips into his forehead, massaged his temples, and exhaled slowly.

"And then he swung at me," William whispered.

"He hit you!" I asked, turning around so I could more closely examine his face. I hadn't noticed a mark earlier. *Maybe he hit him in the stomach?* I wondered.

"No, no. He swung, but I leaned back to dodge it and then grabbed his arm and twisted it around his body. At that point, I knew talking wouldn't help, and I told him to leave," William explained, shaking his head in disappointment.

"Oh my," I managed.

I heard sleet hitting the windows as we sat quietly for a few moments; I desperately wanted to ask what happened next, but I decided it was wisest to wait.

His broken voice spoke into the silence. "Officers McCray and Brown were walking up our front steps when I opened the door. I waved, signaling I was okay. Edward bumped into Officer Brown's shoulder as he walked by and before he got in his car he yelled back to me, 'I never want to see you again. You are dead to me. And tell your wife she can go to hell.'"

"I am so, so sorry, dear," I said, placing my hands on his knees. *What a way to start the new year. God, help us*, I prayed.

"I am just so glad you and the girls weren't here for it," William added before he lowered his head and wept.

CHAPTER 28
June 1956

"Do you have everything packed?" I called to Edward, as I put some last-minute apple slices and celery sticks for him and James into a paper bag. I couldn't believe James had already finished his first year of elementary school, and to celebrate, Edward, Robert, and my father were going north to fish.

"I think so!" Edward replied, coming into the kitchen carrying two bags, one for him and one for James. He stopped on his way out to the car to kiss my cheek and joke about how the snacks didn't have to be so healthy. I smiled because I alone knew peanut butter M&Ms and Pepperidge Farm cookies were packed at the bottom.

While not a flourishing marriage, our relationship was slowly mending. I hadn't suspected Edward was cheating on me since he started his new job, he seemed sincerely dedicated to spending more time at home, and we smoothly tag-teamed with James, household chores, and projects. At times, I felt a nagging sense something was lacking in my life, which I normally attributed to the loss of fervent passion in our marriage, and I often wondered what Edward thought when we saw a beautiful woman out in public. Other times, I wondered if the hole was different, and

I longed for a friend. *That is what girlfriends are for, Margaret*, I would tell myself, but even then, I had no close girlfriends to talk to. To drown out the nagging feeling of loneliness, I focused on James, house projects, and our upcoming plans to finally purchase property on Ocean Isle Beach.

"I'll catch a big fish for you, Mom!" James promised excitedly as he entered the kitchen. Snacks packed, I turned and smiled. He looked more and more like Edward every year. His new Boy Scout wristwatch adorned his left arm, and he was carrying both his knot-tying rope set and his My Spin'n Buddy tackle box. When the kit first arrived, I'd asked James if he wanted to practice tying knots, but he told me it was something he was saving for the fishing trip.

After they left for the long weekend, I decided to visit the ice cream parlor I used to frequent outside the hospital, before going shopping. Ice cream sounded delicious, and I had the day to myself. The smells took me back a decade, and I ordered my favorite: vanilla ice cream in a waffle cone. *So much has changed since the war ended*, I thought to myself as I waited for my treat.

It was my turn to pay, and as I reached into my purse, a man behind me said to the cashier, "I'll pay for the lady's cone."

Surprised, I looked to my left to see who was offering to pay for my ice cream. I nearly fainted.

Ruth

I was overwhelmed with joy at the sight of the grandeur of the sanctuary and the melodious music. Flanked by Abigail on my right and Esther on my left, we began our slow, steady march down the aisle. I had to stifle a laugh when Esther dropped all her petals on the floor before we had even taken our third step and quietly reminded Abigail to only throw out two or three petals at a time. My eyes met Matthias's, and I briefly let go of Abby's little hand to wipe away a tear. My baby brother was getting married.

His soon-to-be bride was my new best friend, and I was thrilled to call her my sister. More, while Matthias remained high on the pecking order in Abigail's mind, Jennifer was a close second ever since she'd asked her and Esther to be flower girls. And, for all our sake, I was thrilled they were going to live only eighteen minutes away.

Jennifer was fiery and passionate, and her faith challenged Matthias to return to church and be the leader I knew he could be. Along with Mama, I was eternally grateful God providentially had crossed their paths the year before in what would be the Glendale Town Center parking lot. Matthias had been assigned to the Glendale site and was thrilled to be working on a project associated with Victor Gruen, a pioneer designer of shopping malls. Jennifer's father worked for L.S. Ayres and Company, and she was exploring with him where the anchor department store would be located. Jennifer's father had sent her to the car that cold December day to fetch his gloves, and the door was frozen shut. Parked catty-corner, Matthias offered to help, and before we knew it, the two had announced their engagement.

Lord, it is amazing how a single, seemingly insignificant event is woven into the colorful tapestry of one's life. Thank you for Jennifer and our friendship. May their marriage blossom, I prayed as I helped the girls sit with my parents before I took my position as the Matron of Honor.

The previous weekend, William had approached me with a mug of decaf tea as I was writing my speech.

"How are you doing?" he asked, as he placed the warm mug in my hands.

"Hello, dear. I think I am done for the night. I have writer's block," I answered, annoyed I couldn't come up with the perfect words to string together. Putting my pen down, I asked him, "How are you?" Before he could answer, I gave voice to my underlying question. "Does Matthias's wedding bring up memories of our wedding for you as it does me?"

He chuckled slightly, shrugging his shoulders. "Oh, sweetie. You know it doesn't bother me anymore. Granted, I wish things were different, but I can't control my family, so I don't spend energy dwelling on the situation."

"Yeah. It is just not how family is supposed to be. It is hard for me not to think about them and our wedding. If anything, it makes me want to go above and beyond to love Jennifer and make their day perfect."

"Family isn't always blood, is it?" he asked, and I rolled my eyes at the truth in his rhetorical question. He continued, "I suppose we should be thankful for them because they are showing you who you *don't* want to be."

"You always see the positive. I envy your ability to view life that way," I admitted. William was without a doubt an optimist, while I would describe myself as a realist. William said that was the polite way of saying pessimist. My reply was always the same: "I would rather not be disappointed." While relations with his family intensified my stance for a season, William certainly helped balance me out.

"My dear, we will likely never reconcile with my family. They do not see life from the same lens, and I am not sure they are even capable right now of being different. And I am okay with that. Like your dad says, 'It is what it is.' We will love them through prayer and by touching base occasionally to test the waters. Now, don't let the negative memories cast a shadow on Matthias and Jennifer's wedding."

"You are so wise," I responded, giving him a playful punch on the arm. "I pray they find the truth so we can reconcile."

"Let's shorten that prayer by removing us from it. 'All these things will be added', remember?"

"Hello, Mags. It sure has been a while," Joe said to me after escorting my shocked, numb body to a nearby table. The chairs were the same metal turquoise chairs from years ago. I stared at Joe. His hair was still dark as charcoal, styled like James Dean, and as much as I didn't want to admit it, his eyes and smile were still seductively attractive. I pushed aside the momentary physical rush and remembered what he'd done to me.

"It's been ten years. Why are you here?" I asked flatly. My ice cream was melting in the bowl he'd requested for me before leaving the counter.

"Not much for small talk?" he answered, taking a bite of his strawberry ice cream and fidgeting with the plastic white spoon. Then, finally, he told me. "Honestly, I wanted to find you." His voice was thick and sincere. "I wanted to apologize for how I treated you, and I wanted to find out what happened."

Is he serious? I asked myself. My heart felt like it was going to pound out of my chest. My hands started to shake, and I felt perspiration under my arms. *After all this time, now he apologizes and wants to know what happened? You don't owe him anything.*

"I know I don't deserve anything from you. To continue in the vein of honesty, I am going through Alcoholics Anonymous, and one of the steps is to make amends with people we've hurt. I'm not into all the religious stuff around AA, but I do agree with most of the steps. You are chief among those I have hurt, and even though I wasn't dealing with alcoholism back then, I wanted to apologize," he continued.

I sat there silent, frozen, my eyes locked with his.

"You don't have to say anything. I just wanted you to know that I know I was wrong, and I am sorry for the pain I caused you," he added and waited for my reply. When one didn't come, he spoke again. "I hope it wasn't a mistake to come here. I meant well, really I did."

Another period of silence passed. I could not speak. My chest hurt, I felt lightheaded, my hands were moist, and my mind was moving so quickly I had to close my eyes for a moment to steady myself. Clearly registering my shock, Joe spoke again.

"I think it's best if I go. If you want to tell me what happened to our child, I'll be in town all weekend. I'll come by this ice cream shop each day at eleven o'clock, wait awhile, and head to the park nearby and sit by that old willow tree for a few hours."

What a fool you were under that old willow tree, a voice chided.

His facial expression changed to one of longing and hope when he spoke the word "child." I inwardly cringed. He stood up, nodded at me, and gently placed his hand on my shoulder as he apologized one more time before walking away.

I sat there, paralyzed with emotion. After a few minutes, I gathered myself together enough to stand up and leave. On the way out, I threw my untouched ice cream in the garbage and continued on with my plan to shop, deciding it was a necessary distraction.

After a fitful night of sleep and two cups of spiked black coffee, I grabbed my newly purchased Chanel quilted handbag and the keys to my Mercedes 190 SL. It was warm outside, and with the top down, the wind and afternoon sun felt fabulous on my face.

While you don't owe Joe anything, you will feel good after speaking your mind to him, I convinced myself, ignoring the nagging feeling that Mother would not approve.

I whipped the convertible into a parking spot and stepped out, feeling confident in my new red dress with white polka dots, especially with the padded bullet bra underneath accentuating my figure. I had skipped the nylon stockings because of the summer weather, and, even if they weren't practical for a walk in the park, the black kitten heels complemented my legs and matched my handbag. Besides, I didn't plan on taking a walk in the park. I planned on speaking my mind and leaving.

And if I was honest, I wanted Joe to regret his decision of leaving me, which is why I went out of my way to look fantastic that morning.

As promised, Joe was by the willow tree. I wanted to maintain a posture of anger toward him, especially because he picked *that* willow tree, but his smile as I approached tugged at me in a physical way I hadn't felt in years. To make matters worse, he looked remarkably handsome in his khaki linen shorts, white shirt, and knee-high blue argyle socks. Even though there was a bench nearby, he lounged on a blanket under the tree with his brown penny loafers next to his bag.

"I am glad you decided to come," Joe said, standing up. "You look beautiful," he added, in a sincere voice.

"I am married, Joe," I simply stated.

"Happily?" he asked and raised his eyebrows.

I stared at him, infuriated he asked and even more disappointed I couldn't answer the question with an affirmative answer.

After a few seconds of silence, he added with a half-smile, "Either way, it doesn't mean I can't compliment a beautiful woman when I see one."

Is he flirting with me? I wondered. *Surely he isn't flirting with me? I am married, and the last time he saw me he was walking out of my life without even the courage to say so!*

Noticing my mind at work, Joe reoriented. "I am sorry for flirting. It is not appropriate, even if I feel a level of familiarity around you. Is it odd I still feel comfortable with you?" When I did not reply, he continued, "Either way, I came here to apologize and to ask what happened."

I wanted to be angry at him. I wanted to hate him.

"Want to sit down?" he asked, patting the blanket.

I sat down, each of us lost in our own thoughts, as a familiar silence descended. While I didn't want to, I too felt comfortable around Joe, just as he did around me. And even though I wanted to deny it, the heart strings we tied ten years ago still existed. I felt my resolve weakening. *How does he still have a power over you?* I wondered.

"So, what happened?" Joe finally asked, softly.

And, as if a cork popped out of a champagne bottle, words gushed from my mouth. I told him everything: about losing the baby, my father's deep disappointment, and the set-up with Edward. I shared how I grew to love him, but then was betrayed by him during the worst possible time – pregnancy. I cried over my mother's death, using his plain white handkerchief to blow my nose. I even told him about my jealousy toward Ruth. But although I felt like clay in a potter's hand sitting next to Joe, I didn't dare risk telling him about the lie. I swore I would take that secret to my grave.

I couldn't remember the last time someone listened to me with such sincerity. I literally spilled the pain of my heart out to him, and like coffee all over a white shirt, I could not take any of it back even if I wanted to. Joe didn't just listen to the words I spoke; he looked through my eyes to my soul. His answers spoke poetically to my heart and his words of affirmation soaked up the pain I poured out. And just as I did a decade ago, I softened under his presence and wondered what it would've been like if he hadn't left for Kentucky. I lay down and stared up at the willow tree. *What would life have been like if he had stayed with you? If you married him instead? The marriage you ended up with certainly isn't a perfect one, even though you pretend otherwise*, a part of me thought. *Stop. You wouldn't have James. He is the best thing that has ever happened to you*, another part rebutted. And there, under the willow tree, I felt like a lost girl who just desperately wanted to be known and loved.

Interrupting my thoughts, Joe's finger caught a tear as it fell from my eye toward my ear. I turned toward him, also now lying down and facing me. Just inches apart, our eyes locked and desired burned within. Maybe it was his smile or the affirming words he spoke. Maybe it was my desperate need for love or the memories from the last time we were under this same willow tree. Or maybe it was the unresolved anger and hurt toward Edward. But just as I had done a decade ago, I let myself give into my carnal desires and leaned in for a kiss.

At first, Joe didn't stop me. Then, between kisses, he said, "Wait, wait. We can't. After all, you are married."

"We fell out of love years ago," I responded, sitting up to check if there were any witnesses. The park, for as far as I could see, was ours alone.

"True, but I don't want you to do something you would regret," he continued.

"Isn't it up to me to decide if I am going to regret it or not?" I questioned, placing my hand on his upper thigh and giving it a squeeze.

"I certainly feel a level of chemistry with you I have never known with any other woman," Joe admitted, shrugging his shoulders. "But I don't want to hurt you again."

I leaned in and whispered into his ear, "You won't." Nothing else mattered to me in that moment than the fire I felt within.

"Either way, however much I want you, the park isn't a great spot."

He was right, of course, prompting me to ask, "Where are you staying? Your hotel would be better than my house."

"I am at the Biltmore," he answered, gathering up his things.

"What is your room number?" I asked, throwing caution to the wind.

When I woke up, I had to remind myself where I was and what day it was. As I thought through the last twenty-four hours and the weekend, I desperately regretted the lunch plans I'd made with Helen. *I hope no one noticed I didn't return home last night. People talk, you know*, I thought, gripped by momentary panic. I stared at the textured white ceiling. I hadn't washed my face the night before, and, since I'd fallen asleep in Joe's arms, I hadn't properly wrapped my hair. I wished I had brought a hairbrush. *What if Edward finds out?* Fear whispered and shame squeezed my heart but were quickly followed by a voice of justification. *No one was watching your house. Besides, Edward hasn't been faithful to you. You don't owe him anything. Focus on the now.*

The sheets felt heavenly against my bare skin, and my dead heart felt like it had been restarted. I wanted to feel this alive every day but knew that the moment Edward returned, the passion would evaporate. I slid over to Joe's body, rubbing my fingers along his muscular, tan arm. After a few minutes he woke and turned over onto his back.

"How is it that you are more beautiful in the morning than you were last night?" Joe asked, pushing a few strands of hair behind my ear.

I met his compliment with a kiss. His body instantly responded. Turning to his side and facing me, he grabbed my leg at the knee and pulled me up against him. The way he moved his other hand from my hair to my neck and then down to my chest sent lightning throughout my body.

He then stopped, and as he took me in full view, he said with a voice dripping with desire, "You are a goddess."

Knowing our time was short, I willingly took pleasure in Joe's body, without the faintest concern of any consequences.

With one last kiss and a promise to return that night, I rushed out of the hotel in the same red dress I'd worn the day before and made my way to Culp's Cafe as fast as I could. Helen was never late, and I similarly was a woman of punctuality. I was so thankful the hotel had a toothbrush and comb to spare, and I gave my cheeks a good squeeze to give the appearance of freshly applied rouge.

"Good morning, dear. Everything alright?" Helen asked as I joined her in line, ten minutes late.

"Yes, I am sorry for my tardiness. I decided to switch handbags last minute because I wanted to show you the new Chanel I found!" I answered, hoping the eagerness in my voice sounded sincere.

"Oh, it is lovely!" Helen exclaimed, accepting the lie as a child accepts candy as she gawked over the new handbag.

A cloud of guilt hovered over me during lunch. *She can't tell. Your hair looks fine, and she won't notice anything out of the ordinary if you act like everything is okay*, I told myself as we sat down. I looked around the establishment, and my mind replayed graduation day when Mother, Father, and I enjoyed a meal together. As I picked at my food, I smiled sadly thinking about Mama. *Even with Johnny's death, life was simpler then. How things have changed. Mama would be so disappointed in you. Helen may prefer to live in ignorant bliss, but that doesn't mean sleeping with Joe and adding to your lie count was right,* shame jeered.

"Margaret, are you excited about the decision to buy on Ocean Isle?" Helen inquired, taking a sip of water.

I snapped back to the present, realizing it was Helen's second time asking. "My apologies . . . I used to come here with my parents, and I was just remembering the time we came here after graduation."

"No need to apologize, dear. I am sure you miss your mother very much," she responded kindly.

"Yes, I do," I admitted and then switched topics, trying to sound genuinely excited. "But yes, I am very excited Edward wants to buy property on the beach. I look forward to family vacations there, and I hope it becomes like a second home. I am especially excited for James. Wouldn't it be grand if he met friends whom he could spend time with year after year?"

The rest of the lunch included our typical shallow conversation. It felt forced to me, but Helen didn't seem to notice a difference. Even if she did, her tendency to self-deceive and hide the truth from her own heart had always worked to my advantage.

With a towel wrapped around my body, I sat at my white and pink vanity and stared at myself in the gold-framed oval mirror. I couldn't wait to visit Joe for his last night in town and my last night before Edward returned. While attractive, my eyes did not sparkle. *You know whose eyes sparkled, don't you?* While it had been years, I could still see Ruth's glowing face. Without even trying, she'd left a little sparkle wherever she went, and I had passionately hated her for it. *Stop looking back. You have something to look forward to tonight,* I redirected my thoughts. I finished my hair and makeup, applied lotion so my body would be supple and soft, and put on a skirt with a striped, button-down blouse.

As I headed toward the door, I glanced at the family photo we'd taken that spring. James looked adorable, and the smiles on our faces would make any onlooker jealous. Yet, beneath my picture-perfect appearance, my heart was cold and missing an unknown, essential piece. And while Edward had been a better husband since his new job, I knew he was restless, especially with the shattered relationship with his brother. He certainly would never admit to his discontentment or to contributing to the discord with William. I often thought about James, glad he didn't have a sibling to potentially quarrel with later in life. And, while I was certain he was happy and knew many positive memories, I wondered if he sensed the distance between his mother and father.

But as I crossed the threshold of the house to visit with Joe one last time, I pushed thoughts of Edward and James to the backburner.

CHAPTER 29
1964

"James Michael, I am not going to tell you again. Turn off that television!" I called out to James for the third time.

Ever since James unwrapped it at Christmas, the Magnavox color TV had been a point of contention. I preferred to keep the doors closed and only open them on occasion, but Edward and James were drawn to the cube like ants to sugar. Be it the TV or the Philips radio, one of the two was always on. The constant noise irritated me, and I was sick to death of hearing about Vietnam and all the bad news surrounding the Civil Rights movement. While an act around Civil Rights had passed, no piece of legislature could change the hate within people's hearts.

"I wish I was old enough to go fight in the war," James said, coming into the kitchen looking for something to eat. While only fourteen, James was already taller than me. He had a thicker build than most of his peers, in part because of all the time spent outside, and a fiery red mop top. Since entering his teens, James increasingly cared about his appearance, and he wanted his hairstyle to resemble that of John Lennon and the other Beatles.

I don't know what came over me that late July morning, but James's desire to join the fight turned my internal temperature up, and my emotions boiled over.

"War is nothing but hell on earth, James Michael. There is nothing glamorous about it, and anyone who tells you otherwise is ignorant or a liar. Your uncle didn't come home from World War II—"

"I know, Mom. You've told me about Uncle John more than a hundred times. That doesn't mean you can stop me from joining the military if I want to."

"As long as you are under this roof—" I started back up before he interrupted me again.

"You can't tell me what to do forever," James shot back, his voice oozing with arrogance.

I stared at him, momentarily wishing for his younger years. At the time, I thought the childhood days were challenging; now, I realized how yesterday's battles paled in comparison to today's. More, I hated it when I saw Edward's pride in James. And then, to twist the knife a little more, James added, "Besides, Dad is okay with the idea."

"Go to your room!" I yelled, then added, "No more television the entire weekend!"

I hated Edward for entertaining James's idea to join the armed forces when he turned eighteen. Edward's attempts to reassure me were futile. "There is plenty of time for James to change his mind," he would tell me. While four years remained until he was an adult in the eyes of the state, I felt like time was slipping by exponentially faster, and I was powerless to slow it down. More, James was defiant – an adjective his teachers had used in parent-teacher conferences for the last two or three years now – and as he grew older, my voice had less and less influence. While intelligent, James didn't excel in school like Edward had, and he was more interested in building things, hunting and fishing, and spending time outdoors. I would normally support those interests, but we regularly fought over them because to James, they often trumped schoolwork, chores, and family commitments.

Just one more week and you will be able to relax on the beach, I told myself. Construction on our beach-front home on Ocean Isle Beach had finally begun earlier that year, and it was scheduled to finish early this week. While Edward had wanted to wait for the island to populate more before breaking ground on a house, he nevertheless decided to write a check for $500 for an ocean-front lot years ago. His decision turned out to be a savvy one, and we were excited to spend our summers in North Carolina.

We crossed the recently constructed swing bridge over to Ocean Isle Beach with the convertible top down; I embraced the sea breeze, hanging my hand out the window, moving it up and down in a gentle wave motion. Originally furious when Edward had first pulled in the driveway with a skylight blue Ford Mustang, I was now thankful for the convertible. My nerves unwound with the smell of the fresh air and the sun on my face, and while I still wished Edward would've discussed the vehicle purchase with me before he'd bought it, I felt like someone worth knowing in that gorgeous car.

My jaw dropped when we pulled up to our 2,600-square-foot, three-bedroom beach home. I was thrilled with the circular brick driveway – something I had to convince Edward to pay extra for – and the landscaping was immaculate. I was halfway out of the car before Edward put it in park. The wraparound porch was gorgeous, and as I opened the double French doors to our new oasis – promptly removing my shoes to not track a speck of dirt inside – I was thrilled with all the natural light let in by the windows. As I explored our summer home, wandering through the open living room and eating nook, I couldn't contain my excitement. I almost cried tears of joy when I saw the kitchen. The white board walls throughout the first floor were beautiful, and the wood floors complemented them well. While we still had to furnish some of the rooms, it was ready enough for us to stay until James started high school.

Edward and James were more excited about fishing than touring the house, and as soon as they'd unloaded our luggage, they disappeared with their fishing rods. I found myself alone with my thoughts in the sunroom off the master bedroom. Sipping tea, I decided to move to the porch. We had no neighbors or expected guests, and I wanted to work on my tan. *Why does it matter? Edward won't notice your skin tone anyway. You'll never have a fairytale romance with him, even with the fancy new house.* Even here I couldn't escape the cloud that seemed to constantly darken my thoughts. I was saddened by the truth and reminded of the past. Edward rarely noticed the small things, and our intimate life was fueled more by obligation than passion. *If only it had worked out with Joe*, the voice continued, and my solo tea party became a pity party. I had never mentioned my rendezvous with Joe to anyone, and while it had been almost a decade, I still often thought of him whenever Edward approached me in the bedroom. Before Joe left,

I made him swear to never contact me again, and he had kept his word. I could not allow one weekend to ruin my entire life; now he existed only in my memory.

As the afternoon wore on, I thought about my mother, my fingers idly toying with the emerald pendant around my neck. Despite thinking she would be disappointed with so many of my choices, I missed her and wondered how life would've been different if she were still around. *Would Edward sincerely miss me, like Daddy misses Mama, if I died prematurely?* I wondered. Father was aging at an accelerated speed; his sight and hearing were failing, and he often made depressing comments about being ready to see Mother again. Although I tried to make light of it, I couldn't deny that his health had deteriorated over the last two years. He was determined for me to know inside and out what he wanted done with his possessions, the house, etcetera. And, as if he had been planning on my birthday this year being the last he'd celebrate with me, Daddy surprised me with a gold pearl ring along with Mother's saltwater pearl necklace and her favorite mink coat. I remember him saying, "It's not every day your baby girl turns forty!" The ring featured a pearl in the center of golden petals, giving it the look of a flower, and he told me I was a bright flower in his otherwise gray life.

Edward also surprised me for my milestone birthday. He had scheduled both hair and nail appointments for me that afternoon, and once I returned home, I realized why. With Helen, Shirley, and Daddy's help, he'd decorated the entire first floor of our home with balloons, pictures from every year of my life, and crepe paper. As I walked in, oblivious to Edward's plan, cheers of "Surprise" rang out. For a moment I stood, stunned, wondering who it was all for. When it hit me, I couldn't stem the tears. Despite everything, Edward was trying to make it a special day for me.

After my traditional birthday dinner, complete with lasagna and Helen's homemade cake, we played the family's favorite card game, Spoons. I was second to spell out S-P-O-O-N, and I joined Shirley as we watched the rest of the game play out. Although his cousins were much younger than he was, James entertained them, to their great delight. We hadn't seen them as much since she and Charles moved to Cincinnati, and she took our brief time together to tell me all about her boys' advanced intelligence and love for baseball, how her third pregnancy was going, and her thriving Mary Kay business.

"You really should consider becoming a consultant. You could even join my team! I bet you would love it. The products are excellent, as you will see soon; I gave you some for your birthday. You will have to let me know what you think!" Shirley said excitedly.

"Can I have everyone's attention?" Edward called out, saving me from Shirley's sales pitch. "I would like to officially congratulate myself for winning, both in Spoons and as a husband. To my forty-year-old wife!" Edward raised his glass, and everyone joined him.

Edward then surprised me with emerald and diamond earrings, which perfectly matched the necklace from Mama. I gasped when I opened the black velvet box; they were stunning, and my eyes brimmed with tears. I was overwhelmed by both Edward's thoughtfulness and by the void in our marriage that couldn't be filled with even the most expensive jewels.

After we said our goodbyes and James was in bed, I took a long bath before retiring to the bedroom.

"How about you put the earrings and the matching neck-lace on," Edward suggested, as I closed our bedroom door.

I obliged willingly, walking to my dresser. After I put the earrings on and fastened the necklace, Edward slinked his arms around me, kissing my neck and resting his hands on my hips.

"They look beautiful on you," he said, giving me a gentle spin so I faced him. With one hand, he brought my mouth to his while his other pulled my body close. After sliding off my silk nightgown, a gift I'd picked out for myself, he picked me up and laid me down on our new king bed. It, too, was deemed a birthday present.

"We haven't consummated our new bed yet," he said, un-dressing himself and moving toward me.

You could use this to your advantage, a sly voice practically sang. And with that in mind, I wrapped my legs around him.

Once he finished, I stayed close to him, pretending I want-ed to, and asked, "You know what would make this birthday even better?"

Relaxed and satisfied, Edward responded with an inquisi-tive, "No, but I have a feeling you're going to tell me."

"A brick driveway at our summer home on Ocean Isle," I said, smiling and running my hand down his chest.

"Okay. We will change the plans and you can have your brick driveway," he responded, with his eyes and smile saying, "you won."

"Thank you!" I exclaimed like a giddy schoolgirl.

"That brick driveway though is going to cost you another kiss," Edward added, laughing and leaning in for a kiss.

It truly was a memorable birthday. And, Helen will absolute-ly love the driveway, I thought as I heard the backdoor open.

Edward and James must have returned. "I better go down and ask how fishing went," I said aloud, as if I needed the pep talk to stand up and leave the sun's embrace.

Ruth

Relieved our long drive was over, I said a quick prayer of thanksgiving as William pulled into the Colony Inn's gravel parking lot and smiled as the children squealed with excitement. With the causeway built just the year before and the Colony Inn earlier in the year, we were all excited to call the Colony our home away from home. School started for the girls in two weeks, and we had decided to spend the last of our summer days on the beach and in the pool.

"When can we go to the pool?" Abigail asked, her legs swinging up and down with anticipation. Esther and Adam joined the conversation, parroting their older sister in her desire to swim.

Our family had grown with the addition of Adam William five years earlier. Especially with the heartache from losing two children, I was eternally grateful to be a mother to two little blessings. While my faith had strengthened during the dark time of loss, when we found out we were pregnant again, my first feeling was trepidation. At thirty-three, I was certainly with child at an older age than all my friends, which only exacerbated my fears. However, mid-way through the pregnancy, I noticed Abigail showing signs that my anxiety was rubbing off on her. Her stomach hurt more often, she was scared of the dark when we put her to bed, and she acted out more when William was gone on Monday evenings for his men's Bible study. Finally, after two weeks of her altered demeanor, I decided one night not to focus on the behavior and instead, try to connect. William agreed it was a good idea and assumed Esther duty so I could dedicate all of my attention to Abigail.

"Abby, dear, you have been acting differently recently. Want to talk about it?" I asked her one night, bringing cookies and milk into her bedroom.

Fixated on the snack, she answered my question with a question. "I can eat a cookie in my room?"

"Yes, tonight you can." I smiled and reached for one myself.

After several cookies eaten in silence, I asked again, "So, darling, what are you thinking?"

Abigail sat on her bed, staring at me, as if wondering whether she should speak or not. "I am sorry for not obeying. I will work on it," she finally responded.

"Thank you for saying that, sweetie. Is there something else I can help with?" I tried again.

"I don't want to make you sad," she responded quickly, and then looked away.

Concerned, I inquired more. "Abigail, my darling, who am I?" We went through our three questions – *Who am I? Who are you? What do you know to be true?* – like we had since she was a toddler.

She smiled and rolled her eyes as she answered the third question, "Mommy loves me." I am sure we had gone through that question set over a million times, but even if she was sick of it, I wanted them deeply ingrained in her heart.

"That's right, honey. Now, please don't keep secrets from me. What's wrong?"

Whispering, Abby responded, "I am worried about the baby in your belly. What if something happens?"

At that moment, swimming in guilt, I felt like I had failed my daughter. I truly thought I had kept my anxiety away from the children, but it was no surprise that she had heard me talking to William or my mother. Those words – straight from my mouth – had taken up residence in her heart. After talking, crying, and praying together, Abigail went to bed in peace. And that night, my head and heart agreed to let my faith be bigger than my fears, if not for myself, then for Abby.

"I have the keys!" William boomed as he opened the car door, jolting me back to the present. He dangled the set of keys to our newly purchased condo from a turquoise plastic square impressed with the number "4." "Who is ready to change and jump in the pool?"

"I am!" three voices instantly responded in unison.

I looked at William, remembering our agreement to visit Baileys Grocery first. "We will get groceries after. Right now, this is more important." He answered my unspoken question, gave me an irresistible smile and wink as he started the car, and leaned over to kiss my cheek before driving to our designated parking spot. I didn't even have time to protest; while momentarily irritated, I let it go and decided we would order pizza for dinner. It was pizza Friday, after all.

We spent our vacation time building sandcastles, hunting for seashells, visiting Baileys Grocery store for food, ice cream and fishing bait, and acting out Bible stories before bed. Abigail stayed up thirty minutes later than her siblings and used that extra time most nights to write down the events of the day in her diary. It was a joy to see her feverishly recount the memories of each day; I knew the journaled thoughts of her twelve-year-old self would be something we would look back on with a smile. The weather was perfect, and during the one rainy day, we drove down Periwinkle to explore the Shell Shack and drop off post-cards at the post office for Gi-Gi and Papa as well as Uncle Mark and Aunt Lauren and Uncle Matthias and Aunt Jennifer.

While time and distance had helped, little things, like mailing postcards to my parents and siblings, still caused heartache. More than anything, our situation with William's family was sad and pathetic, and I just wished it was different. The topic rarely surfaced, and when it did, despite trying my best to stay calm, my heart rate and blood pressure would inevitably rise. Even though I knew I was not actually reliving the events, it was my body's natural reaction, and it took intentionality to capture my thoughts, let go of the negativity, and pray for them.

The last interaction William had had with his parents was when Adam was close to two years old. He'd looked up his parents' phone number in a directory and decided to call to test the waters. There was a sense of hesitation in the air when he called, because we had heard nothing after Edward's visit nearly seven years earlier and after our Christmas letter two years before, which gave a life update, including news on the birth of Adam. The memory of his visit still made me shudder, and their lack of response from our baby announcement was still a source of deep disappointment for William.

After making sure the party line was not busy and agreeing to the long-distance fee, William called on a Sunday night; I was in the room, face down praying, as he dialed.

"Hello?" Robert's voice came on the phone.

"Hi, Dad," William responded.

"Who is this?" Robert asked sharply. Looking up to meet William's gaze, I rolled my eyes at the question, infuriated at his sarcasm. *Well, this call is off to a great start*, I thought to myself and stood up. Grabbing the duster, I started dusting to occupy myself.

"It is William, your son," he replied.

After a few moments of silence, Helen's voice came over the line. "Hi, William," she said, stoic and unreadable.

"Hi, Mother. How are you?"

"I am well, son. How are you? How are your children?"

Behind William, I looked at the wooden-framed mirror on the wall and grimaced, irritated that she had deliberately neglected to ask about me.

"I am good. Ruth is too, and so are the kids," he answered, deliberately inserting me into the conversation.

The dialogue with his mother continued on with the same high-level conversation William would've had with any stranger he'd just met. For a moment, I was hopeful we could start over, create new memories, laugh and talk like family members are supposed to.

"Well, I was hoping we could talk . . ." William began.

After a moment of silence, she responded phlegmatically, "Sure. What can we do to be in each other's lives?"

William breathed a sigh of relief, and I saw a flicker of hope flash across his face. "Okay great, and I am glad you asked. We want to bury the hatchet. I guess . . . could we all just admit things were not handled well from the wedding up until recently?" William said, calling out the elephant in the room in the most general way possible and almost willing her over the phone to agree.

"What do you mean, 'we'? What did *I* do?" Helen responded. "If that is why you called, well, there just really isn't anything further for me to say at this point, William. *She* is the one who can't see eye to eye with us," she continued, her pitch higher than before.

"We don't even know that man on the phone. Get off." We could hear a voice – Robert's – speaking angrily in the background. It was the only contribution he made to the entire call.

"We are sorry for any part we had in causing the discord. Mom, could you please just acknowledge you also contributed to the situation? Your partiality toward Edward and Margaret has been incredibly—"

"Son, I have done nothing wrong. I am sorry your wife and you still feel the way you do. And *partiality*? You are incapable of understanding the meaning of impartiality because your children are too young. You will learn," she said, cutting him off.

And with that, the conversation hit a dead end. Helen's words completely deflated William's spirits, and despite my prayers, all I could come up with were questions. About a month after the call, we mailed a note expressing a few last thoughts William hadn't had a chance to voice over the phone. I thought, just maybe, our words would reach Helen's heart, and she would understand. With every fiber in my being, I believed – or at least hoped – Helen felt something other than hatred and bitterness underneath her armor of pride, and if we wrote just the right words, her kindness would no longer be held hostage.

Father and Mother,

I want to start off by saying we love and miss you, and we so badly want to move on, connected. But how can we have a relationship of substance when you blame Ruth for our division and choose to disrespect us both by refusing to acknowledge her? How can we, with the ever-present elephant in the room? How can we, if you refuse to meet in the middle and admit even at a high level, "we did not handle things well"?

We want you to know that we both forgive you for every lie, painful word, and action or inaction. Regardless if you think you did anything wrong or feel remorse, we forgive you. We want to reconcile, but reconciliation is two-fold. Even having a relationship with God the Father requires reconciliation through both repentance and His forgiveness; the same is true with human relationships. And just like He loves you, wants relationship, and extends His hand of forgiveness through the cross, we love you, want restoration, and want you to know our hand of forgiveness has been, and always will be, extended.

If you are fuming, rolling your eyes, calling us names, and your inner lawyer is taking your defense, so be it. We've long since accepted our state of impasse, and we will continue to pray. But, if you ever have an earnest change of heart, then drop us a note.

With love,

William & Ruth

The silence we received was louder than any reply.

The end of the school year was finally in sight. I was beyond disappointed in each report card and parent-teacher discussion, and I was especially mortified when James was sent to the principal's office, which earned him detention for a week. Outside our four walls or when talking to Robert and Helen, Edward blamed the teacher's style or school. But when speaking with our son, Edward made it clear to James that his behavior was entirely his fault.

"Here we are again, James Michael," Edward said as soon as James closed the back door, late coming home because of his first day of detention. Edward leaned up against the counter, arms crossed. The stark contrast between their outfits spoke of the differences between the two, both external and internal. Edward still had on his charcoal two-piece suit, complete with an orange striped tie and white pocket square, while James wore a crewneck oxford-gray sweatshirt and medium-wash, narrow dungarees with worn knees. Clearly disappointed, Edward added, "Why can't you just be respectful to your teachers and classmates? All the other students seem to behave. You are grounded the rest of the month. No fishing and no shooting."

Showing no sign of agitation or surprise, James simply responded with a "Yes, sir." James and I both knew the punishment held no weight and would not last past the upcoming weekend, because it was more of a punishment for Edward and me than James.

Then Edward mumbled under his breath, "Thank God we didn't risk having another child." It was certainly loud enough for James and me to both clearly hear. I cocked my head toward Edward for a split second, shocked he would voice such a hateful thought, and then my eyes darted over to James. I saw him wince and then quickly return to his usual obstinate, stone-faced stance.

Edward's overall tone was that of anger and dominance, as if he were trying to instill fear into James in an attempt to control him. *The comment about not having another child was entirely uncalled for. Does he think shaming James is going to help?* I thought but didn't dare interject. While I was confident he maintained a calm, collected, professional posture at work – even when correcting those under his leadership – somehow that version of Edward never presented itself at home when James needed any sort of correction, which had increased in frequency as he got older. Instead, to any conflict or disappointment, Edward's default response was anger, asserting control – rather, an *attempt* to control – and the addition of more rules. And, as James grew up, our parental tactics were proving increasingly less effective, widening the distance between us.

Walking closer to James, Edward continued, "The older you get, the more disappointing you become. You better shape up, boy." The two stood face to face, with James standing just as tall as Edward. While Eddy maintained good physical shape, he could not compete with youth and our son's naturally strong build.

"Yes, sir," James said flatly.

Truly worried Edward was going to raise a hand to James, I spoke up. "There will be no dinner for you, James Michael. Now go up to your room and think about what you've done and the disappointment you've brought upon your father and me." I too was frustrated with James, but I was mostly trying to defuse Edward by showing support.

With that, James went upstairs.

"I need some air," Edward said and briskly walked out the door.

Defeated, I slumped down in a kitchen chair. *James will certainly end up joining the military.* My mind jumped ahead a few years. *Maybe it would actually be good for him.*

Tears stung my eyes. James was my baby, whom I still remembered bringing home for the first time; now, he considered our home a prison. I thought back to helping him learn to walk and hearing him say "Mama" in his sweet, baby voice. And here he was, taller than me and not too far off from adulthood. *My boy. Where did the time go?* I asked myself. *He has such a stubborn fire in his eyes, and he seems to want nothing but to leave this small town.* Then, another voice cut in. *Now you can understand how I felt about Johnny.* I stopped and looked around. Was that Mama's voice? *Perhaps you should try praying for him, Edward, and your family*, it gently coaxed. "Pray? You think God would listen to me now, after all I've done?" I said aloud. I shook my head, trying to dismiss the voice. Then, I brushed off the tears from my cheeks and fixed a plate to take up to James.

CHAPTER 30
1967

"I don't want to go to Ocean Isle this summer!" James practically yelled. "It's the last summer I have to hang out with my friends before I join the Army," he added, as he stormed up the stairs to his room.

I focused my gaze on a knot on one of our antique cherry cabinet doors as I counted down from ten while simultaneously massaging my temples, a technique I practiced often to help reduce anxiety. My fingers lost their placement when I heard James yell, "I am not going!" before he slammed his bedroom door. Giving up on the relaxation exercise, I leaned over the stainless-steel kitchen sink and tried to curb the urge to open a bottle of wine before lunch.

The bubbling grape jelly grabbed my attention, and I stirred the Swedish meatballs and turned down the heat. Spoon still in hand, I gave the onion soup a stir and decided to start on the Jell-O. I opened one of the yellow base cabinets, new last fall, and reached for the rectangular box. I had hoped the yellow would add cheer to our kitchen, but the happiness I felt only went as deep as the two-layer coat of paint. *Daddy loved Jell-O,*

I thought, fighting back tears. Daddy had died on Good Friday that year. The Wednesday before, I'd stopped by to check on him to say hello and remind him about Easter dinner.

"Thanks for the reminder, my darling," he said, smiling softly, and then asked, "You know how much I love you, don't you?"

Although I always hated such questions, since his death I took comfort in recalling those often-repeated words, wishing I could've recorded his voice.

"Yes, Daddy. And I, you," I replied, as I had many times.

"I want to talk to you about something." He spoke up as I motioned to leave, even though I had only been there a few minutes. "I know it is not top of mind for you, but I pray for you every day. I've been thinking a lot about your mother and how her faith saved her. And with Easter this Sunday, I just wanted to say, I hope you take the time to remember why we celebrate the weekend."

"I know the background on Easter, Dad. And I don't need saving," I said, my tone shorter than I intended. To soften my response, I added, "You know me, Daddy. I am a good person. You don't have to worry. Now, I need to stop at the store before James gets home from school. Love you." I wasn't going to, but something nudged me to hug him before I left. He held on tight, kissed my cheek, and told me again he loved me before he let me go.

James found Daddy dead on Friday when he went to pick him up for the evening church service.

"Margaret?" Edward asked.

"Hi, dear, welcome home," I answered, returning to the present.

"You okay? You didn't respond the first two times I said hello."

"Sorry, dear. I was just thinking about my father," I explained. He knew how hard Daddy's death had been on me. I was now an orphan with no siblings. Knowing my fragile emotional state, Edward had helped to settle the estate, including selling the house and auctioning off the possessions I didn't want. While he wanted me to, I couldn't bring myself to sell Johnny's DeSoto Custom. Besides the picture of him in his Army uniform, it was all I had left of my brother. And as for the rest of the family treasures, I'd only hung on to a few things: Mama's jewelry and fur coat, and Daddy's fedora hat, which I kept along with his pipe in a memory box in our spare room.

"Okay. I will be in the living room until dinner."

I buried my feelings and focused my energies on dinner, and while delicious, the actual supper time together was hurried and quiet. James's body language communicated he only wanted to retreat back to his room, and Edward claimed to have work to attend to. Edward and I had mastered doing life side-by-side, but I often wondered what it would be like once James, our common denominator, graduated and left the house. Besides logistical discussions, we didn't talk much. Increasingly, it felt as if we were roommates instead of husband and wife. As much as I longed for a deeper connection, I knew, ever since I'd walked in on Edward all those years ago, that I could never fully trust him. And, given the lie that I was living, part of me felt I'd condemned myself to a life of superficialities.

After James asked to be excused and was up the stairs, I brought up our upcoming vacation.

"Yes, I am excited to spend some time on the water," Edward shared.

"Are you sure Helen and Robert can't come? Let's ask again, now that it is only a few weeks away. They should know more now," I suggested, and Edward agreed.

Robert and Helen had told us over Christmas about their plans to visit several places in Florida in hopes to find a winter home. Hence, they did not want to commit to a month in Ocean Isle with us. I thought back to the family meeting we'd had on New Year's Day.

"The winters in Ohio anymore are just too much on your father. We are hoping to find a place to travel to from December to March," Helen informed Edward and Shirley.

"You will be gone over Christmas?" Shirley asked, concerned about Christmastime because her children were still young enough to cherish the spirit of the season.

"Don't worry, we will come back for Christmas . . . unless you all decide to travel to us? We will cover any travel expenses, so you wouldn't have to worry about the cost," Helen said, smiling.

Shirley and I had lost touch over the years. Of course, we loved her and her family and she ours, but physical distance had a natural impact on our relationship. Shortly after she and Charles married, they moved to Cincinnati, and while not far away, it inevitably meant that we spent less time together. While the reason given for the move was Charles's employment, we knew it was because most of his family was there and they preferred the larger city life. For the first five years of their marriage, they traveled to us in Dayton most of the time, because we had James and it was easier for the two of them to travel than the five of us. However, after celebrating their fifth anniversary, she was pregnant or nursing for nearly five years straight. And with two boys and a girl now old enough to be involved and make memories, our visits together were limited to major holidays and birthdays.

After much cajoling, I eventually persuaded James to come with us to Ocean Isle. It was hard to face the fact that my little boy, whom I once considered my world, had grown up and was no longer interested in me. His indifference hurt. I was grasping at straws; the harder I tried to ask questions or make suggestions, the more James distanced himself.

James met a girl, Kimmy, our first week at Ocean Isle, and by the second week, he spent nearly every night with her. I could only imagine what he was getting himself into. As he left to meet her for the fourth night in a row, I wanted to caution him to be smart, but an internal voice mocked me. *You want to tell him to be smart? Isn't that the pot calling the kettle black? You may have been a little older, but you weren't exactly wise in your younger years.* I winced at the memories of Joe, including the last encounter, another secret I always swore I would take to my grave. *His father didn't exactly set a good example either, now did he? Do you honestly think James doesn't know his father was unfaithful? Even if he didn't, he likely has picked up on the distance between you two.* My heart ached, and I wasn't sure if it would ever feel whole.

"He will be fine, Margaret," Edward said quietly, reading my mind.

"I hope so," I whispered.

Edward's facial expression changed, urging me to say something positive before James left to meet Kimmy, and so I called out, "Enjoy your time with Kimmy, James, dear. Perhaps you could invite her to dinner in the next few days?"

"I don't know, Mom. It isn't that serious," James answered dismissively.

"At least consider the offer, for your Mother's sake," Edward added, and I was thankful for his support.

Robert and Helen joined us in Ocean Isle for a long weekend, which I was incredibly thankful for because it gave me someone to spend time with. I was accustomed to time alone, as I hadn't formed any lasting friendships, but I wanted to share our new house with someone. Sometimes I wondered if the lack of companionship was some sort of divine punishment for refusing to listen to Mama's advice to befriend Ruth. Or maybe it had to do with me not inviting closeness, for fear of what I might divulge to a friend.

"The driveway is stunning!" Helen said, arms reaching out to hug me. Her orange-hued shift dress fit the season, and I was certain there were more Jackie Kennedy inspired outfits in her suitcase. She kissed my cheek and added, "My, you have soaked in some sun these last two weeks. Your skin is glowing!"

After the two unpacked, the boys grabbed their fishing rods and Helen and I headed to the local market to pick up groceries for dinner.

I adjusted my summer pillbox hat and brought Helen up to speed. "Her name is Kimmy. We haven't met her yet, but

James has spent a lot of time with her, and he finally agreed to invite her for dinner."

"How romantic!"

I glanced over at Helen, dark black shades covering her face and her bouffant hair held back by a silk summer scarf. She leaned back on the seat's headrest as she soaked in the sun, my favorite part of having a convertible.

"We must make this dinner memorable," Helen started. "Let's have our jalapeno cheese dip to nibble on before dinner. And what would you like to serve for the main course? Pork chops, perhaps? We could pair it with cheesy potatoes and a salad. Or would you rather have cabbage?"

"Let's do a strawberry salad."

"Perfect."

Helen continued on with the meal, what to serve for dessert, and what we needed to buy to mix up Long Island ice teas. I was so glad she and Robert had come; they would provide the perfect buffer when we met Kimmy for the first time. And, Helen would take full ownership of the meal.

Six o'clock came and went. James and Kimmy were late. He'd left after lunch to spend the afternoon with her doing God knows what, and Eddy gave him specific instructions to be back at half past five. Since James repeatedly stumbled in the house past curfew after his rendezvouses with this girl, I'd asked Edward to tell him to return thirty minutes earlier than I really wanted him home. Scanning the kitchen, I was the only one noticeably irked. Robert, Edward, and Helen were enjoying the cheese dip, fresh out of the oven, and I was trying to calm myself down. *Breathe in. One, two, three. Breathe out. One, two, three, four, five.*

Edward called me away from the window. "Maggie, dear. Come join us. As always, Mama's dip is amazing."

I obliged. The three stood around the island, a kitchen addition I just had to have after watching Julia Childs' *The French Chef.* Helen had changed into a pink and yellow patterned, high neckline shift dress, and the men each in a polo shirt. The view of these three chatting and laughing was like a movie scene of the perfect family – a loving mother, who was also an amazing cook, doting over her darling son and hardworking husband, the parents laughing as their grown child told a joke. It was everything I wanted: a husband, money to build such a house, and a family I could call my own. *You know this scene of perfection is just a veneer?* a voice mocked. Yet, I refused to let go of the moment – even if it meant denying reality – and redirected my thoughts. *Kimmy may be a wonderful girl for your boy.* A small smile crossed my face, and I held it there as I walked closer, my smile growing as I admired how the wood floors I picked out complemented the white board walls throughout the first floor, providing a beautiful backdrop for the scene in front of me.

After a few more bites of dip, Edward and Robert sat down and started talking about fishing. "Margaret, dear. Tell me, what do you know about Kimmy besides the fact that she isn't punctual?" Helen laughed playfully, and while she meant it as a joke, I took slight offense to it.

"Not much, actually, except that North Carolina is her home state," I said, embarrassed I didn't know more about the girl James had been spending so much time with. I forced a grin and added, "I am excited to meet her tonight."

"That is how I felt about Ruth."

As if my ears were deceiving me, I tilted my head slightly and blinked my eyes a few times in disbelief. *Did she just say Ruth? I haven't heard that name uttered in years. What year is it again?* I did some quick math in my head. *It has been almost two decades. I never thought relations would remain severed this long.*

Without looking up at me, Helen added with a solemn tone, "I sure hope this Kimmy girl doesn't take dear James from you."

Or, perhaps Kimmy will. Karma and all, fear spoke to my unsettled heart.

"I am sorry I even gave voice to those memories," Helen added with a nervous laugh. "Let's put that thought away and talk about your beautiful home!"

Helen seamlessly transitioned the conversation to the house, and while I accepted her compliments and suggestions, my mind lingered on her comment about Ruth and Kimmy.

She better not take my baby away from me, I thought.

I lay in bed, eyes wide open, staring into the darkness and listening to the gentle hum of the ceiling fan. While not in style, Edward insisted on the ceiling fan, and against my better judgment, I conceded.

"I loved having one in my room growing up. This is our home away from home. Come on. Call it an item of nostalgia. No one will be in our master room anyway," he persuaded, before adding his closing argument. "You got the driveway you wanted."

"Fine. You win!" I responded playfully, waving a white paper towel in the air to signal my surrender.

While an eyesore, I was glad to have the fan. I enjoyed the cool breeze, and the white noise helped me fall asleep. At least most nights.

Kimberly is beautiful. Too beautiful. I wish James would keep his distance; proximity will certainly lead him into temptation he will not even consider resisting. Her long auburn hair was curled, the full locks accentuating her oval, tan face. She was dressed stylishly; the orange, green, and cream stripes on the sleeves and chest of the bold orange mini-dress matched her mini-pants, and her green thong sandals revealed her coordinating painted toenails. While the top was not revealing, the mini-pants showed off her trim, tan legs, and I wanted to smack James across the face when he watched her pick up the fork she dropped when taking the plates to the sink. To round out her outfit, quarter-size green plastic earrings dangled from her earlobes. While Kimmy's golden brown eyes were not a unique color, there was something unsettling about her gaze and smile. Her words and posture were both perfect; yet, there was something deceptive about her, and beyond her intoxicating mix of perfume and youth, my intuition couldn't detect a hint of sincerity in her person. More, her plummy voice annoyed me, and I wondered whether she'd been born with a silver spoon in her mouth. Yet, in addition to James, Kimberly wrapped Edward, Helen, and Robert around her finger, and after she left, their profuse compliments to James made me nauseous.

With Helen's words about Ruth still lingering, another stomach-churning thought surfaced. *I wonder if Ruth detected the same characteristic in you: pretty on the outside, shallow on the inside.*

CHAPTER 31
2015

"Wow! That was a lot." Megan sat in disbelief, eyes wide, completely captivated. "What happened between James and Kimmy?" she asked, clearly curious.

Focused on James, I put my hand to my forehead, stopping the small movement of it shaking back and forth. *It's my fault*, I thought. *I should've never made James go that year.* Regret coursed through my mind and body.

"Do you want to go for a walk? I need to stretch my legs," I asked, buying myself time from answering her question and earnestly needing to stand up.

"Of course!" Megan answered emphatically. "Do you want to drive to a nearby park?"

"Let's just walk around the block."

We left together, Megan holding the door, the aroma of coffee replaced by the crisp October air. The sun's rays burst through the intermittent clouds, and the dance between the two provided a delicate mix of warm and cool. Like a whisper, the breeze gently rustled the leaves still clinging to the trees.

Megan ran to put her things in her car while I waited outside the coffee shop's double doors.

I stood on the sidewalk and watched her. *I wish I didn't need this damn cane. If I could only turn back time.* I looked at my crutch and remembered what James had spewed out when I told him I missed walking without support. *"Given your address, be thankful your legs still work at all. Some of your neighbors are wheelchair bound."* While hardly empathetic, he had a point.

A year ago, almost to the day, I'd lost my independence. I woke up one November morning around five o'clock, and instead of sliding out of bed to dress for my morning walk, I could barely make it to the bathroom. I winced in pain as I hoisted my leg over the bed, and I knew something was wrong. I called James a few times, but after an hour without a call back, I phoned my neighbors, Paul and Pam Gould. While I never agreed with the political signs they put in their front yard, they were kind people and brought me homemade bread or cookies at least once a month.

"Let me make one quick phone call, and I will be right over," Pam quickly responded, then continued, "My mother had similar pain three years ago. She is as stubborn as a mule, and the woman, God bless her, refused to see a doctor for almost three weeks. And boy did she pay for her procrastination. It took her longer to recover! I share that story because I am glad you want to see a professional right away. Like I said, I will be over in just a few minutes." I heard her distinctive, labored voice yell to Paul to get his shoes on before she hung up the phone.

I wanted to wait for James to return my calls, but the Gould couple convinced me otherwise and took me to the hospital. Their insistence proved wise, as James didn't call me back till midafternoon; by then, I was able to give him my diagnosis.

"I need a full hip replacement. The doctor originally hoped for a partial, but after a few more images given my osteoporosis, he determined the socket is too deteriorated for a partial replacement," I explained to James, thankful I remembered to bring the cellular device he'd bought for me.

For a few moments, I had his full attention. He sounded genuinely concerned, but I heard his hands tapping away at his keyboard, no doubt sending "one quick email." Come to find out, he'd immediately begun researching care facilities. After three days in the hospital, and without consulting me, I was relocated to Sunrise Living, an assisted living facility James picked out. He visited a few times between the move and New Year's, but certainly not to converse and play a game of two-handed euchre or Russian Banks. After pleasantries, James cut to the chase: he needed to get rid of everything that wouldn't fit in my new twelve by twelve room and finalize the sale of the house I had called home for decades.

On autopilot, I started walking next to my unencumbered companion. "What a perfect day for a walk!" Megan exclaimed as we started down the sidewalk together. Her statement reunited my mind with my old body taking slow steps on the pavement.

Megan shared how she'd met her husband in a spin class, announced her engagement to her less-than-thrilled parents, and then married him a little over a year after they'd exchanged numbers.

"My parents came around, and they love him now. At the time, I think the issue was twofold: one, they didn't want to let their baby girl go, and two, he grew up Catholic and they expressed concerns. Grandma Ruth stood in my corner though. She, after all, had married a man who grew up Catholic, and she helped my mother, well, calm down, for lack of better words."

Ruth. My body's visceral response to Megan speaking her name for the first time was expected; a pit formed in my stomach, my chest tightened, and my mind struggled to focus on Megan's words. *I wonder if she would've been your advocate, your friend when you needed one? Why did she have to be so perfect?*

To fill the silence, and to share more about her own life, potentially in an attempt to connect, she went on to talk about their travel adventures and dreams. "Of course, we want to have children, however gray the future looks. Sometimes I wonder if we should bring a child into this crazy world. When I shared that concern with my mentor, she told me, 'The Bible doesn't have an asterisk by the command to be fruitful and multiply.' I always get a chuckle when I think of that."

"I wish we would've had more children." The words left my mouth without my permission – and initially, without awareness; the filter between my thoughts and my mouth had slowly deteriorated with age.

"Oh really?" Megan asked.

"Really, what, dear?" I asked.

"You wish you would've had more children?" she repeated hesitantly, her brow furrowed in confusion.

I said that out loud? "Never mind my ramblings. Tell me, do you have any trips planned for this year or next?"

"For our trip next year, we are torn. I want to fly to Bern, Switzerland, but my husband desperately wants to travel around Denmark, Norway, and Sweden, mainly because he wants to attend the International Ice Hockey Tournament. Did you ever go to Europe?"

"No, I never did," I answered as I kept my gaze fixed ahead, making sure there was no uneven pavement. *Stop avoiding the proverbial elephant on the sidewalk. You might as well answer how karma came full circle*, a snide voice derided.

We kept on in silence, passing a couple modest homes. Each one had its own unique curb appeal, one with a fully covered front porch, the steps adorned with a toddler's chalk artwork, and another with freshly painted window boxes filled with white gourds, orange mums, and trailing ivy. The trees firmly planted in the boulevard reached high into the sky, their gnarled, knobby branches reminding me of my own aged, arthritic joints. I recalled how, when James was a little boy, he liked to count the number of rings in the tree stumps at the park. *"Mom! This one's got fifty-five rings! That's ANCIENT!"* he'd say. *"And look at this one . . .!"* What had happened to my sweet little boy? I wondered, then shook myself back to reality.

"James married Kimmy without our permission, which, predictably, led to a rift. I tried to smooth relations over with a letter, but it wasn't received kindly. Well, I take that back. The letter was received fine; it was the phone call after that was damning. Edward pretended he didn't remember James's voice, and that set the tone not just for the phone call, but for their relationship. It was the last time Edward and James spoke."

"I am sorry to hear that. My grandpa's father did something similar," Megan added, her tone lower, sadder, as if she were reliving a memory.

"The apple didn't fall far from the tree." *That isn't a fair statement for William though, now is it?* A softer voice whispered some truth into my reflective, but guarded, heart. "I suppose that statement doesn't apply to every father–son relationship, does it? At least in Edward's case, like father, like son. My interactions with James became few and far between. He checked in every few months, but besides the wedding, I didn't see him until after Edward died. Edward never wanted me to visit him, and I was loyal to my husband's wishes. And, if I am honest, I hated Kimmy so much, I was content with the long-distance relationship. Somehow, blaming her and the scuffle between Edward and James made it all easier when someone asked about my son."

"You wanted to stay the victim? Even at the cost of a relationship with your son?"

Megan's piercing question matched her gaze. I wanted to retreat or defend myself. *How dare she ask such a question? I knew this meeting was a bad idea.*

I looked forward, silent and indignant. We rounded the corner to walk back up the block and eventually return to her car. I tried to focus on the gardens and tree varieties, but my mother's voice tugged at my heart. *She is correct, you know? She just shot an arrow into your Achilles heel. Let it bring you to your knees, my dear.*

I didn't speak until my seatbelt was on; even then, it was only a thank you for helping me close the door. Then, with my prison in sight, my mom's voice reverberated and a sense of dread filled my heart; I didn't want the conversation to stop. Challenging though it was, it was honest and raw, and a small voice encouraged me to let go of the burden of perfection and admit she was correct; admit I had lived as a victim for decades, ever since Johnny died, and I never imagined the consequences I would reap.

A war raged inside my mind, and in the end, my well-exercised defenses won out when she shifted the car into park. I stopped spinning my gold pearl ring and trained my gaze forward. "I hope you have what you need. Have a pleasant rest of your day."

"Margaret, before you go, please forgive my overstep. If it matters, I've become so immersed in your story, I feel like we've known each other for years rather than hours, and I blurted out what came to mind. It is an area I need to improve on, I know."

I nodded my head in silent agreement. *The young, judgmental brat better be sorry*, I thought as I reached for the door handle, but almost as if my mother's hand gripped mine, I hesitated. *Wait, my dear.*

"I cannot pretend to understand what you have lived through and the hurts you've experienced, and I am grateful for what you have shared. In fact, I would still love to hear the rest of your story if you would invite me back. But if this is farewell, I feel compelled to tell you, you can receive freedom. The tension within you is palpable, and based on my own life and hearing the other side of this story, I know there are two responses to pain, heartache, and unrealized expectations . . ."

I held up my hand, signaling her to stop. Evidence to the war within, tears rimmed my eyes. However, instead of facing Megan and receiving what she offered, I opened the door and motioned for the doorman to help me. While I felt her gaze until I was down the hall, I did not look back.

I ate alone that evening; I wasn't in the mood for conversation about the weather, Scrabble, or Alex Trebek. The worn cushion on the oak chair provided no comfort for my aged tailbone, and I became increasingly agitated about the appearance of the pale yellow painted room. What a long way I'd come from my immaculately styled family home, not to mention the Ocean Isle beach cottage. *Just because they painted the room yellow doesn't mean everyone will be chipper. Why can't they at least update the ruffled floral curtains?*

With every breath, my nostrils took in the stale air, heavy with the smell of disinfectant and body odor. I missed the intoxicating aroma of good coffee, home-cooked meals, fresh flowers. And to add insult to injury, the chicken that evening was especially distasteful. The chef, if you could call him that, attempted to hide the lack of flavor with a heavy hand of salt. *Not only are you eating rubber for dinner, but your blood pressure is going to spike too.*

My room provided no solace. I longed for home, but after unearthing and confronting so much of my past, I struggled to remember a house I'd ever considered a true sanctuary.

Guess which side of the story she will side with? She sounded just like Ruth, a darker voice began.

Well, darling, that is not fair, is it? She seemed to earnestly care about what you had to say, a softer one, like Mama's, rebutted.

She was a judgmental little brat.

Perhaps you are upset because her judgment call was accurate.

And with that thought, I called for the nurse. "Hello, Casey. Can you please bring me a diazepam? My legs are twitching awful tonight, and I am afraid I won't be able to sleep without the medication."

—

Megan

As soon as I pulled onto the freeway, I called Mom. While supportive of my educational pursuits, she was not supportive of me spending time with Margaret and expressed as much on the phone. Again.

"I told you she was a venomous snake," Mama said, her voice aggravated. The entire topic annoyed her, even though she was only an indirectly offended party.

Mama loved fiercely. When one of her own was hurting, she shouldered the burden and channeled her energies into helping that individual; her ability to empathize was incredible, but sometimes she forgot she wasn't the one originally hurt. In regard to the family Grandma Ruth had married into, Mama only knew bits and pieces, but from what Grandma did disclose, my mother knew the scars were evidence of deep wounds. While there wasn't much to shoulder, Mom took on the lion's role and never breathed life into the subject.

Mama switched topics to her holiday preparations, which she always began at least four weeks out. "Do you know when you are coming in for Thanksgiving? Is it the day before, or can you two come earlier? Oh, and I would like to review the menu with you one last time."

I knew she hoped we would come the weekend before both Thanksgiving and Christmas to help her clean and finish decorating the house. From scrubbing baseboards to setting the table with holiday-themed china and centerpieces, Mama labored for hours to prepare and host both Thanksgiving and Christmas. Mom and her sister, my Aunt Esther, used to split the role of host for the two major, end-of-year holidays, but that all changed a decade or so ago. Aunt Esther's cancer diagnosis nearly killed both her and my mom. Auntie E first went to her family physician for a persistent bruise, and after a litany of tests, she was diagnosed with Angiosarcoma in both her skin and in her breasts. We all shaved our heads for the family Christmas photo eleven years ago to support Auntie E during her treatment, which we still look back on and smile. Grandma Ruth assumed her anchoring matriarch role, often reassuring the family God was still the sovereign Alpha and Omega. Honestly, I think Grandma's faith was both a source of annoyance and strength for Mom. Ever since her father died, Mama battled fear and anxiety, and she assumed a fighter position against any threat to her family. But the cancer could not be reasoned away. It could not be tossed to the curb, removed from our life, or traded in for something else.

When we all smiled for the 2004 Christmas family photo, none of us could have fathomed Esther would be alive in 2015. But God mercifully had preserved her life and health, and with each Thanksgiving, she, my mom, and Grandma would hold tear-stained tissues while we went around the dinner table and shared what we were most thankful for that year.

While Mama and Grandma differed when it came to their weaknesses, they both shared a "Mama Bear" attitude toward their children, which is why Grandma didn't mention

Grandpa's side of the family much and why Mama rolled her eyes when I told her about my dissertation topic.

Before I'd even applied for my doctoral degree, I had already talked to Grandma Ruth at length about her life. Grandma had had a strong influence on my upbringing, and out of all her grandchildren, I had a penchant for both asking questions and writing stories. When I was ten years old, I initiated and started the first family newsletter, I studied English Literature in college, and my journal count far exceeded my mother's.

Whenever I asked about Grandpa, Grandma was more than willing to share stories about "the love of her life," as she often referred to him. However, once dating and marriage became more real to me, I wanted to learn about her early years of marriage. At first, she shared only good memories, and I had no reason to believe there was anything else to her story. But after a particularly hard break up with my college boyfriend of almost two years, she disclosed more of her past as she offered me nuggets of wisdom.

"You know, sweet child, the man you marry and give yourself to will come with baggage. We all do."

"What baggage did Grandpa have?" I asked, curious, my hand reaching for another helping of freshly made party-mix.

That question kicked open the door to their year of courting and their wedding. After about an hour-long monologue, a few tissues, and another helping of party-mix, I sat there in shock. *How am I just now learning about all this?* I wondered, sifting through memories, trying to recall if any hint of this season had ever been unearthed.

As Grandma refilled the snack bowl, I asked, "Grandma, how am I just now hearing about this part of your life? I mean, it is pretty life-altering. Mom has never mentioned anything about it."

Grandma Ruth lowered herself carefully into the leather desk chair on wheels. While not a traditional kitchen chair, it helped her swivel around to reach easily for a pen or paper on the counter and then back to her round white table. She briefly looked out the window adjacent to the table, and then back to me.

"Oh honey, I hardly ever think about my past. The Lord has been so gracious to me in the present, and there is no reason to look in the rearview mirror and allow bitterness to tempt me."

"Does Mom, Auntie E or either of my uncles know this part of your story?"

"No. All William and I agreed to tell them was that his family lived far away, and they fell into the 'unkind' category of people whom we needed to pray for."

"*Unkind* is a generous adjective," I responded with sarcasm. I instinctively sided with my grandma, and a few more colorful phrases flashed in the forefront of my mind, but I did not voice them.

"Now, now. I let you peer into the mirror of my past, but it does us no good to dishonor his relatives."

"Why didn't you tell my mom more of the story?"

"What good would it have done her or any of our children? They were loved by your grandfather and me, and my parents and family doted on them. Honestly, none of them even asked about their daddy's family until grade school."

"They didn't ask for more details?"

"Not everyone is as curious as you, darling," she answered, taking a sip of water, and smiled. "I suppose they didn't feel like anything was missing in their life. And, after your grandfather died, I never heard from any of his family again. I mailed a Christmas card the Christmas after your uncle was born, but the letter came back with 'Return to Sender' stamped on it. I am not sure if they actually moved or wrote over their name just well enough that the post office sent it back to me. Either way, I did not try again, and I never heard from them either. When I look back, I have to be careful, because I can quickly grow irritated and bitter. Who knows, maybe we will reunite in heaven?"

"That sounds like a movie ending."

"Perhaps."

After that day, I was determined to glean as much information and wisdom as I could from my Grandma. She initially resisted the idea, saying that she didn't have that interesting of a story to share.

"G-ma, please. Think of all the stories from the Bible. What if Moses decided his story wasn't worth sharing? What if Paul didn't think his story was worth telling? I want to hear how God worked in your life and learn from you."

"You certainly are a persistent one."

Knowing I had won, I smiled.

For the rest of my college career, Grandma and I spent invaluable time together unpacking her story. She shared in increments; sometimes it was an all-day affair while baking cherry pies or making fudge; other times she reminisced during a Saturday morning coffee date, and still others she would recall a memory while we took a walk. We didn't move in a strict chronological fashion, and she shared what she wanted, when she wanted. Sometimes I only learned the details of a single day, while others, I recorded her recount of an entire year. Grandma had a stack of journals she referenced, full of documented memories, feelings, and lessons she'd learned along the way. Emotions often dominated the room, sometimes powerfully heavy and other times delightfully uplifting. I would know she was ready to unveil something particularly heavy or complex when she had her rolling pin or potato masher out.

"Good morning, Grandma," I managed to say, yawning one morning. It was barely half past six when I pulled into her driveway, and Grandma already had potatoes boiling and the island was covered with a stack of mixing bowls and unbleached flour, sugar, dark brown sugar, cream, milk, eggs, and spices.

"Wake up, darling. Fix yourself some coffee. We are making Bread Pudding Baked Alaska! I just scooped out the bread pudding and need to fill it with ice cream. You start on the meringue."

What time did she wake up? I thought to myself wearily as I poured some coffee into the prepared mug; Grandma knew I too liked a single pump of simple syrup and a pinch of raw sugar in my coffee, and she had already put both in the mug for me.

Noticing an old photo album open on the kitchen table, I asked, "Are those pictures from Sanibel?"

"Yes. From our last trip with William," she responded, her voice thick with emotion. "The thermometer is in the last drawer on the right."

After a few sips of java, I secured my apron and located the candy thermometer. Then, I put some sugar in the saucepan and added some water. I loved the taste of meringue, and Baked Alaska was one of my favorite desserts. But Grandma knew I was a novice at best when it came to mastering her recipe.

"You want me to help whip the egg whites?" she asked.

"I will try this time," I answered, trying to sound confident.

The last time we'd made meringue, I let the sugar exceed 240 degrees, and we had to start over. But this time, I was determined to reach those firm stiff peaks without aid.

"Perfect, dear! You got it! Your peaks rival the likes of Mount Everest!" she exclaimed.

Once the bread pudding was back in the freezer, I started on the cookie garnish while she drained the potatoes and began talking.

"I remember that afternoon like it was yesterday. At one point, we sent a letter providing a brief update, as if we were strangers, which we were at that point. I asked again about contacting them; for heaven's sake, I initiated almost every time, and they weren't even my parents!" Grandma raised both hands, one holding her potato masher, the other a cup filled with lukewarm milk.

"I am sorry, I need to forgive again," she continued. "You will learn, dear, that forgiveness is not a one-time thing. Anyway, after I asked him about sending a letter, William, tired of the whole situation, told me, 'Ruth, what we want will never come to pass. Let's leave off anything of substance and send a general update. So, we did. We even sent three pictures. This was, what, the early sixties? I was planning Esther's tenth birthday party, so it was 1963. You know what we heard back?"

"What?" I asked simply. I had grown accustomed to Grandma's rhetorical questions, understanding it was almost a cathartic way of expressing her frustration as she relived some of the more challenging parts of her life.

"Nothing."

I winced.

"I could never understand them. If anything, I would think to myself, *Surely they will be humane enough to do x, y or z.* They would always disappoint. William tried again a few months later, asking if they received the original letter. The communication went back and forth a few times; come to find out, Helen received the letter and just chose to ignore it. In fact, she had the audacity to blame *us* for her not sending a response or a gift. She also had no idea how old our children were, and she was daft enough to write, 'I hope to meet them.'"

"Grandma, I can't imagine being treated that way."

Grandma continued, and while she knew I was her audience, I could tell her mind was back in the 1960s. "In the years that followed, we sent a few cards here and there to his parents, but his mother never dismounted her high horse. She occasionally sent William birthday cards filled with over-the-top messages, and then she would either ignore the rest of us or write the bare minimum in a plain card. One Christmas, we received a package, and we thought she'd actually sent something for the children. Negative. She sent a package addressed only to William with his childhood spoons and his childhood nativity book."

"Spoons?" I asked, confused by the unusual contents.

"How in the world would she remember which cheap tin spoons were the ones he ate with?" she asked, raising her hands in exasperation. "The accompanying letter, also addressed only to him, could only be described as manipulative. I remember William's frustration; he felt like she treated him like a little boy rather than a married man with children. And, in any communication, she would make sure to remind him he was her 'son' or 'baby' multiple times. I would have rather drunk vinegar straight than read her hollow comments of 'love to all' or 'hope to see you soon.' I think she wrote those things to make herself feel better; she never ever mentioned anything of significance."

"Grandma, we don't have to continue . . ." I began, my voice barely a whisper. I was torn, wanting to know more, but not wanting Grandma to relive the hurts of her past.

"No, no, it is okay," she reassured me, her voice unsteady.

Pain painted her face, and tears carried traces of mascara down the wrinkled wilderness of pink rouge. Seeing her this vulnerable made me wonder if I shouldn't have given in to my fixation on her past.

"You know, the first and last time she saw her grandchildren was from a distance at William's funeral. Utterly pathetic. When I saw her in the line, I vacillated between hope and fear. Hope that maybe, just maybe, the tragedy would soften her heart and be an avenue for healing. And fear it would be the nail in the coffin." She paused a moment, potato masher raised.

"It was the nail."

CHAPTER 32
2015

Another Thanksgiving had come and gone, and while some neighbors' families celebrated it like the holiday it was supposed to be, I received a card with a cornucopia on it and a phone call perfectly timed to be short. James knew dinner was served at five o'clock sharp, and if I wanted a chance to enjoy the holiday at all, I would attend. So, when my telephone rang at 4:40 p.m., I knew the call was timed to be brief.

"Happy Thanksgiving, *son*," I said, emphasizing "son" in a vain attempt to remind him of the special bond we were supposed to share. I sat on my double bed, fidgeting with the blanket and trying to sound cheerful.

"Happy Thanksgiving, Ma. Sorry I couldn't make it to see you. We hope to come closer to Christmas though."

While I heard voices in the background and knew he would be called away soon, James – for once – sounded genuine and focused on our conversation. I smiled at the thought of seeing him and his children again.

"Oh, you will bring the whole family?" I asked, actually allowing my hopes to float.

"Well, I'll see what I can do . . ." His tone changed. I rolled my eyes and could only imagine the look Kimmy would be giving him if she heard him. He continued, "Jamie and Valerie are both in the *Nutcracker* this year, so I will have to check with their practice and performance schedule."

Because of the unresolved tension between James and Edward, I did not meet James till after Eddy died – and even then, only once when he was a baby – and I didn't meet Valerie till years later. By then, I'd missed their baby, toddler, and most of their childhood years. In fact, Kimmy introduced me as "Miss Margaret" to them. I wanted to smack her perfect, porcelain face, but I restrained myself, knowing if I argued, our time would end. Kimmy knew I had never supported James's decision, and she was well aware of what Edward thought of her while he was alive. The little wench never gave me reason to change my mind, so our impasse remained. Part of me, of course, knew I was allowing history to repeat itself, and I hated myself for it. Just as William had become estranged from his family, I was allowing the bitterness in my heart to poison the relationship with my own son. But I was stubborn and unwilling to admit my faults, and certainly not willing to ask anyone for advice, for that meant facing the truth and opening up to someone. I suppose I feared what an outside observer would say.

"I understand," I lied and looked at the time. "I am thankful you called. Dinner will be served here shortly, and—"

James pulled the phone away from his mouth and called back to the male voice calling to him, "I'll be right there."

Is that Kimmy's father? Does Jamie already have such a deep voice?

"Alrighty, Mom. I need to go help with dinner, and it sounds like you need to go too. Enjoy the rest of your Thanksgiving!"

"Enjoy your Thanksgiving meal as well. Love—"

My salutation was met with silence, as my son abruptly hung up.

Sunrise Living spared no expense during Christmas. The front lawn showcased a nativity scene, and as the days counted down to Christmas morning, three plastic wisemen made their way across the lawn to the stable where the infamous Joseph, Mary, and baby Jesus stoically sat. White lights outlined the roof, adorned every pillar along the front porch, and lined the drive-way like a runway. After walking through the wreathed dou-ble doors, visitors and residents were greeted with a choice of traditional holiday delights, from decorated sugar cookies and thumbprint cookies to peanut butter blossoms or buckeyes, native to the state and a staple sweet in the fall and winter.

I received two pieces of mail that chilly Tuesday morning – the first, a Christmas card from James and Kimmy. While the handwriting was Kimmy's, I was certain James had forced her to mail one. When I opened the card, a letter fell out.

Margaret,

Merry Christmas! We hope you are enjoying the season at Sunrise! I looked at the calendar, and we are thrilled they plan such festive events. James will call as well, but I wanted to mail our card and the formal invitation and ticket to the kids' Nutcracker performance. We are sorry we won't be able to make it to Ohio this year, but I trust you understand the commitment we made to the ballet. We hope you will be able to come. I know my parents, the kids, and James and I would be happy to share the season with you.

Love,

Kimberly

I threw the card and contents on the floor, furious. Then, I picked up my room phone and dialed James, hoping he would side with me for once. Much to my surprise, he answered.

"Good afternoon, Mother," he answered, clearly busy at work. "Is everything okay?"

"No, it is not. You are not coming to Ohio now?" I practically yelled.

"Shit. I mean, shoot. I was supposed to call you yesterday. I'm sorry. Kimmy thought it would be cute to send you the invitation and ticket, but I was supposed to have called yesterday before the letter arrived. I totally forgot."

"You said *you* would come to *me*," I shot back, unmoved.

"I said we would try. Then, Kimmy had the great idea to fly you to us. That way, you could see the kids perform, and we could have—"

"I figured the plan was hers. Anything to keep you from me."

"Mom, stop. I will not let you speak that way about my wife."

"I am your mother!"

"Yes, you are. And Kimberly is my wife. Whether you like it or not, she is my number one."

"I brought you into this world, son."

"You sound like Dad."

A long silence ensued, and I wondered if he'd hung up.

"Look, Mom, I am sorry. I shouldn't have made that comparison. It wasn't fair," James started, his tone softer.

Did he just apologize? I wondered, and he continued, "We have been going to church recently with our neighbors, and it is starting to change my view on things. I want you and Kimberly to have a relationship, but in order for that to happen, you have to own your own shit – *stuff* – I mean, stuff. Now come on, just because the idea is not your own, doesn't mean it isn't a good one."

"I'll think about it," I answered curtly, and hung up the phone.

Looking for a distraction, I turned on the local news. As I listened to the commercials boasting about the holiday sales, I opened the second piece of mail – a Christmas card from Megan, wishing me a joyous season and letting me know she would enjoy meeting again, if I was willing.

You were having a perfectly good day until the mail arrived. Of course the idea was Kimmy's, and of course she would only invite you on such short notice, a voice sneered, increasing my agitation. *What does she think you can do? Just leave on a moment's notice? And, to make it a well-rounded family affair, that girl sends you something.*

I tossed the mail onto the small table and turned the channel to watch an overly predictable Hallmark movie.

I hate this time of the year, I thought, turning off the television after watching prince charming sweep the fair maiden into his arms on Santa's sleigh. I shuffled to my small, sterile bathroom and began to wrap my perm with toilet paper. After covering it with my cap and slipping on my buffalo check nightgown, I returned to the comfort of my pillow. Despite being decades old and losing almost all of its fluff, it was mine. Familiar. Comforting. I rolled onto my right side, placed a cushion between my knees, and tried unsuccessfully to not think. *Perhaps you should consider seeing James, or if you don't want to travel, let yourself see Megan again. It is Christmas time, after all. Perhaps it is time to reclaim the holiday*, Mother's voice whispered.

My eyes opened with a start, but rather than seeing the scene around me clearly, it was as if a haze were in the air or a sheer veil over my eyes. My limbs were heavy, time crept, and I was simultaneously watching myself and within my own body.

"You coming, Maggie?" Edward asked, his voice distant and barely audible.

Looking quickly to my left, I saw Edward next to me, slightly impatient since we were arriving almost fifteen minutes late. He hated to be tardy.

I robotically opened the car door and saw James already at Robert and Helen's back door, letting himself in. James carried a bag full of perfectly wrapped presents, and without realizing I'd picked it up, I carried in my own arms a nine by thirteen dish covered in a hand-sewn casserole carrier. Without actually walking in the door, the five of us stood in the familiar blue kitchen. Shortly after relations with William had essentially ended, Helen redid her kitchen. Again. The previous, mint green color scheme – chosen by Ruth – was a constant reminder to Helen of the woman who had ripped her family apart. While Robert was aggravated by the cost and inconvenience, he agreed to the project, as he equally, if not more, hated William's wife.

Helen was noticeably upset, and I couldn't shake the feeling that I had lived this moment before, although this time, I was watching it through a fishbowl. I listened in on the conversation and heard myself respond, "Do you mind if I see the card?"

I opened the festive, religious Christmas card to see a picture and a note from *her*.

And then, rather than in slow motion, the clock ticked faster and it was as if I were watching a scene on fast-forward. Helen stuck the card and photo back in the carefully steam-opened envelope, sealed it back shut so it appeared as if it had never been opened, and wrote three large letters all over her address: RTS.

Without warning, I was back in my bedroom and time slowed down again. Edward was getting changed in front of me, asking me to join him, but before I could even refuse, his look of desire changed to horror. Feeling a warm sensation running down my legs, I glanced down to see my tan pantyhose stained a dark red as blood dripped, and then gushed, onto the carpet.

I screamed, but no sound came out. I turned to hurry to the bathroom, but I tripped, and rather than my face hitting the carpet, my nose landed on a pillow. Frantic, I looked around, and instead of Edward and our room, I was in my childhood bed and my father was in my doorframe demanding to know why my nightgown was soaked in blood. I could hear Mother's voice whispering, "Come here darling. Please listen to me," but the voice came from different parts of the room, and when I tried to run to her, my legs would not work. While attached to me, they did not move when my brain commanded; instead of trying again, I covered my eyes and shook my head.

I woke up screaming, and eventually, a night nurse ran in to check on me. Turning on a light, and handing me a cup of water, the young woman sat down next to me.

"My baby's gone," I whimpered, and my small frame crumbled into the lap of the stranger who gently rubbed my hair and held me until my sobs subsided . . . Just like Mama had done.

I woke up with a new resolve, and I decided to finish telling my side of the story to Megan.

After unraveling the toilet paper, I fluffed my hair and put my silver-rimmed glasses back on, meeting my gaze in the mirror. *That sweater looks dumpy on you and you look like the old woman you are with that extra layer on*, I told myself. Despite feeling a tad chilly, I made a mental note to take the jacket off before I left my room; I didn't change the dark blue sweater, though, as it was clean and I hadn't worn it in a while. I carefully fixed my face for the day, finishing the look off with a bright red lipstick. Still looking in the mirror, I prepared myself for the phone call and rationalized my decision. *Kimmy will never give an accurate representation of you to the children, and James is her puppet, so neither will he. So, you might as well tell your story to someone who will listen.* I also made a mental note to ask the nurse to run an errand for me; I needed to give something to Megan the next time I saw her.

While I wanted to see James and a nagging thought nudged me to travel, my aversion to dealing with Kimmy was too strong. The decision had been made the minute I opened her letter.

CHAPTER 33
August 1967
Ruth

"Mom! Look! A dolphin!" Esther exclaimed, waking me from a sleep I didn't realize I'd fallen into. Abigail had Adam by the hand and all three were running toward the water to get a closer look at the beautiful creature surfacing briefly as it swam toward the lighthouse.

"Can we follow it?" Abigail asked.

Standing up, I looked back at our things, reached for our room key and my sun hat, and answered, "Of course." William was back at the room taking a nap, and while I was sure he would join us soon, I figured we had enough time to walk to the lighthouse and back.

The sun was warm on my shoulders, and I smiled as I watched Abigail, Esther, and Adam run along the edge of the beach – the water lapping up against their feet in steady intervals – and point out at the Gulf every time they saw the dolphin surface again. As young teenagers, Abigail and Esther insisted they were too old to wear matching bathing suits, yet they were drawn to similar styles. Abigail was adorned in a yellow patterned suit with lime green trim and lime green straps. Esther wore a teal suit with white and yellow flowers. The two looked adorable next to each other. My heart was glad they were growing up as friends; while they fought, as siblings do, they had an inseparable bond I prayed would last a lifetime. They also treasured and protected their little brother, who hated to be called "little" anymore. Adam wore a simple navy suit, not caring at all what I packed for him. He certainly was his father's son: a joy to be around, comical, and worry-free. Using William's Kodak Motormatic earlier that afternoon to take a picture of the three of them, I hoped to capture the moment perfectly so we could look back on it, frozen in time. William loved that camera – a gift I'd surprised him with two Christmases ago – and I was excited to see the results once we returned home.

As we walked, the soft scraping of shell on shell, in tune with the gently rolling sea, was like a heavenly melody, bringing with it a sense of divine peace and contentment. Low tide was at 7:27 p.m., and with the full moon expected that night, we hoped to find some beautiful shells after supper time. William claimed he would be the first in the family to find the rare Junonia shell and even said that morning he was feeling like tonight would be the night. I smiled thinking of him.

"Let's start heading back," I called out to the children.

In unison, they all turned around and we began our walk back. This time, however, our eyes were fixed on the sand to see what treasures we'd find beneath our bare feet. After two weeks on the beach, day after day, our feet had grown accustomed to the shells. We had egg cartons full of cleaned shells and a bag of bleached sand dollars to take home with us. Before we left

Florida, William had found three wooden typeset drawers for the kids. He told them to each pick out their favorite seashells and beach treasures to fill each little spot with, and when we returned home, he would paint the drawers the color of their choice. Hence, the egg cartons and sand dollars. I was certain we had more than enough seashells per child, but I couldn't bring myself to tell them they had to discard any of their precious treasure.

By the time we reached our chairs, William was waiting for us.

"We saw a dolphin, Dad!" Adam shared excitedly.

"Awesome, buddy," he replied. "Any luck shelling, girls?"

"I found some Coquinas, a Turkey Wing, and at least ten Wentletraps," Esther answered quickly.

"You have a good eye, dear. Those will be perfect for your typeset drawer."

Without a doubt, Esther was Daddy's girl. While Abby was athletic like her father, she had different interests than him. Esther and Adam, on the other hand, both enjoyed fishing and hunting, like William. While the three of them spent time together, Abigail and I would shop, bake or discuss something we'd recently read. I was grateful for the close relationships I had with all my children, but the one I had with Abigail was a little deeper than the other two.

I sat down and soaked in the moment as our three little blessings talked with their father about our grand adventure down to the lighthouse and back. Listening intently, William absorbed every word. Once the chatter slowed, he asked who wanted to compete in a sand sculpture competition, guys versus girls. Knowing he just needed to itch everyone's inner competitiveness, all five of us were digging in the sand, far enough apart so we wouldn't sneak a peek at the other's design. The theme, sea animals, was in honor of the dolphin we'd followed down the beach, but building a dolphin was not allowed.

Their imaginations were incredible. Adam and William sculpted a large whale, complete with a semi-open mouth, humpback whale grooves to show the species, two eyes, and two fins. Adam was obsessed with marine life and provided the vision; William was the one who brought that vision to life. The girls both wanted to make a turtle. We were all hoping to see baby turtles make the perilous journey from their nest to the Gulf of Mexico before we had to go back home. So, the three of us set to work making our own unique rendition of a turtle.

William and Adam were the clear winners. While our turtle had bragging rights, it was a clear second next to the humpback whale. The boys declared themselves free of cleaning up after dinner and first in line for ice cream that night.

"Okay, everyone. Let's head back, clean up, and have some dinner. We want to make sure we are ready, come low tide!" I said, folding another beach towel.

It was always a challenge to say goodbye to the island. We woke up at three o'clock that Thursday morning, and with our 1966 orange, white-topped Volkswagen Bus already loaded, we were on the causeway within the hour. The drive back was long, and William insisted on driving straight through.

On the ride back, we made it a tradition to recount our favorite memories from the trip. It did mean, however, we all heard William's story of finding a Junonia for the hundredth time. He'd found it during low tide after our sand sculpture competition and didn't hesitate to bring it up every chance he could that last week. *The Islander* even took his picture and wrote an article about it, promising to mail him next month's publication with him in it.

When we turned onto our street, Runnymede Drive, we all welcomed the sight of the brick, two-story house we called home. While Daddy and Mama offered us their guest house to live in for a few months after our wedding, we decided it was best to have some distance between us. With the future in mind, we used the generous sum they had given us as a wedding gift to purchase a recently built, five-bedroom home within walking distance from the local school and close to our church, Carmel Christian. I remember Mama's tears when we moved out. While I reminded her we were only a few miles away, she answered, "Oh, I know, baby. Change is hard, that is all."

On our street alone, three new families had moved in recently. With the Indianapolis business community close by and the ongoing road construction, Carmel was growing quickly, and with it came changes to Carmel and Clay Township. Alongside other established residents, William volunteered his time and skillset to help the town grow in an orderly fashion; he could describe the changes in such a way that he could sway the mind of any leery, long-time resident. And to our excitement, he provided us with updates on the plans for new recreation areas, swimming pools, fire stations, schools, shopping areas, and more. Also wanting to be involved, I volunteered at the Carmel Clay Educational Foundation and helped raise funds in the private sector to continue the town's dedication to educational excellence.

William pulled our VW Bus onto the long concrete driveway, around to the back, and unhitched our small Sunfish fishing boat before parking the vehicle in our two-car garage. While late, we decided to unload the car rather than save the task till dawn. Once the car was empty, I started a load of laundry and returned to the living room to find the children laying out shells and picking the ones they wanted in their typeset drawers. William would not return to work until Monday and had promised the kids he would paint their drawers before returning.

"Can you paint mine white?" Abigail requested.

"Got it," William answered. "Esther? Adam?"

"Can you make mine stay a wood color, but darker?" Esther asked.

"You want me to stain it? Sounds good. I will pick a perfect stain color when I go to the store tomorrow," he added, turning to Adam. "Alright, buddy, what do you want?"

"I like mine just the way it is," he responded. "I am ready to start gluing."

"Alright everyone," I chimed in. "We can start painting, staining, and gluing tomorrow after breakfast. Now it's time to get ready for bed." We were all running low on sleep after a long day on the road.

The kids ran up the stairs to their rooms. Esther and Abigail shared the larger of the two bedrooms upstairs, and Adam had his own. With one bathroom between the three, I listened to make sure no fights broke out over the sink and was relieved to hear no squabbles.

"Can you tell me a bedtime story?" Adam called from the top of the stairs.

"Sure thing, buddy," William responded, as we both trudged wearily up the red, wool-carpeted stairs.

The girls were no longer interested in hearing a bedtime story, each preferring to read a Nancy Drew Mystery novel. They'd both started reading the collection that summer. Each year, William and I agreed to a summer curriculum for each of our children so they would continue learning. It was light but did include each major subject, with the addition of the Bible; that summer the girls were to read at least ten books each before school started. Abigail and Esther had well-surpassed the goal of ten because of how much they liked Nancy Drew.

"Good night, girls," we said as we tapped on their door before entering to give them a hug. They were both in their respective twin beds, covered in matching quilts my mother had made for them. While my mother could afford almost anything in a department store, she enjoyed quilting and even gave careful eye to the fabric on sale. "We want to be good stewards of our money, dear," she would always say to me. After praying with them, we went to see Adam.

Adam's room was marine themed, with blue carpet like the ocean, blue sheets, and a comforter. An enormous whale picture hung on the wall.

"What story would you like to hear?" I asked him, knowing it would likely be Jonah and the Whale again.

"Jonah," he said, sitting up in his bed, his brown hair needing a wash, but his teeth brushed.

William and I had told the story of Jonah at least a hundred times that summer, but we didn't mind. We both knew we would later miss these days, and that the simple act of telling and acting out a bedtime story was an extraordinary one when our hearts were properly aligned. William was the best actor in the family, and he proceeded to act out Jonah, as I played the narrator. Adam's face lit up, and he laughed and smiled as William was hurled over the boat, sickened by the smell of the fish's belly, and spit out onto the sandy beach. At the end we talked about the story, prayed, and kissed his forehead as we whispered goodnight.

With the kids in bed, William and I retreated to our room. The walls were covered with patterned gray wallpaper and a white, slightly patterned, hand-sewn bedspread covered our bed.

"Being a dad is awesome," William said, already in our queen-size bed, gazing wistfully at me.

Looking in the mirror, we made eye contact and I smiled, blowing him a kiss. I started to undress and reached for my hand-sewn pink pajama bottoms, sliding them on. McCall Patterns fit me well, and I had used them that year for two pajama sets, one for winter and the other for summer. When I was ready and turned around to reach for the matching button-down, sleeveless pajama top, William was holding the top.

"Looking for this?" he asked, flirtatiously.

"Oh, William, give me the top. I am exhausted," I said, half-interested, half-annoyed.

"Okay, okay," William said, feigning defeat, and he extended his arm toward me, shirt in hand. When I crawled up onto the bed and reached for the shirt, he grabbed my arm and spun me onto my back. He was only wearing boxers, his normal bedtime attire, and his chest was sun-kissed from our vacation.

Despite feeling tired, the rush of being spun around and look-ing up at him sent a shiver of desire through my body.

"Are you sure you are too tired?" he asked coyly.

He leaned down to kiss my neck and his index finger traced my face. My lips met his kiss, and I gave in to his touch.

The next morning, I mixed the batter for both raisin scones and chocolate chip banana pancakes, while William whisked the scrambled eggs in our dutch oven cast-iron skillet. The mouthwatering smell of bacon filled the entire first floor, and while delightful, I cracked a window to let in some fresh air. With eight eggs and two tablespoons of butter in the skillet, William counted to thirty several times as he whisked on the heat and whisked off the heat.

"Add the crème fraîche, please," he instructed.

After spooning it in, I poured William and myself a cup of coffee from our Toastmaster coffee maker and set it back on the counter next to the matching four-slice toaster. After adding a little half-and-half and a packet of sugar, I took a sip of the hot liquid gold. *How I love the smell of coffee and the taste of it when it is still piping hot*, I thought, relishing the first sip.

"The eggs are done. How are the scones and pancakes?" William asked.

"The scones are done. The pancakes need about thirty more seconds. Could you please call for the kids to come down?" I answered, eagerly anticipating their excitement. I opened the oven to check the bacon, now ready, and took it out.

Within a few short minutes, I heard Abigail, Esther, and Adam coming down the stairs with a sense of urgency. While still in their pajamas, all three were fully awake and ready to eat.

"Pancakes! Yes!" Adam exclaimed, sitting down in his usual spot. I smiled as I looked at his bed hair. Unlike the girls and even William and me, his hair was a dark brown, almost black. He took after my younger brother.

"Hey now," William started, feigning hurt feelings. "What about my famous eggs?"

"They are my favorite, Daddy," Esther answered quickly, taking her seat, giving him a smile.

"Same here. Especially with bacon," Abigail chimed in.

The white Formica table was laden with orange juice, butter, maple syrup, raspberry lemon jam, salt, pepper, and tabasco sauce. Breakfast was a flurry of eating, expressions of gratitude, and retelling stories from our most recent Sanibel trip.

Once everyone's pace of eating and storytelling slowed, William announced, "I am going to buy paint and stain after breakfast so you three can begin your shell projects later today." Squeals of excitement echoed around the table, as the children eagerly finished their breakfast. "No need to hurry. I will leave soon enough," he added.

With only crumbs left on each Franciscan Starburst plate, everyone was excused, and the kids started to help clean up. A few minutes later, William put on his shoes and grabbed the van keys.

"Miss you. See you all soon," William said, giving me a quick kiss on the lips as I stood by the kitchen sink, rinsing out a yellow mixing bowl. William rubbed Adam's hair as he carried the jam and butter to the refrigerator, and then simultaneously gave each of the girls a side hug and a kiss on the head as they dried the dishes.

Humming contentedly, I blew a goodbye kiss to the love of my life through the kitchen window. As he pulled out of the driveway and gave his customary two-beep honk of the horn, I waved to him, smiling, thanking God for such a wonderful man.

CHAPTER 34

Ruth

The doorbell rang just after ten o'clock that morning.

Abigail was helping Adam sift through shells for their type-set drawers. Esther was in the shower. I was gathering the necessary ingredients to make bread in my Le Creuset Dutch oven, a gift William surprised me with on our last anniversary.

Expecting to see our neighbor who had collected our mail while we were in Florida, I didn't even notice the police car parked in our driveway. I opened the door quickly, ready to greet Mrs. Miller with a smile. Instead, I was met with the face of a solemn police officer. Still on the small porch landing, I opened the screen door and stepped outside. My stomach churned, and I suddenly felt like I was going to lose the delicious breakfast my family had just shared an hour earlier.

"Good morning, ma'am," he said quietly, taking off his hat. "I'm Officer Crisp. I am afraid I have some bad news."

The life-shattering news took only seconds to relay, but my shock made time stand still. Everything slowed, and as my knees gave out, I crumpled to the ground. In the front yard, the twin pear trees' falling leaves seemed to hover, motionless, and the clouds stilled, as if the world were stuck in a freeze-frame.

I caught myself on the wrought-iron railing on the side of the porch, Officer Crisp's arms extending to provide support. I staggered to my feet, an inferno of feelings raging inside.

"No. No. This isn't happening!" I screamed, my voice piercing my own ears. My heart started beating quickly, my pulse pounded inside my head, perspiration formed all over my body, and my hands began to uncontrollably shake.

Hearing my scream, Abigail and Adam ran to the front door, and when Officer Crisp saw their innocent, concerned faces, he looked at me quietly and asked, "Is there someone I can call?"

I bent over the railing and vomited. "God, please! Don't let this be happening," I pleaded over and over again, whispering now.

Abigail opened the screen door, bewildered. "Mama, what is wrong?" Tears started to form in her eyes at the sight of my distress.

"Do you have grandparents nearby, young lady?" Officer Crisp asked gently.

Bewildered and unable to speak, Abigail shook her head up and down as Adam's cries joined my own bitter melody.

I went to Helen's house early that Monday morning, leaving Edward sipping his coffee and reading the paper, and James packing. In one week, he would be gone for basic training. In one week, my purpose in life would no longer live under my roof. I desperately wanted to slow time, but the harder I tried, the faster it slipped through my hands. Determined to send pieces of home with him, I'd asked Helen to help me make his favorite salsa.

As I turned off our street, I yawned. Sleep evaded me yet again; worry was my constant companion, and no cup of tea or stretch sequence calmed my nerves. James was unwavering in his commitment to the service, while all I could focus on was losing him in some godforsaken jungle in Vietnam. I, too, didn't want communism to expand across the globe, but now, with my only son enlisting, suddenly the war was too close to home. Again. And, I worried about his infatuation with Kimmy. She'd had him under a spell since day one. We'd seen her a few more times since that first meeting, and while witty, she seemed too free spirited, and I wondered about her moral compass.

"Margaret, welcome!" I heard through the open car windows as I pulled into Robert and Helen's driveway. Helen held a bouquet of flowers in her hand, just picked from her front garden. "Come on in. I have everything ready."

Helen's bountiful harvest was spread all over the kitchen table. Beyond her cooking skills, Helen was a master gardener. Although I'd made a half-hearted effort to show interest over the years, the best I could manage were a few wilted cabbages and some overgrown zucchinis. That year, she'd grown a variety of tomatoes and peppers. As we picked them, she easily recalled the varieties and talked about all we would need for both the salsa and the canning. Despite her trying to teach me, I never quite perfected the art.

"These little ones are 'Little Mamas,'" she managed to say as she tasted one right off the plant. "That is a Roma, dear. Remember, Romas in one basket, Big Mamas in another," she corrected me, before adding, "I already have the bell peppers and jalapenos in the kitchen."

After all the bell peppers and jalapenos were chopped, I brought up James.

"James will be gone this time next week," I began, hoping she would sense my need to talk about something besides cooking. Edward had no interest in discussing it and always gave the same stark reply: "It is James's decision. There is nothing left to say."

"Oh dear, I know. But let's not focus on it today. Instead, let's enjoy these tomatoes," she quickly responded. Helen had always hated difficult conversations, and if she could avoid one or shut it down, she readily did. "Did you hear that our dear Pope Paul visited the site of Constantinople! It has been centuries since a Roman Catholic pontiff visited."

"Twelve centuries to be exact," Robert called from the other room.

"Thanks, dear," she called back. "Robert knows so much about history. Can you bring that diced garlic to me, please?"

Helen continued on about garlic and why she'd chosen the olive oil she did until the telephone rang.

From the kitchen, I heard Robert answer with his usual even-tempered greeting followed by a curt, "Thank you for informing us."

Helen stopped stirring the tomatoes and peppers when she heard the phone slam down. "Is everything alright darling?"

"It was that woman's father." His voice was void of emotion, monotone even – the usual bitterness and bravado absent – and when his shadow darkened the door frame, I saw his skin had gone pale. "It's William."

"No. No. No." Helen dropped the spoon, tomato remnants flying as it clattered on the tile floor. Her hands flew to her face, covering her mouth and nose as she backed up to the cabinets for support.

"He was killed in an automobile accident. His funeral is Thursday."

⚊⟋

Edward's turbulent mood on Thursday night was frightening, putting me and James on edge. Neither of us had said much that day, apart from what we needed to, for fear of fueling Edward's already raging temper.

We were all emotional, with James leaving for his eight weeks of basic training the next morning. While I was thankful he would be on US soil for another eight to nine weeks following basic training for his Advanced Individual Training, my stomach was in knots anticipating what he would encounter as an infantryman.

Beyond James leaving, though, I knew Edward was facing an internal battle over not attending William's funeral. He feigned indifference the entire week, but I knew he had to feel something. *Perhaps enough time has passed for him to not actually care. I mean, it's been almost twenty years, and time heals all wounds, right?* I told myself. But I knew deep down that blood is thicker than water. Decades had passed since Johnny's death, after all, and I still grieved over him. And somehow, familial relationships heightened expectations and intensified disappointments. *Although he can't show it, Edward is certainly grieving the loss of his brother.*

How can he not? And the fact that he can't show it is your fault, the sinister voiced chimed.

We finished eating dinner, and Edward brought up the few days of leave James would get in between AIT and deployment. "Well, son. I am certain you will excel in training. Where would you like to go during your three-day leave?"

"Actually, Dad, I am planning on visiting Kimmy," James said, eyes fixed on his empty plate.

"You are going to visit *her* instead of us?" I blurted out.

"I love her, Mom," he said, leveling his gaze at me.

"You don't even *know* her!" I yelled.

Ignoring me, James locked eyes with his father. Edward shrugged his shoulders. "Your mother is a good judge of character. And, son, just because you sleep with some slut – or rather, young woman – doesn't mean you love her. She is attractive, sure, but don't confuse lust with love."

"She is not a *slut!*" James snapped back, standing up, hands on the table leaning toward his father, seeming to tower over him. "And who the hell are you to talk? Do you think I don't know about all the sluts *you've* been with?

Ignoring James's comment, Edward slapped his napkin on the table and threw back the Crown Royal to show he was done with both dinner and the conversation. "You will respect your mother's wishes and be home for your leave."

"You don't get to boss me around anymore, *Edward*," James snarled, heading for the doorway to leave the kitchen.

Edward stood up and grabbed James's arm, turning him around. "Show some respect, young man."

"*Respect?* You don't know the meaning of the word. Now I see why your brother wanted nothing to do with you."

And with that last comment, something in Edward snapped. I cried out when he went to swing at our one and only son. Younger and faster, James dodged the fist intended for his nose. As his hand hit the doorframe, Edward cried out, cradling his left hand close to his chest, and slipped to the ground, a slur of profanities leaving his mouth.

James and I locked eyes. "I feel sorry for you, Mama. I'm going to go say goodbye to Gramps and Grams, and I think it is best for me to stay at Dick's. He leaves tomorrow too. I'll write to you."

And with that, he was gone.

—

"Ma'am, your husband has severe metacarpal fractures. We see this a lot when men box, such as your husband," the physician said as he continued to describe the dorsal bend in his bone and how long the recovery would take.

So that is what he told him — a boxing injury? Who is this man you married? He used to be quiet and refined. Now he is a drunkard with a short fuse. "Thank you, doctor. I appreciate your care," I answered when he asked if I'd heard everything he said. In truth, I heard nothing beyond the eight-week recovery time. A condemning voice spoke up as soon as the doctor left. *You know, you caused all this. If you wouldn't have been so insecure, Ruth wouldn't have become the family's enemy and William would've never become the family's black sheep. And now it's too late to do anything about the mess you've made, because William is dead.*

—

Ruth

The shock from William's death was paralyzing, but when Daddy asked about calling Robert and Helen that Sunday night after the kids were asleep, I wanted to flip the dining room table over.

"*Call* them? Absolutely not. They don't deserve to know. I don't want to see them, and I sure as hell don't want my babies to meet them."

"Alright, my dear. It is your decision," Mama responded before Daddy could, resting her hand on her husband's.

"Let us know if you change your mind," Daddy added softly.

My parents were full of tact and grace, characteristics they attributed to age and the Almighty. As they had all my life, they helped me steady my mind when my emotions were stronger than a hurricane's winds.

"You think I am awful?" I asked, head down, buried in my crossed arms.

"Ruthie, you are going through the unthinkable. We don't think you are awful. Like your mom said, whatever you decide. How about you pray about it?"

Ruth

The sun danced through the windows Thursday morning, and for the first few moments between the land of hush-a-bye and the hell of reality, I thought my husband was in bed with me. The memories from the week came crashing down, falling on my chest like a ton of bricks, and I wanted nothing more than to reverse time. I sat up in my old bed at my parents' house, dreading the day's schedule, and walked into the bathroom. I heard William's voice say, *"Let's pray dear. Dear Lord, thank you for the gift of another day . . ."* It was how he started each and every morning. Recalling the memory, I stared in the mirror, a tempest raging in my eyes. *Why, God? Why didn't you sustain him? Why did he have to leave when he did? Why didn't I ask him to stay a few minutes longer? How am I going to live without him, especially with our three children? What will life be like for them?*

No answer came.

I showered robotically, put on the black dress Mama had laid out for me, and hid in the closet we kept spare clothes in, holding one of William's shirts to my nose. No doubt my makeup was ruined by now, from inhaling his scent and from the tears.

"Mama?" I heard Abigail call out. Before I could get up, Abigail, Esther, and Adam were at the closet door.

Without hesitation, they all sat down around me, and we fused together into a close hug. After a few minutes of silence, Esther started singing softly one of the songs she and William sang every morning.

"Holy, holy, holy, Lord, God Almighty. Early in the morning our song shall rise to Thee . . ." Abigail joined Esther and their quavering voices mixed together in a heavenly harmony. Adam's body tensed next to mine, and he did not join the girls in song. The girls' song lifted my spirit, and Adam's resistance fueled my resolve to be strong and face the day. Coupled with the reminder of William's early morning prayer, their voices were as dear to me as the air in my lungs.

"Thank you, you three," I said, composing myself. "I am going to freshen up. I will meet you in the front parlor."

Ruth

As we pulled up to the church, I didn't think I could get out of the car. *This isn't happening. Wake up!* Papa, the name the children called my father, ushered the children out of the car and slid around to the back of the church where family could essentially hide from the crowd. The parking lot was full and cars lined the street. *The entire town must be here*, I thought, dreading all the clichéd – although sincere and well-meaning – phrases. Mama stayed back with me and remained silent for several minutes.

"Well, my dear, you are certainly standing on the threshold of hell." We locked eyes through the rearview mirror. I felt like a lifeless mannequin in my crisp black dress and my wide-brimmed black hat.

"And so are the children," I added. "And for their sake, I must not let William's death kill me too."

I opened the car door and walked with Mama, arms locked, into the church's backdoor, joining Daddy and the children. Pastor Luke prayed with and for us before we entered the sanctuary, and we sat down in the front row. A few close friends reached for my gloved hand and gave it a tight squeeze. With tears in their eyes, Lauren and Jennifer, my dear sisters-in-law, held me in an embrace I knew was meant to pass on strength.

Pastor Luke began. "Hello everyone. I stand here with a heavy heart, with no answer to the question of 'why.' However, we can still be confident of two things. First, the Lord still reigns. And second, William is with Him and would want me to use this moment to tell you about his Savior."

I went numb during most of Pastor Luke's message. I already knew it would mostly be a message about Jesus and God's sovereignty. William used to tease me that my spiritual gift was freaking out. Be it a personal issue or something political, my fears often spiraled, leaving me in a tight ball of anxiety. *Who is going to help me now?* Questions bombarded my mind and fear gripped my heart. It was then that something Pastor Luke said caught my ear, and when I looked up, I locked eyes with him.

"Fear and faith cannot coexist. While faith is not easy to stand on, it is colossally easier to live with. While this stretch in our journey is dark and unwelcomed, I challenge you to run to Jesus and tell Him the problem. Ask your questions. Ask for the strength to walk by faith. This act will be no small wound on the devil's brow." He gave me a tight, closed-mouthed smile. He then continued, again scanning the audience. "I want to end with one of my favorite parts of scripture. In Genesis 32 and 33, Jacob wrestles with God and is then met with Esau's embrace. These two words, wrestle and embrace, are similar in Hebrew. Wrestle is *abaq*, and embrace is *habaq*. They differ by one letter and their pronunciations have a sublime rhyme, as you heard. William's death may tempt you to turn away from God over the unanswered question of why. But, I implore you to turn toward Him instead and struggle. Wrestling with God is hands-on and can be its own form of intimacy. And, if you hang on long enough, the wrestling match will turn into an embrace. Pray with me."

The children and I stood by William's casket, flanked by my parents. We hugged and shook the hands of the mourners, with Papa inviting everyone over to their house afterwards for a meal.

My stomach did somersaults when I saw them at the end of the line. Panicky, I reached for Mama. "Mama, take the kids to the car." Instinctively, Mama scanned the dwindling line and followed my instructions.

"Alright, my little blessings, let's go ahead and head to the house. Is anyone hungry?"

My mother whispered something to Papa, and as I heard the sanctuary's backdoor shut, I felt his arm around my shoulders. We both thanked the final community members in attendance, and I felt him straighten slightly as the two women at the end of the line stood before us. They were dressed in dark clothing, just like they were on our wedding day. The memory assailed me like a punch in my stomach, and on top of the gut-wrenching pain of the day, I felt like screaming. Then and now, Helen looked like she was mourning the loss of her son; the first time, to a woman she despised, and now, to death itself.

"Helen. Shirley. I'm glad you received my message," I heard my father say as I stood there like a statue, eyes locked with my mother-in-law's.

Helen's face twisted; her expression held a myriad of emotions. I so badly wanted to see sorrow or regret, but all I could discern was hate, bitterness, and anger as she stared at me.

"Our condolences to the widow," Helen numbly stated. Shirley nodded to me, eyes icy, and they both turned to walk away before I could open my mouth to reply.

I remained motionless, unable to process their blatant lack of remorse. While I didn't expect warmth, I certainly would've expected something more. *Are they so cold? Are they still so prideful? Are they only here so she can tell people she attended his funeral?*

"Just as Watson said, 'The longer ice freezeth, the harder it is to be broken,'" Papa quietly said as he gave my shoulders a squeeze. He admired the Puritan preacher and especially liked to quote from his, *A Body of Practical Divinity.*

Coupled with Pastor Luke's sermon, Papa's voice rattled my insides, and I wanted to call after them, speak frankly, and be understood. I didn't want this encounter to be our last.

"Helen? Shirley?"

The women paused.

Are you seriously going to walk away? Do you view me with such unbridled animosity? Can this tragedy not be a catalyst for reconciliation? I remember when William started courting me. Helen, you liked me all those years ago. I remember singing, "How Great thou Art" in the kitchen while we baked together and you forever changed the way I take my coffee when you introduced me to Classic syrup. That Labor Day family time was priceless. Shirley, don't you recall telling William to marry me? You were the sister I always wanted. I thought we were friends. Then William proposed, and it seemed like everyone was elated. Everyone but Margaret, that is. Shirley, don't you remember asking us to move to Dayton? We were seriously considering moving, and then our wedding came. To this day, I am not sure what happened. Perhaps we should've tried harder. Hurt had taken root and became bitterness and unforgiveness, and for that, I am sorry. I don't know what the future holds, especially now, but can our relations mend? It's what William always prayed would happen.

I wanted to say all those words. I had said them to the mirror more times than I could count. Instead, I simply called out and offered an invitation.

"Would you like to join us for a meal and meet our children?"

How I wished for a movie-worthy ending: a sudden spark of understanding, of regret, in Helen's eyes, an outpouring of tears as she gathered me in her arms and whispered her heartfelt apologies for all the missed years . . . Instead, Shirley bent to adjust her nylon stocking, and they both continued toward the exit without ever glancing back.

CHAPTER 35

December 14, 1967

Mother,

I hope this letter finds you well. I am sorry I haven't written since I left home. My days are prescribed, and I am investing any free time I have to learn so I can stand out among my company. With training almost over, I will soon have leave before I am shipped off to my station, which is still to be determined. While I know it will disappoint you, I will be spending it with Kimmy.

Give my best to Gramps and Grams.
James

Helen put down the letter and offered her textbook detached statement. "I am sorry he won't be visiting us this Christmas, dear."

Charlie Brown Christmas played in the background, and I heard Linus begin his monologue about the meaning of Christmas. I rolled my eyes and wanted to turn it off, but the milk was ready. Reaching for my porcelain pedestal mugs delicately etched with snowflakes, I poured the two of us a cup of steamed milk to pair with our Swiss Miss packets, marshmallows, and whipped cream. I tried to change the subject to NASA's ongoing goal to put a man on the moon, but Helen was fixated on the dynamic between mother, son, and the son's woman of choice.

"You sacrifice so much for your kids, don't you?" she asked rhetorically. "And no matter what you do, sometimes they take a wrong turn and never course-correct. Is our family cursed? First, William and now my dear grandson?"

I sat there and idly stirred my hot chocolate, wondering if she would, after so many years, finally want to talk about what had happened. At the back of my mind the ever-present worry gnawed away: had she suspected all along that it was my fault? For a moment I felt my defenses crumbling; I was tired of all the lies and so desperate for closeness with somebody that if she had just invited the conversation, I might have told her everything. What did I have to lose at that point? So, I waited for her to bring up William's funeral, to ask the hard questions. But all she did was perpetuate the lie. *What did you expect? Do you really think she could face the truth now that her son is gone, and she has no chance to reconcile?* Deep down I knew that the voice spoke truth; there was too much at stake for Helen to entertain the idea that it could have been any other way.

She shook her head sadly. "What did my boy see in her? I know I told you what she said to me at the funeral: 'Don't you go to your car and cry like a crybaby.' As if she knows what it is like to lose a child."

"Yes, I am sorry she spoke to you like that," I replied, as I had many times before. Truth be told, I wasn't sure I believed Helen. From what I remembered of Ruth, it didn't seem possible that those words would have passed her lips.

CHAPTER 36
2015

Christmas had come and gone. The decorations would remain until after the new year, and I was more than ready for January's tacky snowflakes to replace the smiling Santas and cherub-like Christ-childs that seemed a dime a dozen around the place. I called Megan first thing on the twenty-sixth, and while I could hear enthusiasm in her voice when I asked if she wanted to visit again, she remained calm and collected on the phone, almost professional sounding, like she didn't want to say anything hinting at excitement for fear I would change my mind.

I met her at the same spot as last time, scrutinizing her as she approached. Megan had a little too much blush on, or perhaps she just needed a different color to pair better with her pale skin. She arrived right on time in jeans, snow boots, and a white and black striped top showing under her unbuttoned red peacoat. Her hair looked freshly highlighted and her bangs perfectly cut. I complimented her angel wing necklace, to which she thanked me and told me it was a gift from her husband. I considered staying put, in case I wanted to retreat from the conversation, but the pull for good coffee and a change of scenery was too strong.

Back at the same coffee shop – a welcome escape from my usual surrounds – I inhaled deeper and tried to notice every detail. In contrast to the tacky decorations at Sunrise, the windows were covered in tasteful, hand-painted holiday scenes, the bags of coffee grounds were shades of reds and greens, and festive greenery wrapped in white lights casually draped the counter. White and clear bulb ornaments hung from the ceiling above the condiments counter, the clear ones filled with coffee beans, and the soft voices coming from the speakers still sang both old and new seasonal tunes. We sat at a table, this time in a corner near the wall of windows.

"Thanks again for deciding to meet with me. You didn't have to dive right back in, either. I know how hard Christmas is for you, and after what happened last time, well, I didn't know if I would ever hear from you again," Megan said cautiously.

"These drawings are so detailed," I said, pointing to the windows.

"I always wished I were able to draw. Or sing. Really, I wish I could sing. I would be such a good singer if I could sing," Megan answered, picking up on my hint to forget about our previous engagement.

What she said registered as odd, and my expression looked at her inquisitively.

"My husband always laughs when I say that. I just mean, I enjoy being in front of a crowd and dancing to music. I should say, 'I would be a good performer if I could sing,' but the other way is funnier. Or it is between my husband and me, at least." She laughed awkwardly.

I forced a slight smile and stared blankly at my coffee mug. Her jolly demeanor both agitated me and made me jealous.

"Okay, well, let's keep going," she said with a more poised voice and journalistic approach. "Jealousy and pride can certainly create a division in a family. How sad when the ones you are supposed to love and stand by unconditionally become, well, almost enemies, and vice versa."

"Yes, I suppose that is one way of putting it," I feebly answered.

"What happened with James?"

James. I paused at the sound of his name. *He should be here right now instead of with her. But no, his daft wife had to upset another holiday.*

What a disappointment he grew up to be. Impatient. Arrogant. Whenever he spared me a few moments to call or visited out of obligation, his tone was hurried, as if I were an interruption to his otherwise more interesting life. If I happened to repeat myself, his words were as piercing as a ruler snapping a desk, and although he would politely apologize, I knew he was not sincere. And, God forbid I ask a question about the black rectangle he gave me at Christmas two years back. I wanted to remind him so badly of how I had patiently taught him to eat appropriately, get dressed, and brush his teeth. Alas, my words would fall on deaf ears. *Until recently,* a soft voice reminded me. I shook my head, refusing to allow myself to hope that he was capable of change. *He probably started off a New Year's resolution early or some friend gave him a holiday challenge.*

As hardened clay is to melted wax in the sun, were my words to James versus Megan. She sat patiently and listened intently. I wasn't sure how much time had passed since her question, but she did not rush me.

"After his time in the Army, they settled in North Carolina, close to her family. I suppose the Irish Proverb is true: 'A son is a son 'til he takes him a wife, a daughter is a daughter all of her life.' Admittedly, I have hated her ever since he chose her over me all those years ago when he returned to the states after he was wounded."

"He was wounded?" she asked, eyebrows raised in concern.

I waved my hands, not wanting to talk about his injury yet. "I will get to it," I said. "Regardless, to this day – this Christmas in fact – she has kept my baby from me."

A part of me wanted Megan to feel sorry for me. To take my side. To see how horrible Kimmy was. Yet, another part of me was sick of the facade and the exhausting battle, and a smaller part wondered if Kimberly was truly as bad as I made her out to be.

"I can see how you would feel that way," Megan answered sincerely. It seemed like she wanted to say a few other things, but instead, she asked, "Did relations improve between James and Edward?"

"At some point I wrote an apology letter for Edward and signed his name the best I could. I desperately didn't want the kind of relationship Helen had with William, and while I wouldn't have chosen Kimmy for my baby, I wanted him in my life. At least in the beginning."

"But did you want *her* in your life?"

If she hadn't asked the question so softly, if she wasn't the only one who seemed to listen to me, if she wasn't the only one whom I'd ever spoken to so openly, I might have walked away from the conversation again. Something held me in my chair, and I surrendered.

"No, damn it, I didn't. I *don't*. I hoped he would divorce her and come back to me. But he didn't. I suppose I turned out to be more like Helen than I wanted to be."

Megan had put down her tablet, head resting on her hand. I couldn't read her. *Does she think you are terrible? Is she thinking it's all just some kind of divine karma playing out?*

"I know I played a part in the impasse between William and Helen," I admitted, digressing from the topic of James.

"Yes, from what I've learned, you instigated the divide," she said matter of factly.

I winced at the accurate judgment call. For so long I'd played victim to the circumstances I had created. She had been correct all those weeks ago, and I did not want to admit it.

"But Margaret," she continued gently. "Helen was her own person, capable of making her own judgment calls. You are not responsible for her choices. She chose to believe you without question. She chose to not seek to know the other side, she chose not to offer an apology where one was warranted, she chose to brush the issues under the rug. You can't rebuild a relationship while living in denial. Or in your case, I don't know if you have a chance at having a relationship with James if you still reject his wife."

"Yes, I suppose you are correct." I sat back in my seat and glanced at the patrons waiting for their drinks. The bustle of the baristas behind the counter, busily preparing various creamy calorie-laden concoctions, provided a welcome distraction.

"A mentor once told me I could always try to brush decisions under the rug, but I would never be able to escape the consequences."

Well, isn't that the truth? I thought to myself as I nodded in response. *I wonder if James could ever forgive me?* And as if my mom was sitting across the table from me, I heard, *You need to apologize and try.*

Megan circled our conversation back. "So, what came of the letter to James?"

CHAPTER 37

1968

James was coming home. As I read his letter, alternate waves of relief and shock swept over me, my tears flowing freely onto the page.

Mom,

I suffered a shot to the leg last month — I believe, I have lost track of time — and I will be returning to the states in the coming weeks. The wound is not fatal; however, I am not sure if I will recover fully.

I will write again when I have more information.

James

Nixon claimed to have a plan to end the war in Vietnam, but his promise no longer mattered to me. It had been 228 days since James saw his first day of combat, or so I thought based on his deployment information, and now he was injured fighting a war half the country was against. To say people would be thankful for his service was a far cry. The support for his sacrifice was lukewarm, at best. But that was irrelevant to me; I wanted to give my son the welcome that he deserved. The welcome that I'd never been able to give my brother so many years ago.

Edward's shadow darkened the door of the kitchen, and before he had a chance to pour his coffee, I started talking about a welcome home party.

"We will hold no such gathering," he said, his back to me, arm reaching for a coffee mug.

"What do you mean? His return will be cause for celebration, and we need to make sure he feels loved, especially in his condition," I countered firmly, infuriated by Edward's response.

"Margaret, do you even know if he will come back here? He said he would be coming back to the states, not coming back *home*. And if he does, what mental state he will be in?"

Those two questions hung in the air, as if mocking my excitement. *Why would he not come home? What mental state?*

As if reading my mind, Edward continued, "You think he will come back here when he has a girl to see? And, he may not be in the mood for celebration after seeing combat."

He placed a limp hand on my shoulder in an attempt to offer some comfort before he left for his lounge chair, where he would drink his coffee as if it were any other day.

A few weeks passed, and word came again from James. Thankfully, his leg was spared amputation, but he'd been told it would be a long, slow recovery. He relayed this information with his usual stoicism, not trying to elicit sympathy. In the same matter-of-fact way, he delivered the final blow: upon his return he would be returning to Kimmy, not us.

My head spun when I read the words, *"I will send word when I reach North Carolina. Hopefully you, Gramps, and Grams can visit shortly thereafter."*

Now, wrapped up in Mama's fur coat, I lay on the bed in the spare bedroom. I wanted to blink and wake up to a new reality. *When will life return to normal? How could James not return to me? How can he pick that woman over his mother!* I asked myself over and over.

Johnny's picture hung on the wall over the old wooden desk from my parents' house, and Daddy's fedora rested on the nightstand next to the bed.

"Mama, Daddy, I wish you were both still here," I said aloud. "What am I to do? Even if I agree she isn't good enough for my son, Edward should not have called Kimmy a slut. Edward was mad and worried, that's all. James should know his father says things out of anger. Why can't he get over it, if nothing else than for my sake? What should I do?"

I so badly wanted to hear Mama's voice in that moment, but instead, I thought of something from one of Ruth's letters. *"Pretending to be at peace never resolved a conflict."* While I hated to admit it, she was right. However, Edward would never apologize. In his own eyes, he was justified. *I certainly don't want the relationship Helen had with William. And for them, it is too late to make amends.*

"Well, I will just write Edward's apology for him and hope James accepts it," I said aloud to Johnny's picture and the photograph of Father and Mother on the wooden desk.

Ruth

I woke up on Easter morning, and for a split second, as I had done a hundred times, I thought William was next to me. It had been eight months since William's death, yet it still felt like half of me had been buried alongside him, and I couldn't imagine life without an ever-present cloud. Yet, I knew that part of him lived on in me. It was only weeks after the funeral that I discovered I was pregnant with our fourth child. Of course it had been unplanned, and in my stronger moments, I liked to think that it was God's way of telling me that I needed to keep going and pull through. Not just for me and the kids, but for this new life that wholly depended on me. But as much as I tried to regulate my emotions, they swung back and forth like a pendulum, weighing down my heart and soul; I would feel joy because of the kicks growing stronger and stronger with each passing day, and in a split second, grief and sadness because this child would never know William.

The pastor's message that Sunday must have been written by William and hand delivered by an angel, as it seemed to be addressed directly to me.

"Our Lord and Savior, Jesus Christ did not shy away from His emotions. Instead, He allowed Himself to lament. Taking time to lament is uncomfortable, but it is necessary if we hope to span the chasm from death to life. Invite God into the pain rather than growing numb, and He will help you reach not just a point of acceptance, but also a point of thanksgiving for who you will become as you walk through the fire set before you."

As Pastor Luke concluded his message, I desperately wished I wasn't sitting in the front row —the location we had long ago claimed as our family's regular spot. Tears streamed down my face, and I couldn't quite reach my purse for a new hand-kerchief. After grabbing it for me, Abigail wrapped one arm around me and the other around her sister. Following her lead, I wrapped my left arm around Adam, and allowed the other one to rest on my very round belly.

The music filled the sanctuary, and in combination with the message, my children, and the kicks coming from my womb, I heard the Lord whisper the precious sequence of questions we had repeated countless times to our children. But this time, I allowed myself to listen and respond.

Who are you?

"I am Ruth, a child of the king." I whispered the familiar phrase my grandfather used to tell me.

Who am I?

"You are God," I sighed, sitting down and hunching over, my body starting to shake. I felt Abby's youthful but strong hand gently rub my back and then wrap around me as she sat next to me. I could sense the other two sitting down too.

And what do you know to be true?

Jesus still loves you, I heard William say. I nodded my head and responded to the question with conviction: "Jesus loves me." My throat was thick, the taste of salty tears on my tongue, but my soul felt lighter and the tightness in my chest was gone. As I let myself finally surrender, one of my favorite verses came to mind: *You will walk through this fire, but you will not be burned.*

"You okay, Mom? Is the baby okay?" Abby asked.

"Yes, darling. We are both okay. We are all going to be okay," I answered and squeezed her hand three times, our family's way of expressing in a non-verbal way, *I love you.*

$$\sim$$

1969

Months went by and James did not respond to the apology letter. For weeks, I eagerly awaited the mail, and each day returned to the house, fuming. I was convinced the lack of response was Kimmy's fault. Eventually, I retrieved the mail without anticipation. Then, one quiet Sunday night, the phone rang; I jumped at the sound, and Edward shook his head and laughed a little.

"It is just the phone, darling. You keep reading about the best looks of the season, and I will see who is interrupting my story about James, David, and Russell."

He set down the paper and finished off his whiskey before walking toward the den across the hall. I smiled and picked my *Vogue* magazine back up to finish reading about the latest medical facts on hair. While the talk of the nation was putting a man on the moon, I was more interested in the spring fashion trends and how to care for my aging hair. Apollo 9 had launched the week before, and Edward talked about the mission as if he were going into outer space with the three astronauts he referred to by first name. Eager to be a part of history, Edward already told me we would be vacationing to Cape Canaveral to witness the launch of Apollo 12.

I saw my husband stiffen when he answered the phone, and I immediately knew who was on the other end. Magazine still in hand, I practically ran to the office to hear the exchange, eyes wide and hands in prayer position, silently pleading with Eddy to be calm and mature.

"Hello, Dad. Are you there?" I heard my baby say.

"Well, hello James. It's been so long I forgot what your voice sounded like," Edward answered sarcastically.

For a few seconds, the silence was louder than the ring. *Maybe he is going to ask to move home? Maybe he is just trying to find the words to tell us it didn't work out with that girl and he wants to move back?*

Instead, reality punched me in the gut. "Kimmy and I are getting married next month. She, or we, wanted to call and invite you both."

She wanted you to call? I could hear my heart pounding in my chest, and my palms began to sweat as I grabbed the phone from Edward.

"Hello, darling. How are you? What did I hear you say?" I blurted out, twirling the phone cord, trying to remain calm. I eased myself into the black leather chair tucked under the desk and stared at the unused fireplace.

"I am marrying Kimmy, Mom. I wanted to let you and Dad know so you could make plans to attend the ceremony in a few weeks," he answered defensively.

"Well, son," I began, "you don't have to rush into marriage. It is a big decision." In an attempt to remain calm, I switched my focus to the floral curtains and began counting the number of blooms. *One, two, three . . .*

"Yes, it is. Let me know if you can make it. We mailed details out today to you both and Grandpa and Grandma."

After a moment of silence, James spoke up. "Mom?"

While crumbling internally, I didn't want to further injure our relationship, so I rattled off the answer I thought he wanted to hear. "I'll look for the invitation. Your father and I will come, of course."

The phone's long, agitating beeps sounded off, each one shooting into my head and heart. Edward, either indifferent or furious, I could not tell, finally hung up and muttered something close to, "Well, I am damn sure not going to that wedding," then left the room. I could hear the familiar clatter of bottles as he poured himself a drink. I stared off into the abyss of petals and heard one word repeated over and over in my mind. *Karma.*

Robert, Helen, and I sat in cushioned blue chairs on the right side of the aisle. Eyes fixed on my son, I thought back to his childhood days when I was not just his hero, but the only woman in his life. Now, wearing a pill-box hat with a flowing bouffant veil, a new woman took my place. While I never expressed any praise, her high-waisted empire line gown was beautiful, and each of her three bridesmaids wore a different color, complementing both her and the flowers.

I squeezed the small, rice-filled pouch given to us upon entering the sanctuary. A white ribbon held a dainty note explaining the meaning of showering the couple with rice, and I read the words *"a symbol of prosperity"* over and over again as I heard James recite the traditional vows, untying any cords of loyalty to me with each word and knotting every heart strand to his bride instead.

Whispering, Helen commented to me about everything from the short Protestant service to the medium-cooked prime rib to the tacky figurines atop the three-tiered cake. In her eyes and mine, nothing was how it was supposed to be. I knew the entire event reminded her of William, although she never voiced the comparison.

The whole day was awkward. I avoided anything more than pleasantries with Kimberly's parents, and even though I desperately didn't want history to repeat itself, I couldn't help but think of how Helen had been with Ruth's parents. Kimberly's parents asked every question they could think of before finally excusing themselves; I just couldn't bring myself to show any interest in learning more about the parents of the woman who was taking my baby from me. As I watched James dance with her, I scowled, feeling bereft, as if no one cared about the mother of the groom. Finally, James reached for my hand to dance, and beyond our three minutes on the dance floor, we hardly spoke. He never asked about Edward, and I did not relay his excuse for not attending. We both knew the excuse was rubbish anyway.

After a few more songs from The Beatles, The Temptations, The Archies and the like, Helen and Robert – easily the oldest couple in the crowd – said they were ready to go and slowly shuffled over to James to say goodnight, timing their exit for when Kimmy was busy with other guests. I pretended to be engrossed in conversation with one of the venue's employees. James looked in my direction as Helen and Robert made their way back to me, and I waved. I didn't want to intrude on his conversation, and more, I saw Kimmy practically skipping back to his side. He shot me a puzzled, disappointed look, but as I turned around and walked away, I reasoned he would understand some day.

⌒

2015

"Why did Edward not attend the wedding?" Megan asked.

It was an obvious question to ask, I thought, as I stared out the decorated window and started to count the number of snowflakes drifting by, a task as futile as trying to rewind time.

"He said he didn't feel well the morning we left, claiming there was pressure in his chest and abdomen. At the time, of course, I thought he was just making excuses, especially because he never packed a bag. And if any part of me believed him, I assumed the pain he felt was a result of stress. Come to find out, it was likely an early sign. He died from a heart attack two Sundays after the wedding."

"Oh my goodness, I am so sorry," Megan offered, clearly shocked at the news.

"1969 and 1970 were hell for me. I lost my son to his wife, my husband to the grave, and both my in-laws died in 1970, eight months apart. Robert died of a stroke, and it was all too much for Helen, who'd had to bury both her son and husband in a matter of a few months."

"Oh dear. Margaret, I am sincerely sorry."

The sweet girl sitting across from me reached for my hand, tears in her eyes. *Would Ruth have been this kind to me if I would have let her?* I wondered. *Of course not,* a dark voice answered.

You were the black mark on her wedding, and she would've never forgiven you. For goodness sake, you played the same Debbie Downer role at your son's wedding too. You can't help but screw everything up. I winced at the familiar words.

"And to add to the pain of loss, Kimmy had a baby eight months after their wedding. You can add up the reason for their shotgun wedding. New life is supposed to ease the pain of loss. For me, however, it stung all the more because I had a grandbaby that I would not be able to watch grow up."

"Did you ever consider moving to be closer to James?" she asked, and I thought back a few decades.

1970

Without any family left in Ohio, I decided to put my big girl panties on and do something daring for the holidays. With enough life insurance money and inheritance from Robert and Helen to sustain me and a few generations, I tossed caution to the wind and flew to the Windy City for Thanksgiving.

Once through security, I found my terminal. Sitting down, hand on my purse and a small bag tucked under my seat, I adjusted my new, mauve, form-fitting dress and unbuttoned my navy, wide-lapel blazer, internally rating each person's outfit as they walked by. Once the TWA Convair 880 arrived, I watched the flight attendants walk toward the gate perfectly in sync. Their blue, pressed uniforms looked impressive. Each one looked like a model, with shoulder length or shorter hair, polished shoes, painted nails, and flawless makeup.

After boarding the plane, I stretched my legs and reached for *To Kill a Mockingbird.* I had not read the novel since it had won a Pulitzer Prize almost a decade ago, and I decided it might be the catalyst to an interesting conversation with whomever sat next to me.

A young blonde stopped at my row. She politely said hello, and as she sat down I noticed her dark bell-bottomed jeans, white Go-go boots, and the sweater coat trimmed with fur she draped over her legs. Unlike many girls her age who went bra-less beneath tie-dye shirts, she wore a fitted camel blazer atop her skin-tight, white T-shirt that left nothing to the imagination. *At least she is wearing a bra*, I thought to myself. I was sure her pearl earrings and necklace were real, and I wondered what her father did.

"Harper Lee is an amazing author, isn't she?" the strikingly beautiful woman said, breaking the barrier between 3A and 3B.

Our conversation carried on until we were halfway to Chicago. She was visiting her boyfriend for Thanksgiving. As if seeing the wheels turning in my mind, she quickly added that she would be staying with one of his female friends.

"He attends Moody Bible. He wants to be a pastor," she explained, her tone a mix of glee and pride. "We are actually going to be serving Thanksgiving meals to the homeless in Chicago this weekend. My mother was not thrilled with the idea, but my father stepped in. And now, here I am. On my way to the Windy City."

A pastor's salary isn't going to pay for the lifestyle you come from, I immediately thought, noticing her elegant Datejust Rolex.

"Well, I hope you have a wonderful visit. I am going to dive back into this book," I answered her, opening my book.

Despite my efforts to savor every word, my mind drifted to Ruth. I hated thinking about her, especially after decades had passed, but the attractive, bubbly blonde next to me was an unwitting trigger. I couldn't help but wonder if she was still alive, or if I ever crossed her mind. I wondered if she knew Helen and Robert were dead. *Not much you can do now, is there?* The question crossed my mind sharply, and I willed myself to finish the chapter.

The black Lincoln town car pulled up to the hotel at 140 E. Walton Place, the Chicago wind lashing me as I made my way to the entrance. A welcome wave of heat welcomed me into The Drake Hotel's lobby, and I felt important as I checked into my suite, which I had decided was a necessary luxury, despite being just a party of one. Once settled in my posh room, I laid out my clothes for the next day and decided to find some warmer accessories the next morning.

Chicago's Magnificent Mile made it easy for me to spoil myself. I shopped to my heart's content, especially enjoying Saks 5th Avenue and the twinkle lights adorning the elm trees outside the store's sturdy black doors. Taking in the John Hancock Center and visiting what would be the Willis Tower, I began to wonder if I should leave it all behind and embrace the fast-paced city and all it had to offer, especially the food. I enjoyed German cuisine at The Berghoff, a chicken pot pie at The Walnut Room, and a steak at Gene & Georgetti.

But once back in my room, surrounded by name-brand bags, lush bedding and the option for room service, I felt utterly alone. Despite the hustle and bustle of city life – the cars, people, sidewalk performers, and the like – I knew no one here and had no one to confide in. More, I dreaded the next destination. While I wanted to meet my grandbaby, the thought of seeing Kimmy made my stomach lurch. As I packed for the next morning, I crafted reasons to excuse myself from her presence as well as ideas to see her out the door.

A logistical benefit to visiting Chicago before traveling to meet my new grandbaby and see James was the direct Delta flight from Chicago to the Raleigh-Durham Airport. As I had done two weeks before, I settled into my seat and reached for *To Kill a Mockingbird*. Adjusting my corduroy cap and tucking my thick Burberry scarf into my blue suede handbag, all new, I decided I was not up for chit chat on this flight. While my fly-mate – an overweight gentleman several years my senior – was polite, he too seemed uninterested in small talk and was snoring before we reached our flight's peak altitude.

I was elated when I saw only James at the airport.

"Mother, welcome," he greeted, giving me a side hug and reaching for my carry-on.

"Hello, son. It is so good to see you. Do I have the pleasure of one-on-one time with you as we drive to Garner?" I asked, fully expecting an affirmative response.

"We can certainly carve out time for just us, Mom. But Kimmy was excited to see you too. She is waiting in the car so I could leave it running. I didn't want the car to be too cold for you."

"My grandson is with her, I assume?" I asked, excitement in my voice.

"Yes, but he was asleep when I parked, and it would be best for all of us if we don't wake him," he replied with a slight laugh.

My heart sank, and I excused myself to the restroom to compose myself before facing the dingbat who took my son. I adjusted the mandarin collar on my winter dress and held my head high as I gave myself a pep talk. *Put your big girl panties on and show her who a real woman should be. Remind your son what a mother should look like and enjoy the brief time you have with little James Junior.*

Kimmy complimented my teddy fur coat when she stepped out of the car to give me a hug. Instead of returning the gesture, I acted as though she was offering to take my bags and passed her my purse and suitcase instead. I couldn't help but smile at the taken aback look on her face, but I was confident my exaggerated thanks covered up my true intentions. Insisting I sit in the front seat, Kimmy climbed in the back next to the covered car seat. As we drove to their small town, the two quietly asked questions about Chicago and shared stories about Jamie. *They already nicknamed him? Her idea, no doubt.* I rolled my eyes, gazing out the window at the boring snow-covered landscape on our way to Garner, wishing for a daughter-in-law I knew I would never have.

〜

Their gray, split-level home was modest, to say the least. Brick covered the two lower levels, and white siding was on the top. The burgundy outdoor shutters needed repainting, and I felt an almost irrepressible urge to adjust the colored lights on the bushes. The station wagon barely fit in the one-car garage, and once inside, I couldn't decide if Kimmy was a poor decorator or if they simply could not afford artwork or updated furnishings on James's mason's salary.

As Kimmy took my grandson – whom I had still yet to meet – to his nursey to finish his nap, I examined the kitchen with a critical eye. The entire room was painted an outdated Smurf blue – everything from the cabinets to the fridge to the countertop.

"Can I get you some water or something to drink?" Kimmy asked, her voice overly friendly, as James carried my luggage to the extra bedroom.

"Yes, please," I answered, noticing the matching blue kitchen towel and curtains.

"There is a lot of blue, isn't there?" Kimmy asked and awkwardly laughed. "We decided to save for a future home instead of pouring too much money into this one. We love it, even if she is old at heart. Anyway, let's go sit in the living room."

Leaving the land of the Smurfs, she led me to a large room that served as both their family room and dining room. The blue patterned couch and matching chair pulled in the color of the kitchen, and the ruby-red Berber carpet coordinated with the fake flowers on both the side table and buffet as well as one of the three pillows. Large prints and wall plaques covered the ivory wall behind the couch. One of the framed prints featured a hot air balloon with red stripes, another a blue humpback whale, and the third, a print of the King of Hearts. Surrounding the framed prints, I examined a cherubim with a trumpet, a large letter G for our shared last name, and a giant key. *How random,* I critiqued as I tried to maintain a poker face.

We sat down, she in the chair and I on the firm couch. For a few long minutes, we sipped our water in silence.

I finally asked, "What does your father do again?"

What I meant was, *How can parents let their daughter live in such a shack?* Hearing my intention, James swiftly came to his wife's defense as he stepped off the final step, returning from the guest bedroom on the upper level.

"Eugene works at Duke University, Mother," James answered in a no-nonsense tone. "He manages the grounds, which you, as my mother, should know. But wait, you and Dad never cared to find anything out about my better half."

I stared at him, pretending to be hurt. "Darling, I simply forgot. Forgive your aging mother."

How dare he speak to me like that, especially in front of her? I thought.

"No worries at all," Kimmy interjected, looking at James with wide eyes and a pleading smile. "My parents forget details all the time. Anyway, yes, Pops works at Duke. He loves his work, the people, and it affords us several perks."

"Oh, how nice. Like what?" I asked, feigning interest, feeling James's steely gaze on me.

"Well, for starters, we are able to watch Duke football and basketball without paying for the tickets. We love that, don't we, James?"

"Yes. Yes, we do," he answered, taking a seat on the other side of the buffet across the room. I saw his body relax, and I tried to also.

"And, the main benefit we have enjoyed for years is that our family friend, Professor Trip, generously lets us stay at his house on Ocean Isle, where we met."

"Oh, your family does not own property there?" I asked, nodding my head in understanding. Now that I knew a little bit about her background, I understood why they were living in such a modest home; at least her parents weren't withholding funds from her and James. With Edward dead, all James would have had to do was ask, and I would've helped him afford a larger home and some updated, tasteful furnishings. In fact, I had offered to do just that in exchange for a visit from James, but each offer was met with rejection.

"Kimmy and I will own property if you don't sell the house you and Dad built." James answered my question, his words laced with attitude and the same derision he heard Edward use about people he didn't like, especially William.

After Edward died, I'd mentioned selling the Ocean Isle property, as I didn't see myself visiting there alone, and I didn't know if James would be interested in a house that would remind him of his dad.

"Let's talk about it later. I need to start dinner before Jamie wakes up," Kimmy interjected, again trying to calm the waters. "My parents will arrive around half past four with scalloped potatoes and a cherry pie. Jamie has been napping longer in the afternoons, but they should at least arrive before five o'clock."

"I will help you," I told them both, and stood up, following her into the blue abyss.

Home a few days earlier than planned, I lay on my left side in my own bed, a blanket folded and tucked between my knees. I tried to focus on counting sheep rather than replaying memories of the disastrous time in North Carolina, but despite my attempts, the recent events played like reruns in my mind.

It started that very first night when I realized Kimmy had turned my son into a vegetarian. Surveying the ingredients laid out for the chili, I asked if she was using chicken or beef. Much to my surprise, she informed me they were vegetarians and started lecturing me about the health benefits. I could not believe my ears. *My James, a vegetarian?* Did she not care at all about his opinion or what he liked? Interrupting her hundredth reason why being a vegetarian was a good decision, I assured her James liked his chili with ground beef and steak chunks. At some point between me searching through their fridge and freezer, James entered the room, but rather than tell his wife he wanted meat, he informed me he no longer ate meat. I buttoned my mouth and politely excused myself to my room.

While unpacking, I heard James Junior waking up. Anxious to meet him, I tossed the clothes I was holding back into my suitcase and headed for his room. Opening the door, I peered in to see my six-month-old grandson sitting in his crib.

"Hello, little one. I am Grandma Margaret," I introduced myself as I pulled back the curtains.

He stopped crying and stared curiously at me. Atop his oval face were spikes of auburn hair, and I wiped away a tear as I gazed into his large eyes.

Memories of James as a baby came flooding back. I remembered when he sat up by himself for the first time; filled with pride, I clapped and cheered as he looked at me with a toothless grin before tumbling over onto a baby blanket. *Oh, to return to the days when he needed me. . .* Melancholy gripped me, reminding me of my advancing years. *Father Time is a thief. Those precious days of learning to sit became waving goodbye on his first day of kindergarten too quickly.* Before I knew it, he was dressed in a sports coat and slacks for his First Communion ceremony. Then I blinked, and he'd joined the U.S. Armed Forces. *And now, the house is perfectly quiet, a fitting stage for the illusion of your perfect life.* Not wanting to admit that my life held more past than future, I shook away the sadness and smiled at my grandbaby.

"Can I pick you up?" I asked through the crib bars.

That was when Kimmy interrupted our precious moment.

"Looks like someone is awake. I see you met Daddy's Mommy," Kimmy said in a baby voice as she reached into the crib. "How about I change him first? I don't want your first interaction to be changing his diaper!"

Laying him down on a simple changing table, she reached for a disposable diaper.

"Oh, you are using *disposable diapers?*" I questioned critically.

"Absolutely! The clean-up is much easier," Kimmy began before her voice shifted to baby talk again. "We couldn't imagine what a huge poopy diaper would be like without them, could we, Jamie?"

"Cloth diapers are certainly more breathable. I used both the Boater and the Safe-T Di-Dee for James. Both snapped on, and we never had issues," I remarked. "There are diaper services too, which I would certainly pay for."

"Breathable? I thought the waterproof covering for cloth were made of plastic. Either way, I appreciate the offer."

James Junior, now on her hip, clung to Kimmy's knit sweater while his big eyes looked back and forth between us.

"I insist," I pushed, annoyed she had not jumped on my generous offer. "I really think it would be best for James Junior."

"Really, Margaret. I am happy with our choice. Thank you though." Her tone was polite, yet definitive. "Now, the corn-bread will be ready shortly. Want to play with Jamie before dinner?"

Defeated and desperate to hold my grandson, I replied, "Of course," before meeting her hopeful expression with a closed mouth smile.

As the stay went on, tension amplified when Kimmy asked if I would join them for their church's Christmas-themed musical. I humored them for a while and pretended to be interested as she talked on and on about the musical as if it were a Broadway play. A few hours before her parents arrived to pick us up, I put my plan into motion, detailing the sudden onset of a terrible headache; I even ensured there was enough time to take a nap in hopes it would go away. Neither James nor Kimmy was moved when I informed them that, regrettably, I would not be joining them.

A day or two later, a polite shortness replaced Kimmy's sweet demeanor after I asked harmless questions about James Junior one morning. "Are you going to let him cry that long?" "You want me to burp him that hard? Honey, I am not going to hit my grandson." "James sounds so much more masculine than Jamie, don't you think?"

Our relationship reached an impasse on December 23.

"When do you plan to baptize James Junior?" I asked that morning, as Kimmy handed me a poinsettia mug full of coffee.

I saw her body stiffen under her gray, white, and black buffalo check jumper, and she answered me as she walked back toward the coffee pot to pour her own. "Oh, did James not tell you? We will not be baptizing *Jamie* as a baby." Her voice emphasized the nickname, Jamie, and her strong tone bothered me.

"So you want *James Junior* to go to hell if he dies as a child?" I snapped back without thinking, mimicking the emphasis she put on my grandson's name.

"Margaret, I have had enough!" Kimmy yelled, fire burning in her eyes. Her left fist made contact with the counter, and she pointed her teaspoon at me like I was a child. "You have patronized me since you stepped foot in my house, and until now I have let all your demeaning words, questions, and glances slide, but I will *not* let you talk about my son that way."

Heavy footsteps on the stairs signaled James's approach. Before I had a chance to reply, he appeared in the doorway, a velour burgundy robe wrapped around his body. His eyes looked slightly bloodshot from the whiskey consumption from the previous night, a look I was all too familiar with.

"Are you going to let her talk to me like that?" I asked him, forcing tears to fill my eyes, trying to play the victim card even though a quiet voice urged me to apologize.

"I could hear you two from upstairs, and she is right, Mother," he said firmly, wrapping his arm around her shoulders. "I should've said something sooner."

"Should've said *what* sooner?" I inquired, standing up now, my feet feeling hot in my faux fur purple slippers.

"Mom, I feel disappointed in the way you have treated Kimmy. While I am at it, I am flat out angry for the way you have treated her since you first met her. You have been nothing but a monster."

"James, what on earth are you talking about? I have sacrificed so much for you. Don't tell me you are disappointed in me. You only have one mother, you know? I would love nothing more than to have a relationship with all of you," I answered, trying to sound sincere about the last three words. A wave of guilt rushed over me, but I resisted its call to apologize.

"Your hypocrisy makes me want to throw up," Kimmy said, exasperated. "I literally cannot handle it anymore."

"Is that seriously all you are going to say?" James asked, choking back tears, shoulders slumped in defeat.

I stared at him, and suddenly he was six years old again. I was making pancakes, and he was rattlingly off the Build-Em Cars and Emergency Speedsters he wanted from Santa. Eddy was reading the paper, his coffee likely flavored with Jack Daniel's. But rather than hearing his sweet voice call me "Mommy," I heard James's angry adult voice.

"Mother, you have outlasted your stay. Please pack your things. I will take you to the airport."

Those last three sentences reverberated in my memory. Hot, angry tears dampened my pillow, and I finally sat up and reached for the box of tissues on the nightstand. I dabbed my eyes, blew my nose, threw the sodden tissue on the floor, and reached for another.

The voice of my mother told me I was in the wrong. *Sweetie, stop defending your actions. You witnessed Helen live her whole life without William. And you only have James! Do not repeat history.* Yet, the other voice was louder. *Kimmy was rude; she changed James. You know him better than she does, and he will come around. He wants a relationship with you; you could hear it in his voice and see it through his tears.*

CHAPTER 38
2015

And there it was. The truth. The ugly and honest truth spoken for the first time in its entirety. And to whom? To Ruth's own granddaughter. Her spitting image, nonetheless.

We both stared at each other. The admission sucked the air out of my lungs, and panic surged through my body. "You know, I've always believed in the idea of karma for others, but I never imagined myself on the receiving end of it. Or perhaps it drips with irony that I instigated the divide between Helen and your grandfather and then made the same mistakes she did with my own boy?"

Megan's answer about not believing in karma sounded muffled as I went back inside my own head, the full weight of guilt upon my heart and an inferno of feelings raging inside. I was again confronted with my wrongs and faced with a crossroads: accept my shortcomings or continue to work to make myself comfortable with what I had said and done to both Megan's grandmother and my own son. At that moment, I resolved to stop avoiding reality, especially because the consequences were unavoidable. A montage of memories flashed through my mind again, and I felt like I was talking to Ruth herself, clinging to her dainty hands and asking for forgiveness. "I am so, so sorry. I am sorry I lied. I am sorry I tarnished your wedding; it should've been your perfect day."

She tried to interrupt me, but I wouldn't let her. "No, let me finish." I closed my eyes, holding my aging hands slightly above the table, anxious but determined. I continued, "I am sorry for turning everyone against you, and then when you and William tried to salvage a relationship with us by addressing the issue, I remained against you. I was terrified Edward would leave me for good and that Helen would never speak to me again. But what did it cost me? A lifetime of guilt, superficial relationships, and the need to jump from one distraction to another. And, it undoubtedly fed into how I viewed my son and his wife." I let out a long sigh and confessed, "I hated who you were because it reminded me of who I was not. Mama warned me not to act on my jealousy. That's what it was. Jealousy. I wish I would've listened to her."

"Margaret?" the blonde woman in front of me softly said in a questioning tone, bringing me back to my senses; it was Megan, not Ruth. All the same, her words that followed were a salve to my soul.

"Thank you for sharing your story. Granny shared her story with me, but it was never from a place of anger. I mean, she still got upset recalling her past, but until her dying breath, she only ever wanted to be your friend." Megan paused, her face creased in thought, her eyes glossy. "You know," she continued, "she had things in her life people wouldn't be jealous of. She had a miscarriage too. And a stillborn baby, which really rocked her."

She is gone too? I suppose she had her own share of sorrows, just like everyone does, but I would have never guessed we shared some of the same losses. We had more in common than I would've ever guessed . . . and now it's too late to try to reconnect. I closed my eyes, looked down toward my print pants, and wiped away the wetness forming under my lower lashes. My inner negative voice, fainter now, wanted to speak, but I silenced it. Looking up at Megan, I said sincerely, "I am sorry for missing out on that friendship and for ruining what might have been between my son, your mom, and those in your generation. You all share a last name but are complete strangers."

"Yeah, in many ways you are right. And while we can't go back and change the past, you can start where you are today and change the ending. Starting with James and Kimmy," Megan said, smiling, then added, "and me, if you're willing. I am Ruth's granddaughter, after all, so part of her lives in me. It may feel like it, but it's not too late."

EPILOGUE

2015

After saying our goodbyes and best wishes for the New Year, I lifted Megan's wrapped gift from my purse. Instructing her to not open it until she was safely home, I handed her the copy a nurse made me of my mother's journals I'd once dismissed as notebooks full of prayers. I had only recently excavated them from my belongings, the desire spurred on by my time with Megan, and I hoped the copy would help her understand both me and my mother better.

Back at Sunrise, the smell of coffee still permeated my clothes, and I mulled over our conversation. Something Megan had said as she left stuck with me. After I wished her a lifetime of happiness, she replied, "Thank you. Remember, though, far more is at play in our lives than temporary happiness. I will pray you can forgive yourself and reconcile with James."

I grappled with her words and the experience she had afforded me, breathing deeply as the healing power in sharing my story washed over me. I felt a sense of closure with my past, and while I could not forgive myself yet, I saw the power of it. The life in forgiveness. The breath of it. The mystery of it.